Praise for *Black Dog* and the Hellhound Chronicles

"With an unrelenting pace, wildly imaginative details and moments of shocking emotion, this is a book—and surely a series—that is going to earn an eager following."
   —*RT Book Reviews* (top pick, nominated for Best Paranormal Romantic Suspense @ RT Awards)

"[D]efinitely a keeper. The pacing is speedy without being too rapid, the character design is intriguing . . . and the story is a clever riff on the tried-and-true revenge motif. . . . Lots of promise here; make this one a series to watch."
   —*Booklist*

"A fast-paced read perfect for lovers of dark fantasy."
   —*Kirkus Reviews*

". . . Kittredge employs an enjoyable variation on the standard urban fantasy worldbuilding."
   —*Library Journal*

"This is a fascinating world, with a well-developed supernatural setting that includes Kittredge's version of Hell. I highly recommend it for readers of urban fantasy."
   —GeekMom Blog

"The combination of the world and the action kept me turning pages late into the night with this one."
    —All Things Urban Fantasy

"Always providing a fresh and unique perspective on commonly used tropes and archetypes, Ms. Kittredge herself weaves her own sort of magic with words on the page. . . . *Black Dog* is the perfect start to a (hopefully) long and happy relationship with the new Hellhound Chronicles series."
    —Literary Escapism

"Caitlin Kittredge has a way with words, she teleports you to this world she has created and then vibrantly paints it for you."
    —Once Upon a Twilight

"Kittredge has created a very interesting world with very intriguing characters/creatures, and I think it will only get better from here."
    —Dark Faerie Tales

GRIM TIDINGS

Also by Caitlin Kittredge

Hellhound Chronicles

Black Dog

Black London Series

Street Magic
Demon Bound
Bone Gods
Soul Trade
Devil's Business
Dark Days

Young Adults

Iron Codex Trilogy

The Iron Throne
The Nightmare Garden
The Mirrored Shard

GRIM TIDINGS

HELLHOUND CHRONICLES BOOK 2

CAITLIN KITTREDGE

HARPER Voyager
An Imprint of HarperCollins*Publishers*

GRIM TIDINGS. Copyright © 2016 by Caitlin Kittredge. All rights reserved. Printed in the United States of America. No part of this book may be used or reproduced in any manner whatsoever without written permission except in the case of brief quotations embodied in critical articles and reviews. For information, address HarperCollins Publishers, 195 Broadway, New York, NY 10007.

HarperCollins books may be purchased for educational, business, or sales promotional use. For information, please e-mail the Special Markets Department at SPsales@harpercollins.com.

FIRST EDITION

Harper Voyager is a federally registered trademark of HarperCollins Publishers.

Designed by Paula Russell Szafranski

Library of Congress Cataloging-in-Publication Data has been applied for.

ISBN 978-0-06-231693-6

16 17 18 19 20   OV/RRD   10 9 8 7 6 5 4 3 2 1

You may bury my body
Ooh, down by the highway side
So my old evil spirit
Can catch a Greyhound bus and ride

—ROBERT JOHNSON,
"Me and the Devil Blues"

GRIM TIDINGS

CHAPTER

1

‖‖‖

My blood landed on the snow, each drop leaving a crimson crater in the frozen white. I coughed, and felt the drowning-on-dry-land pull of a collapsed lung. Pain shot up my forearm from a triangular slash of auto glass buried between my radius and ulna bones. Wrapping a torn piece of my jacket around my opposite hand, I grabbed the shard and yanked. The electric shock of nerve pain blurred my vision and pushed a strangled whimper from my throat. Good thing nobody was around to hear me.

A few dozen yards behind me, a black muscle car lay on its roof, mangled beyond recognition. Steam escaped from the radiator, melting snow and revealing the black rocks that had bashed the car to scrap when we went off the highway and into a ravine. Gas dribbled from a rent in the tank, running out even faster than the torrent of dark blood from my arm.

There was too much—too much pain, too many smells, the too-loud roar of my heart beating against my eardrums, the blizzard around me, and the blood rushing through my body on its adrenaline-fueled joyride, all competing for volume.

If I'd been on my own, I would have let myself pass out. But I wasn't, so I forced myself onto two legs from a crouch, slogging through the deep snow back to the wreck. "Leo," I croaked, staggering to the driver's side door. It was bent almost in half, like a giant child had given his toy an angry kick.

The seat was empty, but there was blood on the steering wheel. I touched it with a finger, sniffing. It was Leo's. So where the hell was he?

My head was starting to clear after the titanic jolt I'd taken when I'd been thrown from the wreck, and I started to get frantic as my thoughts sped up to their normal RPMs. "Leo!" I screamed, and a gust of wind blew snow down my throat for my trouble. It would be dark in the next half hour, and we were twenty feet below the highway, invisible to anyone who might want to help and vulnerable to anyone who didn't.

He'd be all right, right? I asked myself. It wasn't like either of us could die from something as mundane as a car crash. He'd probably just gotten his brain rattled and wandered off.

We'd been alone on the highway heading east, the pavement pure white and the landscape devoid of any other living soul. The blizzard had started soon after we'd crossed into Iowa from Nebraska and we'd passed the orange beacon of a highway patrol sign telling us the road was closed about twenty miles back.

Leo had tapped his fingers on the steering wheel, in no particular rhythm. Nobody would stop us, if they even noticed the black car gliding through the silent storm. Human eyes had a way of sliding right over people like Leo and me, relegating us to shadows or something imagined out of the corner of their eye. Leo's fingers were tattooed, small black card suits, triangles and Cyrillic alphabet delineating each pale joint. I watched them, curled inside my coat on the passenger side, watched him. He'd traded in his black suit and white shirt for a black canvas jacket as we got deeper into the massive ice chest that is the Midwest at the onset of winter, but otherwise his face was just the same as when he'd been alive. Black hair short at the sides and longer on top, sharp cheeks and chin, deep black eyes that hadn't looked like they'd belonged in a man's face even before he'd died. More fingers of ink crawling up his neck to nearly touch behind his ear.

Finally, he turned down the scratchy God-'n'-Jesus program that was the only thing coming in on the radio and looked over at me. "What's up?"

We didn't talk much, and that was fine. I wasn't a person who needed a lot of conversation and neither was Leo. Right that second, though, I did feel like the stuff we weren't talking about was sitting between us like a third passenger.

"Just thinking about what's in Minneapolis," I lied. Well, half-lied. It just wasn't *all* I was thinking about.

Leo's mouth twitched. "More bullshit, I imagine." A wind gust pushed the car into the oncoming lane and Leo righted it. This car would never go off the road, never break down, never need a fill-up. If you could get past the part where you were a slave of Hellspawn or something much worse, being resurrected as a reaper definitely had its perks.

"Hellspawn aren't good at much else," I agreed, shifting my leg to tuck it under me. My body was complaining after hours in the car, and I was tempted to suggest we pull in somewhere and find a motel to wait out the storm. We didn't even really need a motel, I thought as I looked at Leo again. He didn't have a problem keeping me warm.

Stop that, I told myself. Leo and I had fucked, and I wouldn't mind doing it again, but harboring fond memories of our time together wasn't going to do either of us any favors. Not now, because everything was different and one-half of a couple dying a brutal death has a way of taking the gleam off any relationship.

Silence for another ten miles. I just hoped I could get out of the car without saying something that would bring up a lot of shit neither of us wanted to deal with. How Leo had died. How he'd come back as not just a reaper, but *the* reaper—supposed head honcho of the whole soul-stealing business. How he and I were going to Minneapolis to find . . . what? Somehow I doubted the rest of the reapers would be waiting with a muffin basket and a corner office. They hadn't been under anyone's thumb in the almost hundred years since I'd joined their little pyramid scheme from Hades, and in my experience the only thing they liked more than taking human souls was dickering with each other over who got to be the boss, since all reapers were created equal. Until now.

Leo was different, supposedly. Supposedly, *I* was different now too.

I didn't feel different. I just felt tired, and wished I could let go of what was chewing on me long enough to sleep for a few dozen exits along the interstate.

The worst thing I wasn't discussing with Leo, I hadn't even told him in the first place. I hadn't told anyone, just let it keep me up at night until I was even paler than usual and the circles under my eyes could have been used as a racetrack. I let it get me jittery and paranoid, watching every time a car followed us for too long or a tall shadow followed me into a truck stop.

I hadn't felt this bad since the first few decades I was a hell-hound, back when Gary, the reaper who'd found me at my most vulnerable and made me the offer I'd been too stupid to refuse, had decided to make fucking up my life his personal project. Back then I'd barely let my feet touch the ground, drifting from one whistle-stop to the next, through the Dust Bowl, up and down the west coast and across the broad face of the Rockies. I thought I could escape, that if I just ran far enough eventually a creature made to hunt people down would lose my trail.

Told you I was stupid back then.

Eventually, I got better at my job and Gary lost interest in tormenting me. Eventually, the guy who held my note now would do the same. At least I really hoped so, because unpleasant as Gary was, an angel on a power trip was a whole new level of shit.

Sure, Uriel had pretended he was making a request when he came to me with his offer, doing an exchange, putting us on the same footing. But unlike the backwoods kid who'd accepted Gary's offer in 1919, I wasn't stupid anymore. I knew I had to do what Uriel had asked of me, and that as polite as he was doing the asking, I had absolutely no free will in the matter.

5

Not if I wanted to keep him away from Leo.

"Getting dark." Leo tilted his head from side to side. I watched the cords of his neck flex as his spine crackled. Even the king boss of reapers got tired of the road, I guessed.

"We could be in Minneapolis by sunup if we push through," I said. Leo grunted, and I wondered if that wasn't the response he wanted. Was he worried about what we'd find too? The Leonid Karpov I'd met in Las Vegas, when he was a Russian mob cleaner and I was a burnt-out Hellspawn minion, didn't get worried. Not even when everything fell apart. Not even when Lilith, Gary's boss and Hell's resident bitch on wheels, stuck a knife in his heart and held it there until it stopped twitching.

If Leo was worried . . . suddenly, the hot dog I'd had a state and a half ago threatened to come up. "Pull over if you want," I whispered, digging my fingers into the vinyl of the seat, leaving little white scratches.

"Nah," he shrugged. "No point in putting off the ass-fucking we're probably gonna walk into, right?"

My stomach eased a little. "Right," I agreed. "If you're into that."

Leo turned to me, his mouth turning up a little at the corner. His face was cold—I think if I had been merely human, I'd have probably peed my pants when he came after me in Vegas—but he had a great smile. Warm, entirely human. I tried to return it, knowing I looked like a junkie on the wrong end of a three-day bender.

"It'll be okay, Ava," he said. "You know that, right?"

I opened my mouth, and then out of the corner of my eye a black shape loomed out of the white. It stood in the center of the highway, completely still as the car bore down on it.

It looked human in the moment, but I wouldn't swear to anything.

"Leo!" I screamed, jolting upright in my seat. He didn't say anything, just jerked the wheel hard, laying on the brakes so I felt myself come off the vinyl. I had the absurd thought I should have worn a seat belt, even though nothing this side of a Hellspawn weapon could dent me for long.

For two seconds, I was weightless. Then the brakes locked up and we smashed the guardrail in a sideways drift, undoing it like a twist-tie. The car took a rock and flipped, and we made two more bone-crunching revolutions before we came to rest at the bottom of the hill.

Somewhere in there, I went through the shattered windshield and landed twenty feet away like an errant Frisbee. I blacked out for a while, and when I came too it was dim twilight, and I smelled gas. I did the basic checklist you learn when you've been beat to shit enough times—can you see, can you move your arms and legs, does your head feel like it's been cracked open? I coughed blood, tried to look for Leo, then when I couldn't find him stood in the lee of the wreck, trembling against the wind, and feeling ice chip tears scraping my cheeks.

Leo wasn't the only person here. Whoever had been in the road had seen the whole thing.

Maybe it was just a confused hitchhiker, or a drunk trying to make it home. But I doubted it. I just didn't have that kind of luck. So screaming for help was out, and nobody was coming to the rescue.

Standing there panicking was going to kill me. I had to find

Leo, be ready to protect him. And to do that, I needed to be ready to fight.

I staggered around to the broken side window, crawling back into the car. I hit at the glove compartment with my good hand until the door opened, raining the contents onto my head.

If I became the hound, I'd probably heal up, but my arm was hurt so I'd also be lame, and even running away would no longer be an option. That just left me, little Ava in her fucked-up little body. It'd have to do.

I flipped the top off the first aid kit Leo had insisted on when we got on the road. I'd thought it was dumb then, but a lifetime of never knowing when you'd get hit and bleed had turned him into a regular Boy Scout. I got the gauze roll and wrapped my arm up tight, biting it through with my teeth. The rest of my cuts weren't going to make me lose enough blood to be a problem, but my vision was starting to black out and every breath felt like I was sucking through a straw with a hole in it. Broken ribs I could handle, but if I was running on half the oxygen I needed, that wouldn't help Leo. All it'd make me was a wheezing appetizer for whoever was up there.

I fumbled in the kit again, ripping at the front of my bloody shirt so my skin was exposed down to the V of my bra. I grabbed the long syringe, meant to be loaded with adrenaline if one of our hearts stopped, and pulled out the plunger with my teeth, spitting it to the side.

"This is going to suck," I told my fractured reflection in the side mirror, and jammed the syringe directly into the flat, square bruise the dashboard had left on me when it collapsed my lung on my way out of the car.

For a split second the world turned to fire, and then with a tiny hiss of air, I felt my lung inflate.

Tossing the syringe aside and retching from the pain, I pulled my coat back on and crawled back out into the white. Now that I could breathe again, I could smell again, and I followed the faint blood trail away from the car, losing it every so often in the wind. I came to the banks of a small lake, barely distinguishable from the snow around it, and finally got a strong enough hit to fix on a direction.

"Leo!" I screamed again, over the howling wind. No answer. I struggled through the drifts, which were well past my knees, and finally saw him. He was on his back, head turned to the side and eyes closed like he was sleeping. If it hadn't been for the great red bird's wing of arterial blood staining the snow under him, I would have believed it.

My entire body lurched, like I'd just hit a wall. "Shit . . ." I ran, falling into the snow next to him. I felt for a pulse, realizing belatedly that I wasn't even sure if he'd have one anymore. "Leo." I shook him. "Leo!" Fast as I'd toughened up, all my steel was gone, and I started shivering again.

A perfect sliver of glass had embedded itself in Leo's neck, under his smooth jaw where the carotid artery nestled. It had neatly bisected one of his tattoos, slicing him open with the precision of an autopsy.

I put my head against his chest, listening for a heartbeat, but there was nothing but the static of the wind, just like the car's crackling radio as we finally moved out of a station's range.

"Don't do this," I whispered against his chest, but he still didn't stir. He was cold, the only warm spot the gentle waft of steam from his cooling blood on the ground around us.

I lifted my head, looking for any sign of civilization, but we'd been on a lonely highway and this was a lonelier spot still. I looked back at the distant slope to the road, at Leo. I was going to have to carry him. There was no other way.

The lake was surrounded by a little stand of wind-whipped trees, barren now in the onslaught of freezing wind. As I struggled to get Leo up, my feet skidding in his blood, a shadow passed between the gray skeletons of the tree trunks, popping up as suddenly as the figure in the road.

I froze, even though it was useless to try and hide. Leo and I were the only things that stood out from the landscape for miles.

The shadow moved, and behind it another appeared from the trees, and another. They didn't move in the flicker-and-fade, snap-shot way of spirits or revenants, scavengers just looking for a meal. They were solid, but way too fast to be anything that had our best interest in mind. I leaned down to Leo's ear again. "If you can hear me, you need to get up," I murmured. "We are in serious trouble."

The three figures were nearly clear of the trees, moving in the flying-wedge shape that anyone who's ever watched a nature show about pack hunters is familiar with. The one in the lead twisted its head sideways for a second, looking back, and I followed its eye-line to see the dark shape from the road standing at the top of the slope, watching us.

I stared back at them, not because I was frozen in fear—my heart sending throbbing pulses through my bruised ribs, scream-ing at me to get moving—but because for just a moment, as the snow cleared and gave us a look at one another, I felt something familiar.

It wasn't a sting of recognition—more like déjà vu. I'd seen something like him before, that tall skinny black figure standing so very still, a stillness that humans just don't possess.

Then a gust of snow blinded me and when I looked the figure was gone, and the shadows with it.

I wondered what I'd done to deserve a break for a change, and then a cold hand clamped down on my wrist and Leo was staring up at me, croaking, and scrabbling at the glass shard in his neck. When I pulled it out, it made a little sucking sound, and fresh blood gushed out. I clapped my hands over it, the hot blood making my frostbitten fingers prickle.

"I wasn't sure you were getting up," I said, hoping Leo would think the tears on my face were just melted snow.

"Me either," he said, his voice raspy from the cut in his neck. The blood started to slow, and in no time at all—considering the slash would have killed a regular man in thirty seconds or less—stopped altogether.

I slumped against Leo, and before I thought about it, I'd wrapped my sticky, red-stained fingers around his. He pulled my hands closed, putting them inside his jacket where his skin warmed mine. "You're shaking," he said quietly.

"I'm cold," I muttered. Leo put his hand under my chin and lifted my head so I was looking at him.

"You stayed with me."

"'Course," I said, squirming that he could see just how upset I'd gotten. "Who else is going to look out for your dumb ass? You can't even drive."

Leo pressed his mouth against mine. I tasted the sharp old-penny tang of his blood on my tongue, and kissed him hard, warmth building between our bodies until we both fell back with a groan, our respective injuries twinged.

Leo grimaced. "Let's get back to the road and get the hell out of here."

I helped him up, and we leaned on each other. "I'll always be here," I told him quietly as we picked our way up the rock slope. "No matter what happens."

Leo gave me a flash of that smile again, as we started limping down the shoulder of the interstate to the next exit.

I looked back once, but shadows and their master had gone, not even a footprint to show they'd been anything but a bad dream.

L eo and I checked into the first crummy nonchain motel we
saw off the exit—the closer to the interstate you get, the fewer
questions people generally ask. The clerk barely looked away from
the talk show squawking on the lobby TV when he checked us in.

Leo let out a sigh when he flopped back onto the shiny bedspread. "Home sweet home."

I helped him take off his jacket and shoes, pulling an extra
blanket over him. The first night we'd ever spent together was in a
motel room just slightly worse than this. I'd just killed Gary, was
masterless, alone, and had no idea what was coming next. I never
expected Leo to stick around.

As I watched his chest rise and fall under the blanket, sleeping
off the crash, I still didn't know what I expected. Everything had

gone so much further sideways then I could have imagined when I sank my teeth into Gary's throat.

Leo and I had this little slice of time, sure. But when we got to Minneapolis, it was all going to change. He was the top of the reaper food chain, and I was still a hellhound, just another dog in a pack of thousands.

I looked out the steamy window and saw blinking neon across the parking lot. Pulling my boots and coat back on, I slipped out into the blistering cold. Making sure the door clicked shut quietly enough that it didn't wake Leo, I stomped through the slush toward the bar. After the day I'd just had, I deserved a drink.

The bar wasn't anything special—and "nothing special" was a hilarious understatement. Dive bars are all the same. They're dark, they smell like stale beer and bleach, every surface is sticky, and there are between four and ten chronic alcoholics holding down the booths and stools.

I let the wind blow me inside and kicked the door shut. The kind of people who'd brave this weather to get drunk on cheap domestic beer wouldn't pay me any attention—I blended in with the pitted walls and buzzing beer signs to the point of invisibility.

I asked the bartender for whiskey and he gave it to me without a word, accepting my cash with a grunt. I downed it, and two more just like it, finally starting to feel warm again. Before too long I'd go back across the parking lot and crawl into bed with Leo. We'd be in Minneapolis tomorrow, and whatever happened there wasn't anything I could control. A fourth whiskey should make me stop worrying about it.

I held up my cloudy glass to the bartender, who finally deigned to lift a shaggy eyebrow. "Maybe slow down, sweetheart."

I glared at him until he shrugged and refilled my glass. One of the drunks at the far end of the bar got up and walked crookedly over to an old jukebox against the far wall. He popped in two quarters and after a minute "That Old Black Magic" drifted from speakers that looked older than I did.

The point between my shoulder blades tightened up. I don't know much, but I did know for a fact that no jukebox in Hick-town, USA had a ready selection of Glenn Miller. Especially not *that* song.

When the drunk sat down next to me, I was ready for him. You lose a fight two ways—and not being willing to use whatever you have at hand as a weapon is one of them. I tightened my fist around the pitted tumbler of whiskey. "In three seconds you're going to be wearing glass splinters in your face, so how about you get out of mine?"

The drunk let out a low sigh that sounded like rocks dragging over bigger rocks. "You always had a way with words, Ava."

My world tilted for a second, Glenn Miller going fuzzy. Nothing to do with the booze either, dammit. I took a second look at the scarred, bald head sunk down inside the drunk's padded jacket, the white lines where skin had been inexpertly knitted back together from eye socket to collarbone gleaming under my gaze.

"Wilson?" I said softly.

He turned to face me, the one milky eye rolling off in its own direction. To say Wilson was ugly was to say that truck stop speed made a person a little jumpy. He'd been torn apart by shifters and put back together by sheer force of being too mean to die. He used to be Gary's chauffeur, errand boy, and general punching bag, before I made Gary dead and Wilson unemployed. You'd think he'd at least be grateful enough to leave me alone, but Wilson was a miserable bastard long before a pack of shapeshifting hillbillies rearranged his face.

"You look like shit," he said.

"You'd know," I told him. I didn't let go of the tumbler. I'd jam a shard of it into my own throat before I went down under Wilson's teeth and claws.

"We need to talk," he said. I cocked my head.

"You been practicing since I cut your chain?" I said. "Last I heard you preferred grunts and hand gestures."

Wilson's good eye fixed me. "Something has happened."

"A lot has happened," I snapped, slamming back the last of the whiskey. "One of those things? I don't ever have to waste another second looking at your face just because the same jackass holds our note. So have a nice life, if that's even possible for you."

Wilson grabbed my arm and held me in my seat. I tensed, and he tightened his grip, so hard it would leave bruises. "Stop that," he growled.

"You started, you stop it," I said, matching his tone. "I swear if you do not let go of me they will be cleaning both of us off the walls." The second way you lose a fight is not being willing to get your ass kicked. I never had that problem with Gary and his pack of guard dogs.

Wilson let me go, and smiled, which was the most terrifying thing I'd ever seen him do. "Good," he said, pulling himself upright and brushing off the worn-out canvas jacket he wore. "I'm glad to see you haven't lost your edge, darling."

I backed up fast, off my stool and out of range. "You're not Wilson."

He dipped his head in assent. "Sit down. We do need to talk and your propensity to cause a scene won't help with that."

I sighed, shoving my face into my hands to muffle any involuntary screams. I just wanted to get drunk in peace. Was that so much to ask? "Men's room, now."

I slammed open the door decorated with a wood cutout of a guy in a trucker hat pissing, and locked it behind me and Wilson. A dim set of bulbs flickered above us, and when my eyes adjusted Wilson's ugly mug was gone, replaced by one of the few faces I wanted to see even less.

Uriel wrinkled his nose. "It reeks like a Boston gutter the morning after St. Patrick's Day in here."

"Welcome to the mortal realm," I said. "It smells bad."

"I apologize for using your friend's guise like that," the angel said. His shiny shoes squelched on the grimy tile floor and he made a face.

"Wilson is not my friend," I snapped. "And I don't want your apology, I want you to leave me alone."

"We both know that's not feasible, Ava," Uriel said. He turned and adjusted his tie in the mirror. He was wearing a pale gray suit and a white shirt, the kind of soft tones favored by CEOs, TV preachers, and the favored host of the Kingdom of Heaven.

"You *said* you'd leave me alone," I ventured. Uriel straightened up and gave me one of his patented Ken-doll smiles, so fake it squeaked.

"I said once our business was concluded you and I could part ways. Not before."

I sighed, slumping against the dripping sink. "I don't know if you noticed but I've been through a lifetime's worth of shit since our little business meeting. A lot's changed."

"Strange, I'd think you'd want to help me," Uriel said. "After what Lilith and Gary and the Fallen have put you through. An employee of the Host is better than a slave of the Hellspawn, in my book."

"So I'm your fucking executive assistant now?" I said. "You want me to fetch fugitive fallen angels, or just coffee? Got any typing and filing for me?"

Uriel tilted his head at me. "Ava, I'm not Gary. I'm not going to make you fetch anything."

I spread my hands. The bathroom was tiny enough to make me feel trapped, even if I hadn't been within arm's length of an angel. "Then what? The deal was, I find the rest of the Fallen for you white-shoe assholes and in return you never, ever accost me in a men's room. Why are we even meeting? If the Fallen catch wind of this it's gonna be lights-out for me and I don't appreciate it."

"I wouldn't be here if it wasn't an emergency," Uriel snapped. "I am not an idiot. Something has happened, like I said, and you're the person I need looking into it."

"Why me?" I said. "I'm sure you've got a lot of worker bees up there in the Kingdom who are more competent than I am."

"Lots of underlings, yes," Uriel said. "Competent, a few. But none who have your skills and contacts—and none who are the Grim Reaper's personal hound."

I rubbed my forehead. "Please don't call him that. Not unless you want me dead of secondhand embarrassment."

Uriel reached up and tapped the bare bulb in the ceiling fixture until it stopped buzzing. "You've been alive a long time, as far as humans understand time."

"Just over a hundred years," I agreed.

"In that those years, you once encountered a serial killer called the Walking Man, yes? He worked the Midwest in the 1940s. Kansas, Nebraska . . . all those flat places where everything looks the same."

My breathing slowed as my heart rate picked up, just another defense mechanism you pick up when you live in a world where the slightest display of fear is an invitation to be beaten, or worse. "Yeah," I said softly. "I know all about him."

"Well, he's back," Uriel said, pulling open the restroom door. "And since you're one of the few people to see him and live to tell about it, I'd like you to look into it. For all our sakes."

I lunged forward and slammed the door shut again. Uriel lifted one of his perfect eyebrows. "Problem?"

"You can't just drop that bombshell and walk away," I said, bracing the door with my good arm.

"I don't see the problem," Uriel said. "Please let me out. I feel like a thousand showers can't erase the miasma I've picked up in this bathroom."

"You know damn good and well there's more to the Walking Man than a scary hitchhiker on the side of the road who likes to hack up motorists," I said. My fast heartbeat was making my voice sound high and hysterical, and I gulped down a deep breath. "And if you know that then why the hell are you messing around with him? Leave him in Tartarus where he belongs."

"I am 'messing with' him as you say because the Walking Man

in fact escaped from Tartarus and I'd dearly like him back." Uriel fixed me with his clear, unreadable gaze. His eyes weren't dead, like a demon's, but they missed human by a mile. It was like staring at the surface of a pond that never moved.

"Hundreds of human souls did a runner when Lilith broke that place open. If you want me to help, be honest with me, because I figured out that the Walking Man wasn't human a long time ago." Even saying it out loud filled me with shivers all over again, like we were standing back out in the cold.

Uriel sighed. "Lilith packed Tartarus so full of human souls partly to power the engines of Hell, and partly to obscure that which isn't . . . exactly mortal, shall we say?"

"She always liked to have eight or nine knives ready to stab you in the back," I agreed. "So she hides the Walking Man in among the riffraff for . . . what? Her own personal amusement? If you're so worried," I said, "you must know what he is."

I waited, not breathing, to see if Uriel had the answer, not at all sure I wanted it.

"There are parts of Tartarus so deep that even I don't know about them," he said. "Whatever he is, he doesn't need to be walking around here on earth."

"For once we agree on something," I said. Uriel cocked his head.

"May I exit now?"

I got out of his way. "Go nuts."

Uriel stepped out, the door swinging back in my face. When I shoved it open again he was gone, like I tried to blink the exhaustion out of my eyes and when I opened them he'd vanished, like he'd never been there.

The whiskey hadn't helped with the whole wanting to sleep for months thing, and I started for the parking lot. Even Uriel's bad news couldn't put a dent in the fatigue weighing me down.

Healing up from catastrophic injuries always took it out of me too, which is why the person waiting in the shadow of the snow-bank outside was able to step behind me and slide a hand over my mouth.

I didn't scream, just opened my jaw wider and bit down, my teeth tearing through flesh and hitting bone. Blood spurted, the hot red kind that meant whatever had hold of me was something with a beating heart. Whoever it was let out a surprised grunt, but they didn't let go. We stumbled backward into the bulwark of snow, me throwing an elbow into their gut that did absolutely no good. I felt the sting of a needle in my neck, and whatever the syringe held was even colder than the air around us. Ice spread through my veins, and everything was still and cold and white, silent as freshly fallen snow.

CHAPTER

3

|||||||||||||||||||||||||||||||||||||||||||||||||||||||||||||||||||||||||||||

BUCHENWALD CONCENTRATION CAMP
DECEMBER 1944

Even the snow was gray. Not turned gray by the churned mud beneath it, crisscrossed by boots and jeeps until it was a vast plain of frozen sludge. It was like the flakes fell from the sky already muted and stained. In this place, even the snow had given up.

I'd begged Gary not to send me. Give me a dirty trench in a French farmer's field, a clear night in London with rockets falling— even the ghettos packed wall to wall with humanity, crushed together by sandbags and barbed wire, spotlights and dogs, were preferable to this. Gary had just smirked at me, brushing a piece of lint off his vest. "We all have our duties, Ava. There's a war on."

Wilson chuckled at me, downing his fifth or seventh pint. Gary favored a rickety little pub in Knightsbridge for handing out assignments, which were fast and furious these days—every third-rate warlock who could draw a halfway decent summoning spell was itching to sell his soul to rake in more power before it all came crashing down.

"Not for much longer," I muttered. Unlike most of the hounds, I occasionally glanced at a newspaper. The Third Army was pushing across the Rhine and deep into Nazi territory, like a knife blade sliding closer to your heart inch by inch. Soon enough, all those German warlocks and Italian *brujeria* begging Gary to trade with them were going to turn off like a faucet. I kind of hoped I was around when it happened, just to watch that tight little smirk fall off his face.

"All the more reason to collect while we can. Herr Colonel Kubler has had a nice run with the bargain he made." He flipped his ledger shut and stood up, fixing his tie in the mirror behind the pub's bar. "Need I remind you that if he meets his end by bullet or rope before I can collect, then I get nothing?"

I looked down at my shoes. They were covered in dust from the last time we'd all had to dash for the nearest bomb shelter. We were resilient compared to the people who huddled all around us, but nobody, including Gary, wanted to end up on the wrong end of a V-2. "No," I murmured.

Gary smacked me on the rear with a ledger as he gestured to Wilson, who slammed down his glass and grabbed Gary's coat, scurrying after him like a pedigreed terrier. "Good girl," he said. "Enjoy your time with the master race."

I fought the urge not to itch all over as I slogged through the gray, slushy snow, keeping my head down. I'd snagged the uniform from one of the bicycle couriers who spent all day pedaling between the vast acres of the camp complex, their leather satchels full of communiqués and cables for the officers. The bicycle courier herself was in her underwear somewhere south of the complex. If she were lucky, maybe somebody from the town out of sight behind the curtain of snow would pick her up. If she wasn't lucky, well. Not my problem. Her uniform, crisp and spotless though it was, was made of wool that itched like fire ants and smelled like a wet dog.

Colonel Kubler was a science officer. That much I'd found out from going through the duty rosters in his camp section. The low block of buildings was set off from the others, behind its own fence. The guard shivering outside the gate barely looked at me before waving me through. I tried not to look around either. If I let myself see the filth, smell the overwhelming stench that rolled out from the deep trenches gashed in the earth even though everything around me was frozen, see the hunched, skeletal forms in pale uniforms that had been striped at some point in the distant past, I knew I wouldn't be able to move. I'd stand there paralyzed while the hound took over, like a moth transfixed by an open furnace. Then nobody would be safe, and the people who didn't deserve it would be food the same as the uniformed Germans in the building I stepped into, stamping the snow off my feet.

No brow-shirted guard jumped up to greet me, which was a little odd. The closer the Americans and the Red Army got, the jumpier these assholes became. This Colonel Kubler would never have promised his soul to a reaper even a year ago, but now the writing was on the wall. The war wasn't going to last, and when it was over the warlock who made the best deal would be the only one left standing.

"Hello?" I called out cautiously. My German was for shit but it wasn't like I was here to take notes. Hello, good-bye, the reaper you gave your soul to says it's time to pay up—that about did the trick for the Nazi's mother tongue.

The whole place was quiet, which in and of itself made me shiver a little. These places were scream factories, and even when they didn't have a fresh crop of prisoners inside they bustled with normal everyday sounds of a field hospital.

I looked up at a small creaking sound and saw the wire-caged light over my head swinging gently back and forth, like a stiff breeze had just passed by.

Nothing would have made me happier than to turn tail and not stop until I was back across the Rhine, but Gary would be furious and if nothing else, this Kubler deserved to have his soul pulled out through his nose. A lot of warlocks thought it was possible to cheat a reaper, and I never got tired of seeing the looks on the faces of the ones who really had it coming when I darkened their door.

"Herr Kubler?" I called, starting down the hall. Still quiet, just me and the buzzing lights and the soft drip, drip, drip of melting snow off my overcoat. "Hello?"

"They've gone."

I spun to face the open door and the soft voice emanating. Inside was a small office that looked like a tornado had touched down. Colonel Kubler didn't look nearly as impressive as the photo Gary had shown me. Without the black SS uniform and the hat to hide his bald spot, he looked like any other skinny old man who probably touched your arm a few times too often when he talked to you and spent half the time trying to sneak glances down your blouse.

I let the leather satchel slide out of my hand, keeping my grip on the brushed steel knife I'd used to pin down stray souls ever since I came to as a hellhound, in the mud at Gary's feet. He'd leaned down and held out his hand and told me I didn't have to die. And like an idiot, I let him pull me up.

"Lucky I'm not here for anyone else," I said. Kubler blinked at me when I switched to English, but then he did as well, his voice coarse and reedy as a broom scratching across a floor.

"They are still here," he whispered. "But they have all gone."

"Much as I'd love to spend my time chatting, I think we both know why I'm here," I said. "You are way overdue on the deal you signed. You going to come quietly?"

Kubler started to laugh—at least I thought he was laughing. When it turned to a rusty cough, and a spray of bright red dusted his white lapels, I took a step closer, squinting in the flickering light.

"Alas." Kubler favored me with a bloody grin. "A bullet," he said. "Meant for another. But you have missed your chance all the same. I am not long for this world, and my soul remains my own."

He started to laugh again, until I crouched down and peeled back his lab coat, revealing the starburst of blood and powder burn in his side just above his hip bone. "Gut shot?" I said. Kubler gasped, his neck twisting a little in pain.

"What would you know about it?"

"I'm not a doctor like you," I said, pulling the knife from its leather case. The case was soft and smooth under my fingers, even though the leather was mottled and dark from being in my bag, my back pocket or tucked against my skin for over twenty years. "But I have been around a lot of dying people, and gunshot wounds are usually quick."

Kubler tried to back up, but he was trapped between his bookcase and his desk. A few files slithered off the top, raining onionskin paper around us that landed and sopped up his blood. "That is unless you take a slug in the guts," I said. "Then it can take hours. Worse if you rupture the intestines. Then you can go septic waiting to die. I've heard the pain is indescribable. But that's not the point. The point is, it takes hours."

I leaned in, pressing my free hand against Kubler's wound. He let out an animal cry, but I was stronger than him and his struggling didn't do much more than smear blood up to my wrist. "Lucky for you, I've got all day."

He started to laugh at me, and coughed up blood. A droplet landed in my eye, staining half my vision red. "My soul remains my own. Yours, I'm not so sure about."

"Me neither," I said, sitting cross-legged and tapping the knife blade against Kubler's metal desk. He grimaced at me.

"*Vas?*"

"Oh, I'm waiting," I said, tapping out the beat from "In the Mood". "As long as I stick you before you expire, I still collect. But I think we can afford to wait a little longer."

For the first time, Kubler's face slackened. He was yellow, in the whites of his eyes and the pale skin around his lips. The bullet must have nicked his liver. "You cannot . . . you would torture me?"

I shrugged. A clock was ticking somewhere, and Kubler's rusty wheezing filled up the space between us. He glared at me, his eyes burning, but he could barely keep his eyes open.

"You think Hell will be a misery for me?" he gasped finally. "I am *in* Hell. Stuck in this place, with the trenches full of animal corpses—the living ones and their stink . . . the cow mewlings and screamings . . . after this place, Hell will be a comfort."

All at once, our little waiting game got tiresome. "Those *people* you keep out there in the mud and the shit," I said quietly, "will have the comfort of knowing that they'll never have to see your face again, because you died like a coward begging for the pain to stop. And those trenches you throw their bodies into were a hundred times too good for your corpse."

I leaned forward and stuck the knife between his ribs. I aimed up and into his heart, shuddering as the wasted, tattered thing that was all that left of most warlock's souls flowed into the knife. "And by the way, I've seen Hell," I whispered in Kubler's ear as he groaned. "They still have a few surprises waiting for you."

The blade glowed for a few seconds, like I'd heated it over an open flame, and then quieted.

I shoved the knife back into its case and stood, swiping the last of Kubler's blood off my face. The whole hospital was still eerily silent, more like a morgue than a medical center. Nothing good happened in this place. Nothing good had set foot on this ground in a long, long time.

I stepped into the hall, heading back the way I came. I couldn't wait to be out of this place. It was one of the few times since Gary had found me that I was actually glad I wasn't a human being anymore. Warlocks could do plenty of depraved shit to each other, but there was something so impassive about the camp and the German personnel in it. They were just people, just going about their job like it was any other slightly inconvenient, grimy assignment. I didn't think the girl whose uniform I'd stolen would have shown any more emotion if she'd worked collecting garbage. This place must have been a dream job for a necromancer like Kubler—all the bodies he could want and then some. But there should be bustling Teutonic efficiency, not silence and chaos. Nobody had even investigated Kubler's cries.

Close enough to the door to feel icy wind around my ankles, I heard a scraping sound behind me. I made myself turn around slow, like I was only curious, and I belonged here. I didn't need a passel of Nazis on my tail on top of everything else.

The girl was also wearing a uniform, canvas that had at some point been crisp and white. She even had one of those little nurse's caps hanging askew from her rumpled curls.

I paused, waiting for her to speak first. That's another important trick of blending in where you're not supposed to be—don't be the chatterbox.

"Where . . . is he?" she ground out. I squinted to get a better look at her in the flickering electricity. Red spilled down the front of her uniform like she'd dumped a glass of punch on herself, and her skin was so white it gave her uniform a run for its money. She took a fast step toward me, and I realized what the whispering sound had been. She was wearing only one shoe. The stocking on her bare foot was ripped and bloody, bruised toes leaving little rusty half-moons on the dirty floor.

There's a misconception about predators, that we're all created equal. But that's not true at all—some stay on top of the food chain being the baddest on the block, but the truly canny ones, the survivors, learn how to tell when they're outgunned and beat a retreat, staying alive until they wear you down and pounce.

The nurse wasn't bloody because she was sick or someone had beaten the shit out of her. She wasn't limping toward me because she needed help. Her dime-size pupils and the red foam leaking from the corner of her mouth told me everything I needed to know, and that thing was *Run for your life*.

I shot my gaze sideways, down a corridor lined with swinging doors, little round windows like the kind on submarines glowing from within. Light was a good sign. There might be humans down there I could use as roadblocks.

The limping nurse hissed at me. We locked eyes in that split second of violent calculus that happens when a lion meets an antelope. Then I turned and ran, and she chased me, a guttural scream ripping out of her throat.

I smacked at a few door handles as I ran past, but they were all locked. The nurse was snapping at my heels by the time one gave and I shoved inside, slamming the door in her snarling face. The handle rattled and banged. She wasn't giving up.

I was inside some kind of exam room, all the instruments neatly laid out on a tray and a tilting white table shining under a bare bulb. The nurse screamed on the other side of the door, beating the flats of her hands on the metal.

"Simmer down, lady," I muttered, yanking open drawers and cabinets to try to find something to defend myself with. The little glass vials on the shelf were all in German, and I picked one with a skull and crossbones printed on the label, fingers shaking a bit as I fumbled a syringe. Whatever was wrong with that nurse, I wanted to be far away from this place when it spread.

I heard a creak behind me, a rusty hinge bending, and before I could turn, my skull exploded into a thousand pieces of glass. I was knocked out so fast I didn't even feel myself fall.

I was immobile when I came to, and I really hoped it wasn't because I'd had my brains bashed hard enough to paralyze me. I moved my arms and legs, feeling hard leather straps holding me down, cold metal under my back and aching head. I thrashed against the restraints and managed to bruise my wrists and ankles for my trouble. Of all the places you want to find yourself tied down, a Nazi hospital isn't top of anyone's list.

"Quiet." The voice came from beyond my field of vision, which admittedly was about as crisp and clear as a dirty windshield on a rainy night. Everything was blurry, and every time I tried to move my eyes my vision slipped sideways.

"Ungh," I said to the invisible voice.

"Please," it replied. "I apologize for the pain but you must be quiet."

I lay back against the cold table, feeling my heart thudding. "I hate to break it to you, but if your plan is to torture me quietly that's not going to work out."

"Nothing could be further from my mind," the voice said. It was male, clipped dry syllables that came from somewhere in this neck of the woods, but not the immediate neighborhood. Not a German. Maybe a neighbor.

"Then why all this?" I said. Raising my head up felt like somebody had taken a hammer to the side of my skull, but I did it all the same. A face swam into view. He was painfully thin, sallow in the dim light, black hair swept back from a high forehead. He looked down at me without blinking.

"I thought you were a German at first," he said, indicating my uniform. "Then I thought you might be sick."

"Sick like I'm covered in blood and chasing folks looking for more?" I asked. He grimaced.

"I'm sorry I hit you," he said. "You are an American?"

"Born and raised," I said, relaxing into the dizzy waves bearing me up. Born and raised and died and was born again as a monster was just long-winded.

He moved away and came back to put a cold cloth across my forehead, then undid all his good work by shining a light into my eyes. It felt like being sliced across the face with a butcher knife. "Jesus!" I snapped. "Do you mind?"

"You have a concussion," he said.

"You really are Sherlock Holmes," I sighed. "What did you hit me with?"

"A bedpan."

I glared at him. "Better and better."

He leaned over me to unbuckle my straps. He was wearing a plain white shirt, not the ragged pajamas most of the prisoners in the camp had to make do with, but it was ancient, yellow at the armpits and collar. His pants weren't any better, worn at the knees and so filthy they were stiff. "Are you a POW?" he asked. "I have not met any female GIs. The men they keep far away, in a satellite camp with the Russians."

"I'm not a prisoner," I said.

"Then you are a spy," he said, nodding to himself. "And you could not have chosen a worse time to slip inside these fences."

"And what about you?" I said, sitting up and feeling the back of my head. It was tender and a little bloody, but I was basically whole.

"I am a doctor," he said. "They brought me here and made me assist the staff with procedures." He held up his hands, turning the long fingers this way and that. "There are few skilled surgeons in the camps. Most are at the front lines or sitting on their fat asses in Berlin, ducking bombs and drinking tea."

Something crashed out in the hall, and I watched the doctor's whole body get taut. "Are we safe in here?" I said.

"For now," he murmured. "Until they find a way to open that door."

"And 'they' would be . . . ?" I lifted an eyebrow. He sighed, running water over his hands and forearms to get rid of the speckles of what I assumed was my blood.

"One of the reasons I was brought here."

I saw the plain tattoo just above his wrist bone, spidery letters and numbers inked out in a hurry. My head pounded again. "Where's your family?"

"Gone," he said. "Except for my daughter. We sent her to England ahead of the invasion. I have not seen her in four years." He turned away, wiping his hands on the same cloth he'd pressed on me.

"And they force you to operate on people?" I said, looking back at the door. From somewhere beyond the flat metal painted with bubbling white paint I heard a shrill scream, cut short like the voice's owner had run into a wall.

"Oh no." The doctor let out a small laugh, bitter as hemlock. "I only assist, clean up, occasionally perform autopsies. The Wehrmacht would never let a filthy *Juden* put his hands on them, especially if those held a scalpel."

"I'm Ava," I said impulsively, sticking out my own hand. I usually made a point to stay away from people at all costs, but I had a feeling that without this guy I was pretty much lunch meat anyway.

"Jacob," he said. "Dr. Jacob Gottlieb."

"Where are you from?" I said. I slid off the table and tried standing. The ground rolled under me, but soft swells, like I was on the deck of an ocean liner. I could handle it. I'd had more trouble walking after a long night of bourbon sours and cheap cigarettes than from Jacob's little Babe Ruth impression with my head.

"Krakow," he said. "I was a chief surgeon. Youngest at my hospital."

"Tennessee," I said. "I was a bootlegger's apprentice. My grandmother was very proud."

Jacob gave that dry laugh again. "Won't she be worried about you, here among the enemy?"

"She's dead," I said. "And she never worried much when she wasn't."

We both jumped when someone banged on the door, and kept banging. Not the frantic, hungry pounding of the nurse but the desperate hammering of a person whose brain was still working and was running on sheer terror.

I glanced at Jacob, who'd grabbed up his bedpan again. "We don't have to open the door."

His jaw knotted and I waited. I wasn't particularly inclined to open up to whoever was out there. If they were running around free, chances were they weren't in the same boat as Jacob but were wearing this uniform voluntarily.

"Jacob," I said as the banging increased, a man's voice pleading in German to be let in. "Really. I'm happy to leave us locked up tight."

He sighed and lowered the bedpan. "I can't. No matter how much they've taken from me here I'm still a doctor."

He pulled back the bolt and spun the handle. I waited, looking into the blackness as the door swung open.

CHAPTER

4

I came to with the cold water snap of fear, my animal brain driving me into consciousness whether I liked it or not. It was dark, the kind of deep velvety black you only find in a windowless room. I took in a damp, slightly musty scent like an old wool blanket over my face, and the almost claustrophobic warmth, and did the mental math that arrived at *basement*. Old, too, judging from the thump and grind of a boiler heating things to sweat lodge levels.

My arms were suspended over my head, wrists wrapped in some kind of chain. The chain forced me to stand on tiptoe, soles of my boots rasping against the concrete as I struggled for purchase.

"Leo?" I whispered. My throat was hot and close from disuse. My head pounded, and even though it was dark, lazy white pinwheels spun in front of my eyes. I shut them again and fought a hot spurt of vomit trying to climb its way out of my stomach.

A light snapped on, one of those big caged bulbs that buzz and snap like a hive of bees. It didn't do my head any favors, but if they were watching me at least I'd get some answers.

The boiler room door swung open and a man in a suit stepped it. He didn't wear a suit the way Leo did, all black, understated, thin tie, jacket just a little wrinkled at the edges because he was comfortable in it. This guy wore his blue wool blend with pinstripes and gold cuff links the way some guys wear a gold chain with a bunch of diamonds—to show off.

I'd known a lot of guys like him, and I'd hated every last one of them.

"Comfortable?" the man asked, and when he smiled I figured out why my stomach was churning from more than the ketamine hangover. He was a reaper. Same plastic smile, same too-perfect face, same hair that looked like a cheap wig.

"I'm fantastic," I said, rattling the chain with my numb arms. "How did you know this was my favorite stress position?"

"I apologize," he said. "But until we've figured out a few things you understand we have to be careful."

"I understand nothing," I said, "including where I am, who you are, or who told you that tie was a flattering color."

He touched the bright blue and gold striped silk reflexively, and favored me with a look like he'd just smelled garbage on a hot day. "Gary always said you were a handful."

"Gary's dead," I snapped. "You here to get payback? If you are can you just go ahead with the waterboarding and the car batteries or whatever and save the preamble?"

While we'd been having our chat I'd been testing out the chains. They were stronger than I was, and wrapped around an I-beam that was equally strong. The room was empty except for a few old desks and chairs piled in a corner and a grimy safety poster dated 1967 hanging next to the huge round hatch that led to the innards of the boiler.

"I'm not supposed to do anything but talk to you," the reaper said. He tilted his head slightly. "I'm Owen. Can we clear up a few things?"

"Where's Leo?" I said, trying to keep my feet on the floor.

"Careful," Owen said, indicating a ring of black dust around my prison with a shiny patent leather shoe. "Those are black iron shavings."

I sighed. "That supposed to mean something?"

A smile chased over his thin mouth before he straightened his tie again. "I forgot that Gary liked to keep his dogs . . . insulated, shall we say." He toed the pile with his other foot. "Black iron shavings repel hellhounds and other types that were, shall we say, formerly human. Stay in your electric fence and we won't have a problem."

"Oh, you already have a problem," I said, rattling the chain for good measure. "Bigger than you know."

"I'll keep that in mind," Owen said.

"Why am I here?" I said. "*Where* am I?"

"You're at Headquarters," Owen said, and the way his slick Trust-Me-I'm-Important voice dropped I could hear the capital *H*. "Minneapolis. As to why, you know why. You and that fellow you ride with have been making some big claims. Claims you have no business making, and it's my job to get to the bottom of all this nonsense."

I shut my eyes and inhaled, the smell in the air almost making me choke. "I'm not the one that's been saying anything. This isn't Leo's fault either."

Owen reached up and patted my face. I thought about biting him. "It's adorable that you're defending him. He hasn't been nearly that complimentary about you. In fact, he's barely spoken."

He went to the door and opened it, showing me a glimpse of dank hallway. From far away, wavering through the low-ceilinged corridors, I heard a scream. Owen cocked his head. "Looks like he's got something to say now, though. Think about what I've said, dog, and you may save yourself some pain."

"You need to let me go," I blurted. "You don't know what's going on here and you're gonna make things really bad."

"Good doggy," Owen said grinning as he pulled the door shut. "Stay."

"Come on," I breathed as I was plunged into the dark again. "Stupid bastard," I said to nothing as I tugged hard at the chain. Owen was like all the reapers—arrogant enough to think nothing could hurt them and dumb enough to believe that was actually true.

I wrapped one fist around the chain and took a deep breath. Even though I was what you'd call durable, I was hardly invincible, and this part always sucked. I held my breath and jammed the base of my left thumb hard against the chain, pushing until I saw stars and the joint popped out of true. I bit down hard as I folded my thumb under my other four fingers and slid the whole mess free of the chain. I bent double as I pushed my thumb back where it should be and managed to only let out a tiny, ladylike scream.

And then I did it with my other hand.

I didn't move any further, since I didn't want to get shocked to shit by some magical fire line that Gary had never bothered to tell me about. I tried to quiet myself, to think like Leo. He'd know what to do if he was in this room, and not somewhere down the hall getting screams yanked out of him one fingernail at a time.

He wouldn't panic, because Leo never panicked. He never showed fear. I took a shaky breath and made myself stand up and work the cramps out of my arms and back from being hung up in the chain. I didn't need Leo to save me. I'd survived this long, survived Lilith, survived Gary. I could get us both out of here.

If I could just get past this damn barrier.

"Watching you try to think is painful," a voice said, and a small flame flared in the dark, sparking the end of a cigarette. Uriel exhaled and approached the line, grinning at me.

"It took you fucking long enough," I snapped, massaging my thumbs. Uriel glanced up and the light came back on, casting its sickly, gout-colored light. It did nothing to diminish the glow that always seemed to wrap around the angel, even in the darkest, most filthy places on Earth.

"Looks like you and I have more to talk about," he said, gesturing with his cigarette.

"Yeah," I said. "Like you're an angel who smokes."

"I like smoking," Uriel said. "It helps with the smell in places like this. As to this little tableau, I don't think you want that idiot with the bad tie knowing you have an angel in your pocket. I'm only here because I need you to not die until our business is complete."

"I can take care of Owen," I said. "But I can't get out of this room, so how about you flap your wings and turn around three times or whatever it is you do and break this spell?"

Uriel laughed and then reached into the inside pocket of his suit, tossing me a lighter. "Ava, these reapers have been cut off from the Pit for over a century, thanks to Lilith and your old buddy Gary. Do you really think if you could repel hellhounds with something you can find on the floor of a metal shop nobody would know about it?"

I hung my head, glad the angel couldn't see my face turn red. Uriel watched me step over the line of iron filings on the floor and smiled approvingly. "What's the lighter for?" I asked. He exhaled smoke from his nose and smiled.

"Consider it divine intervention."

The lightbulb hissed again and Uriel was gone. I tested the door, which wasn't locked. That was reapers for you—so convinced they were better than the hounds they didn't even bother to think we could figure out doorknobs.

I stepped out into the hallway, easing the doors shut with a soft click. No reason to make myself an even easier target for Owen and his buddies.

The screaming had stopped, and I felt a twist in my stomach. I didn't know if Leo *could* be dead again, and I didn't want to find out.

Thick metal doors like what I'd been locked behind were recessed into even thicker walls as the hall went on, each door marked with the symbol for a fallout shelter, the yellow faded to almost white. Knocking steam pipes ran along the ceiling over my head and water swished through thin copper lines, like I was inside some kind of vast circulatory system, the belly of a living, breathing beast.

Footsteps rang out and I shrank myself into one of the door-ways, hunching up against the cement. A female reaper wearing a deep red dress and shoes with heels sharp enough to puncture whatever neck she was standing on opened the next door, giving me a brief glimpse of a white-tiled shower room, at least four more reapers milling around, and a figure strapped into a chair in the middle of the floor. Leo's shirt had been pulled open to show a swath of his heavily tattooed chest, and his face was swollen and bruised on one side.

I fell back again as the door slammed shut. How the hell was I supposed to take out five reapers in an enclosed space? I'd barely managed to get the jump on Gary, and I'd had help. I'd also had fangs and claws on my side and that wasn't happening while I was running on no sleep and had what felt like a gallon of horse tran-quilizer working its way out of my system.

I wanted to punch the door I was standing against, but breaking my fist wouldn't help me, or Leo. I squeezed Uriel's lighter hard enough to leave an imprint on my palm, letting the sting even me out and make me focus. The door was marked BUILDING MANAGER, and I tried it. This place was ancient, but maybe there would at least be a broom handle or something in there I could arm myself with, since the reapers had taken everything from my knife to my hairbrush.

The office was just as dusty and gross as the rest of the basement, but the rusted metal shelves were a treasure trove for a hellhound disarmed and down on her luck. I swept the ancient lightbulbs and a stack of nudie mags off the shelves as I fumbled through the tool kit. I grabbed the longest screwdriver and shoved it up my sleeve and tucked a box cutter in my back pocket. An old metal thermos sat next to the toolbox and I grabbed it and an armload of sloshing chemical bottles.

People are scared of reapers and things like them. It's a survival instinct as old as walking upright—steer clear of the things in the dark. They're hungry and strong and they can't be hurt. But if you're already in the dark, if you have to live there too, you learn that monsters can bleed just like the rest of us.

I stepped out of the building manager's office, holding the thermos in one hand and Uriel's lighter in the other. I carried the rusty bucket I'd found in the corner, flipped it over, and stood on it, flicking the wheel until a flame sprouted. Holding it to the star-shaped head of the sprinkler, I really hoped that the city of Minneapolis was on top of their fire safety inspections.

For a sick heartbeat, nothing happened. Then I was rewarded with a spurt of water in my face and the tired honking of a fire alarm somewhere on an upper floor of whatever Cold War rock pile I was in.

The first reaper to come out the door was a pudgy guy in a polo shirt and jeans. He could have been someone's dad on the way to pick them up from practice, except for the dead-eyed fury on his face. I slipped the screwdriver from my sleeve and popped him on the bridge of the nose with the handle as he lunged at me. While he was moaning and grabbing at his crushed face I flipped the screwdriver around and jammed it into his shoulder, slipping it under the collarbone and taking his arm out of commission when I hit the tendon.

Dad Reaper's buddy was fast on his heels, and I grabbed up the bucket as the water streamed around us, swinging it in a wide arc. He threw up an arm to block me, but the water pooling around our feet made him slip and I didn't miss again. The rusty metal left a nasty gash in his temple. "Hope you got your shots," I muttered as I shoved open the door to the shower room. "Leo, hold your breath!" I shouted into the chaos inside, and then tossed the thermos at the feet of a trio of shocked reapers.

Stick around for almost a century, and you learn a lot. Like how some of the most noxious stuff on earth can be mixed up with just a few household cleaners. The woman in the dress came first, choking and swiping at her eyes and mouth as she stumbled into the hall. Greasy fingers of smoke warred with the sprinklers in the hall. I pulled up the rag I'd found in the building manager's office around my nose and mouth and dove into the mess inside the shower room.

Leo was sitting with his chin tucked against his chest, trying not to breathe. His eyes were watering and the line around his lips was turning white. I pulled out the box cutter and sliced at the thick layer of tape holding his wrists and ankles in place. It was getting hard for me to see now, and every time I tried to breathe it felt like a small but very angry horse kicking me in the chest.

"What did you do?" Leo wheezed as I helped him up. He leaned on me hard as we stumbled through the gathering water toward a blurry red square that I really hoped was an exit sign.

"Saved your ass," I said as we shouldered through a heavy door and into a blast of air that was both breathable and so cold I felt the sweat and sprinkler water on my face crystallize. "You're welcome, by the way." Outside, we both collapsed in a dirty snowbank. Gotta love Minneapolis in the dead of winter. Cars swept by in two fast lanes throwing up sand and more snow. We were in one of those industrial wastelands where nothing except warehouses, strip clubs, and bodegas stays in business. One of each sat across the street, complimentary neon offering a place to get a payday advance and a gaggle of XXX GIRLS to blow it on.

Leo coughed, and then leaned over and vomited into the snow, flopping back with a low moan when he was done. "What the hell, Ava? I lie down at that motel hoping for a nap, maybe a little vodka and a hand job to ease the pain of going through a fiery car wreck, and I wake up tied to a chair in Satan's locker room."

"You're pushing it with the hand job," I said. "And at least you didn't wake up hanging from the ceiling being yapped at by the Hellspawn's answer to Gordon Gekko."

Leo's face hardened, underneath the bruises and the crescent-shaped cut beside his eyebrow where someone wearing a ring had hit him. Owen was wearing a big crop of chintzy gold rings, I remembered.

"Did they hurt you?" Leo asked. I shrugged.

"Nothing a few dozen Valium, a hot bath, and a bourbon won't cure."

He shook his head, nostrils flaring. "I'm going to kill every last motherfucker in that place. This was my favorite shirt."

I stood up, brushing wet snow off my legs and butt, and offered a hand to Leo. "You have a dozen white shirts."

"Yeah," he said, accepting my hand. "And this one was my favorite."

Leo's weight almost knocked me back into the snowbank. He grunted when he leaned on me, and I could tell a couple of his ribs were broken. "We can't stay out here," I said. The wind cutting between the dark buildings around us made my teeth rattle. I aimed Leo at the intersection, punching the crosswalk button with my free hand.

"I'm fine," he insisted. "Just give me a minute to get myself together."

"Freezing to death for the second time in two days is not going to help us," I said. "Now get your stubborn ass indoors."

Leo grinned at me. "Yes ma'am," he said. Even with the bloody mess the reapers had made of his face, I felt myself smiling back.

I was headed for the strip club—at least they had booze in there—when a beater pulled up to the curb, spewing black smoke and Motown. The driver threw open the passenger door. "Get in!" she shouted.

Across the highway, I saw the first signs of movement outside the big gray box that the reapers called home. I nodded at Leo and helped him onto the big front seat. The inside of the car was as wide and plush as a champagne booth in the strip joint behind us, and I barely got the door shut before the driver hit the gas.

"You don't want to be standing there when they get their act together," she said. "Trust me."

"*They* would be . . ." I said, trying to gauge whose car we'd just gotten into.

"Reapers, stupid." The driver pressed her foot down to the floor, roaring through corridors of snow punctuated by streetlights and burned-out warehouses. Aside from the eye shine of the occasional bum or very, very determined hooker, we were alone in the blackout. "Well, some of the reapers. Who d'you think?"

"The Easter Bunny, maybe," I said, and she shot me a glare.

"Guess you think you're pretty funny."

I returned the look. "Guess I do."

"Ladies," Leo muttered, his voice gravelly with pain. "Can we keep it down to a dull roar?"

The driver shook her head, dislodging a few pitch-colored strands from her short Mohawk. They fell in her face and she huffed angrily. "Typical. I risk my ass to get you out of there and y'all are just as pathetic as the rest of us."

"The only thing you're risking now is a busted axle." I winced as the car bounced over a mound of dirty ice cast off a truck tire.

"You just hush until I make sure none of those suits is following us," she snapped. We drove around for another twenty minutes, taking random turns through the wasteland and finally getting on the interstate, heading north.

"Are we being kidnapped?" I said. "Surprise party? Where are you taking us?"

"He's the one, right?" the driver said. Her eyes never left the road, and her knuckles were so tight on the wheel I could see the bones. "The new Grim Reaper?"

"I sure hope so," I said, watching as the speedometer climbed past 70. She showed me her teeth in that masking smile that never really hides fear.

"Me too."

"So where are we going?" I asked again, trying for a softer approach. She was so twigged I was half-scared we'd go flying off the shoulder and end up in a snowbank until some unfortunate state trooper found us come spring.

"Safe house," she said. "The empty suits at Headquarters might not have been happy to see you, but we are." She turned her eyes to me, and there was white all the way around. "We all are."

CHAPTER

5

Jacob was the one who finally moved, pulling the door in a swift motion and hopping back. A sobbing man fell into the room, blood splashing the front of his brown uniform like a sash on a beauty queen.

I didn't move until Jacob slammed and locked the door again; then I nudged the sobbing man with my foot. "You know him?"

Jacob nodded. "He's a soldier. He's a bad soldier. That's why they keep him here sitting at a little desk signing the party members in and out."

I kicked the soldier again. "Stop crying!"

He clearly didn't speak English, but the kick got the message across. He gulped and looked up at me, looked to Jacob. "*Wer ist sie?*"

"All right," I said, going back to my search of the drawers and cabinets for anything I could use against what was happening outside. "What's with those people outside? The short version."

Jacob was bent over, examining the man in the uniform. He wasn't really a man, I saw as he sat shaking, his close-cropped head in his hands. He couldn't have been more than seventeen or eighteen. A couple of months ago he'd probably been happily heiling his way through a Hitler Youth meeting, with no idea that the Fatherland was being crushed around him like a tin can in a vise.

"How about you give *me* the short version?" Jacob said, turning the man's head from side to side and shining a small light into his eyes. The soldier flinched, and Jacob squeezed harder until he stopped struggling. "I have been here for two years and never seen an American who wasn't a prisoner at death's door, and now that you are here, everything is going to Hell."

"There are no scalpels in this place?" I demanded, deciding to ignore his comment. I tossed the instrument tray to the floor. It clanged, and the soldier whimpered. "Not even a damn pair of scissors?"

"They lock up the instruments so we don't steal them," Jacob said mildly. "Who are you, really? Why are you here?"

He reached for gauze and a needle and thread, gesturing at the soldier's arm. "Roll up your sleeve."

The soldier shook his head violently. "*Nr. Ich werde nicht von einem Tier genäht werden . . .*"

"Hey!" I drew back my foot. "You want one that actually hurts? Shut your Nazi trap and let the good doctor work."

Jacob's mouth twisted into an almost smile as he poured disinfectant on the soldier's wound, wringing another shriek out of his thin, bloodless mouth. "You are a liar, but I confess I like you. What is your name?"

"Ava," I said. "Like Gardner, not Braun."

"One of those dying prisoners was the first," he said. "An American. Many of them arrive sick, and Kubler uses most as fodder for the anatomy lab, or for his hypothermia tests. But this man was different. He was . . ." Jacob trailed off, his eyes narrowing as the dimensions of the soldier's wound became clear.

"Now, I'm not a doctor like you," I said as the twin half-moons of purple, bloody squares dribbled a little fresh blood, "but that's a human bite mark."

Jacob hissed something under his breath, jumping back from the soldier as the man bared his own teeth in a stiff, bloody grin. His gums were bleeding, his nose, even his eyes were pooling with runny red tears. He let out a long croak, unfolding from the floor like he was spring-loaded.

Jacob wasn't fast enough. Nobody who was only human would have been. The soldier grabbed him by the throat and they both crashed into the exam table, Jacob ramming the thick roll of gauze into the soldier's snapping jaws before they could close on his neck or his face.

"They change!" he shouted as the soldier let out an anguished roar, a welt of thick, black blood oozing from his mouth as he vomited. "The doctors that the GI attacked, and now—"

He trailed off as I landed on the soldier from behind, wrapping one arm around his neck. I couldn't use the knife, even now. It held Kubler's soul, and if I didn't come back with that, I might as well just leave myself for whatever was outside the doors.

The soldier jolted upright, swinging around and trying to shake me off, but I pressed down with all my strength, using my forearm like a bar to press down on his windpipe and the fat veins of his neck that got blood to the brain.

He sank his teeth into the meaty part of my forearm, but I held on. Even when he ripped and pulled at the flesh, I held on. If only one of us was walking out of here, it was going to be me. I'd be damned if some Nazi grunt got me to buy the farm after I'd survived this war, five years of blood, mud, shit, and more dumb warlocks than any one person should have to encounter in their life.

After a good thirty seconds, he finally started to slump, and I used the tiny slackening of his fury to shift one hand to his forehead, bringing his neck around with a crisp snap that filled up the tiny exam room.

Jacob let out a slow, shaky breath as the soldier's body toppled, and me with it. I was pumping blood like a fresh oil strike, rich and red as the armband on the asshole I'd just dropped. "I'm so sorry," he said, backing away from me, fingers already scrabbling through the door. "You saved my life. I'm so sorry to leave you to this fate."

"Jacob," I said. "Jacob!" louder when he was still trying to fight his way out of the room in a panic.

"You'll change," he said, almost apologetically. "And then you'll be one of them."

"*Jacob.*" I gritted. "I would really like to not bleed to death, so could you at least toss me that gauze?"

He tilted his head to one side, watching me. I glared at him as we just stood there, the adrenaline screaming through me like a hot shot, his heart throbbing in his neck so hard I could see it jumping under his yellowed collar.

"What is happening?" he said after what felt like a century.

I stood up and ripped the gauze from his hand. Vertigo slammed down on top of my head, and I stumbled against the table, wrapping up my arm tight as I could. The bleeding had mostly stopped, but I was missing a chunk of skin and muscle. It'd be a couple of days before I was right and even longer before I could turn into the hound without being lame. "Son of a bitch," I muttered as I tore off the end of the gauze with my teeth.

Jacob muttered something that sounded like a prayer and I threw the gauze back to him. "Yeah, all right, I'm not human," I said. "But on the bright side, I'm not trying to empty you out like a canteen, so I suggest we both find the silver lining and get the fuck out of here."

After a long second he nodded, and I unsnapped the soldier's holster, pulling out his pistol. Only four bullets sat in the clip. "Perfect," I muttered as we gingerly opened the door.

"Are you a good shot?" Jacob asked, sticking so close to me he might as well have been growing out of my shoulder. "Americans are crack shots, yes?"

"You've been watching too many cowboy pictures," I whispered, pausing in the lobby where the nurse had attacked me.

The hallway was still deserted, but there was a sound coming from outside now, a rising and falling drone of screams and cries. "It's spreading," Jacob whispered. "There are thousands of people out there. Innocent people . . ."

"I'm sorry," I said as I peered through the frost-covered window to the outside. "But there's nothing we can do."

Jacob squeezed his eyes shut, sliding a hand over his face. "I can't do this. I was meant to die here. I just . . . I don't want to die like this."

"Jacob." I grabbed his sleeve as he started to back away. "Don't you quit on me now," I said.

He slumped. "Why do you care? You are not one of us. Those people, the sick ones—they are not either, not anymore. And they will take the lives of all the people trapped here with no more thought than you killed that man in the exam room."

"I died," I said. It just came out, as the shapes moving beyond the door lurched and groaned, one pressing bloody hands against the glass. We pulled back, pressing ourselves against the wall. The grip of the gun was sweaty in my hand. "I died," I said again. "And they haven't managed to keep me down yet."

I reached down with my free hand and squeezed his. "I'm not going to die here, and I'll try my best to make sure you don't either."

Jacob stared at the bloody hand prints on the window, but his fingers squeezed mine in return. "They're strong," he said. "Fast. Anything they haven't bitten, they'll chase down like a pack of wolves." He met my eyes. "Do you know what they are?"

"It doesn't matter," I said. Better than admitting I had no fucking idea what was happening. Hellspawn didn't do this—Gary would have a conniption if he got a spot on his tie, never mind bathe in blood. Demons didn't have the need to cause mass chaos when they had the Hellspawn to do it for them. Vampires turned victims with venom, more like a venereal disease than whatever this was. That left deadheads, corpses raised by a necromancer, but Kubler was dead. All of his walking corpses should have dropped with him.

We stepped outside, and I almost fell over Kubler's body. What was left of it, anyway. The crowded yard behind the barbed wire was swarming with the same languorous, bloody monsters I'd seen inside. Jacob flinched as a few turned their eyes on us. The eyes were pure black—or so clouded with blood from ruptured vessels they looked black. I crouched slowly, not breaking off eye contact.

"Get as much blood as you can," I said, gesturing at the pile of ground meat and entrails that used to be Kubler. "Cover yourself."

Jacob did as I said, retching as we both smeared the sticky, cooling blood over our faces and hands, down our fronts. While I was at it I ripped off the red armband. It fluttered into a pile of bloody snow and got trampled underfoot.

Beyond the fence surrounding the hospital, I could see more shadows in the gray half-light. Some were shuffling as if they still had control over their limbs; some were lying on the ground, quivering as the people still upright walked past without even looking at them.

"Where will we go?" Jacob whispered. "The guards . . ."

Sirens began to wail from outside the fence and a Klieg light snapped on, sweeping the yard and lighting it up brighter than the sun. Snowflakes twirled in the cone of light, turning red where they touched the bloody ground.

"The guards have bigger problems than us," I said. Like the universe wanted to back me up, a burst of automatic gunfire clattered through the freezing air from far off in the camp.

Sticking to the rough hospital walls, Jacob and I eased past the mob of creatures. I didn't want to think about what could be going on here. Deadheads were fast and hungry like these, but if they bit you all you were going to do was bleed, not turn into a pissy cannibal yourself. No vamp I'd ever met could rip a person limb from limb, even on their best day. I was still left with a big fucking I DON'T KNOW blinking over these things' heads, and I didn't like it.

By the time we'd made it to the fence, we were both almost weak from the tension of moving slowly, freezing every time one of the things turned our way and sniffed the air. Jacob grimaced at the sight of the wire. "You can fit. I am not so small."

I shrugged out of the thick linen shirt I'd stolen. It was ruined anyway, so I wrapped it around my fists, trying not to wince as the barbs bit through the layers into my palm. I used my foot to push down the bottom strand and jerked my chin at Jacob. "Go."

Jacob bent down, trying to fold himself in half and sliding under the top wire. He looked back at me. "What about you?"

"I'm right behind you," I said. It wasn't a lie until I felt a hand clamp down on my shoulder hard enough to pull my collarbone back. "Jacob, run!" I screamed, as I landed in the freezing mud.

He ran. To his eternal credit, he ran and didn't look back. He didn't freeze, or try to be a hero. I would have grinned if I wasn't spending all my effort on breathing after getting slammed to the ground. I'd been right. Jacob wasn't going to die here. He was a survivor. Like recognizes like.

A foot tucked under my shoulder and rolled me over. The spotlight lit up a man's face, hard-carved with sharp cheeks and chin, like someone had hacked him out of wood. He looked at me, steam rising from his mouth as he breathed hard in the snowy air. "And who might you be?"

I lashed out with my foot. He was a big bastard, at least six and a half feet, so I didn't bother aiming for the groin. Kneecap is much more accessible when you're on the ground, and he let out a startled grunt when I made contact.

I managed to get up, but he grabbed me again, slamming me into the fence. The sensation of a hundred hot pins digging into my back and thighs as the barbs bit my skin forced me to make a sound, and he smiled.

"You're not one of them," he said, looking at me with his head cocked, like I was some kind of rare creature he'd caught in a trap. I wondered if I was about to lose my skin.

"No," I whimpered. "I'm not a Nazi."

He pressed me harder against the wire, and I hate that tears were leaking out of my eyes. Men like him wanted me to flinch, wanted me to cry and beg. Usually that was the quickest way out of whatever mess I'd found myself in, but this time the man's eyes were dead. Nothing was going to get me out of this. I knew that kind of man by sight too.

"That's not what I'm talking about," he sighed, almost in my ear. His breath was hot and he smelled—not like offal and blood, but something strong and herbal, which chilled my nose and all the way down the back of my throat. "You're so small," he said. "Like a bird. I see birds caught on this fence. Their feathers get so heavy with blood they can't fly away." He pushed again, and I felt one barb dig into the back of my head, all the way through the scalp. The man moaned into my hair.

"You're a lucky bird," he said in my ear. "You're not the species I like to catch and eat." Faster than my heart was beating, he wrapped one massive scarred hand around my throat. "But I'll pull your wings off just the same."

I clawed at his hand, but I might as well have been trying to tear apart a chunk of cement. My nails tore at the tattered sleeve of his uniform shirt and I saw through the black borders closing in that it wasn't tan, like all the good little Aryans in the place—it was dark green, stained and faded.

One of those dying prisoners. An American. Many are sick when they come here but he was different . . .

At the realization spreading across my face, he grinned wider. "That's right," he said. "Nobody here but you and me and the monsters."

I kicked at him, feeling the wire tear chunks out all up and down my thighs, but he slammed his knee into mine. The wire shook under me. "Stop struggling," he snapped. "Only the foolish ones struggle."

A shape moved up on my left, and I thought it was just a blood vessel rupturing in my field of vision until a hand reached across the wire and pressed into the man's ruddy forehead.

Jacob squeezed his eyes shut as he murmured, the man's skin under his hand turning a molten color like it was metal in a forge. The man cried out, letting go of me and swatting at Jacob's face as he swung wildly, catching him on the side of the temple. When the connection broke, Jacob fell onto his ass in the mud and the man lunged for me again.

I emptied all four shots from the Luger into him, three in his chest and one thunking into his scalp. He staggered, like he was drunk, his head dipping to his chest. Nothing came from the wounds. The bullet just left a small black dot on his forehead from the powder burn.

"Come on!" Jacob shouted in my ear, grabbing the barbed wire and pulling it up as much as he could. I squeezed underneath, not caring that I was raising a fresh crop of welts across my buttocks and back. Jacob yanked me up and we ran, up a rise and into the thick woods that surrounded the camp, snow up to my knees, then past it. We ran until Jacob stumbled over a downed tree trunk and fell headlong into the snow. He floundered up, coughing.

"We have to keep going," I wheezed, even though I'd fallen against a tree myself, heart thudding. We were so far away we could no longer see the lights from the camp except for faint bars of the spots painted on the clouds above us. Above the shouts, I could hear the howling of dogs and the frantic yelling of soldiers behind us.

"Guess we're not the only ones who got out," Jacob said, clambering to his feet. He tried to put weight on his ankle and whimpered. "Dammit."

He sank back and sighed. "You better run. I'm not going to make it far on this, in the middle of the night, in the snow."

I shook my head, reaching down and stripping off my bloody stockings. Jacob's eyes widened slightly. "What are you doing?"

"Calm down," I said, thrusting the stockings at him. "You're a doctor, right? Make yourself a splint."

I broke off a branch from the fallen tree as Jacob did the same, aligning the two pieces of wood on either side of his ankle. "Not that this'll do any good," Jacob said. "I still can't outrun a pack of dogs."

"Let me worry about that," I said, turning the sharp end of the stick toward my thigh. I drove it into the puncture wound left by the barbs, widening it and causing fresh red blood to spurt, landing in fat, steaming droplets on the snow.

"Stop that!" Jacob cried, lunging for the stick, but I was already done. I tossed it to the side, letting the wound bleed freely, putting my scent in the air for the dogs.

"Do me a favor," I said to Jacob, wincing as the deep wound stung in the cold air. "Don't ever tell anyone about this. Especially about me."

"Who would I tell?" Jacob spread his hands. "Even my teacher at the temple who showed me that trick would find this hard to swallow."

"Good trick," I said. Jacob shrugged.

"It's just an all-purpose way to banish a *dubbyuk*. An evil spirit who looks like a man." His head snapped up again as the dogs howled again, closer. "Are you one of them? Is that why you weren't infected when you were bitten?"

"An evil spirit?" I said. "No, I'm flesh and blood. More or less."

Jacob grabbed me suddenly, pulling me into a hard embrace, and then let me go. "Look after yourself."

"I always do," I said. "This is both of our lucky days, Jacob. And I mean it—don't tell anyone about me, or this night, and especially not about the thing that looked like a man back there."

He nodded at me, then turned and limped into the forest. I ran, leaving a trail of fresh blood for the dogs, hoping for different reasons that I'd never see Jacob or the man at the fence again.

CHAPTER

OUTSIDE MINNEAPOLIS
NOW

The sedan bottomed out in a rut, undercarriage scraping icy dirt. The jolt brought me back to reality, and I saw a lone farmhouse rising out of the icy, stubble-ridden field beside the road. The windows were lit up, the only light as far as I could see. When the car rolled to a stop and I got out the freezing wind pulled all the breath out of me.

The driver jerked her head, wrapping her arms around herself as another gust almost pulled me off my feet. "Inside," she said. "Where it's safe."

"Sure," Leo muttered to me as we followed the girl through the furrow cut in the thigh-high snow leading to the front door. "Because when I think safe house, I think *Texas Chainsaw Massacre*."

The front door swung open and a guy literally twice my size, both high and wide, stepped forward. A thick braid curled over his shoulder and his forearms were the size of my legs. "Hold up," he grunted.

Leo raised one eyebrow. The swelling on his face had gone down, but the bruises and cuts were going to be there for a while. I wouldn't have tried to stop him. "It's pretty cold out here, pal."

The tree trunk lifted his massive arms, indicating Leo should do the same. "Gotta search you."

"Listen, Cujo," Leo sighed. "You're not working the door at a strip club in the Bronx. Chill out."

"Gotta search you," the tree trunk repeated. His eyes, already tiny in the folded flesh of his face, narrowed even more. Leo folded his arms in response.

"I would love to see you try."

"Come on," I said, pushing past him. I was going to freeze to death in the time it took them to decide who had the bigger metaphorical penis. "You can search me," I told the tree trunk. He shook his head.

"No need. You're not one of them."

I would have lifted one eyebrow, if they weren't both frozen solid. "One of what?"

"Reapers," the girl who'd picked us up supplied helpfully. "In case you hadn't realized, nobody around here is their biggest fan."

"Hey, lady, you brought us to this lovely slice of the ass-end of nowhere," Leo said. "How about next time, if you don't want me around you don't pluck me off the side of the road?"

"How about you thank me for saving your sorry hide?" she shot back, putting a fist on her hip. Her Mohawk dipped and bobbed like she was a fighting rooster.

"Thank you, random woman I've never seen before, for saving me and being so fucking modest about it too," Leo said, spreading his hands. "Now what the fuck am I doing here being fondled by your gimp?"

The tree trunk growled—actually growled, like a bullmastiff—as he patted Leo down. Leo submitted as apathetically as possible, making the guy raise both of his arms and bend over to pat down his legs.

"He's clean," he announced.

Our driver turned on him again. "If you're the Grim Reaper where's your Scythe?"

"Whoa, now," Leo said. "Buy a guy a drink first."

She grabbed Leo by his lapels and pushed him into the nearest wall, so hard his head impacted the plaster and gritty dirt sifted down on my head. "I look like I have time to joke around with you, slick?" she snarled, shaking Leo like a chew toy. "Here's a hint in case you're slow—I'm not joking and neither is anyone else. Now are you him or not?"

Leo shook his head, blinking plaster dust out of his eyes. He'd never stopped smiling. If that girl was smart, she'd realize she'd caught something much worse than her by the tail. Based on the way she was snarling and the vein popping out of her temple, though, I didn't think smarts were in play just then.

"Listen, honey," Leo drawled, sounding every inch like the Brooklyn boy he'd been once upon a time, "I don't know who hurt you, but your attitude problem ain't cute. It's not making me weak in the knees or hard in the dick, so how about you get your hands off my thousand-dollar jacket and we try this again, using our words?"

She slammed him again, harder, and I reached out and tapped her on the shoulder, my finger pinging off the rivets studding the shoulders of her leather jacket. When she turned, I hit her.

There's not much complexity behind a good solid right hook. You want to get the power from your feet and hips, swing your whole upper body into the blow, make a good fist, and follow through. If you do that, no matter how small you are, hit the right spot and you're going to put a dent in whoever pissed you off in the first place.

Still, it was a dumb thing to do. Aggressive and impulsive. I didn't go around hitting people just because they made me mad. At least I hadn't before I met Leo and started caring whether or not people wanted to hurt him. If you hit someone, with that perfect right hook gained from decades of fighting dirty, you'd feel better for the few seconds they staggered and their mouth blossomed with blood.

Then the girl caught herself on a side table piled high with sodden mail and empty pizza boxes, and let out a low snarl as she came back at me. That's the part where you get your ass beat, and the stupid decision you made when you lost control and hit them in the first place launches you into a world of hurt.

I braced myself for the ass-kicking, but Leo stepped between us, leveling a snub five-shot revolver at the girl's forehead. She pulled up short, panting, her lower teeth coated with blood like she'd just torn out someone's throat.

"Here's a tip," Leo said. "You're going to keep a gun between your seat cushions, make sure it's where you left it when you get out of the car. And you," he said, looking sideways at the tree trunk. "You're gonna pat down another dude, don't be all delicate avoiding the junk."

"That gun isn't even loaded," the girl snapped. Leo actually let out a laugh.

"Honey, my old gig was carrying a gun for a living. I can tell it's loaded just by the weight." He pulled the hammer back. "Now I'm guessing none of you assholes can hit anything smaller than him"—he jerked his head at Tree Trunk—"so this is probably loaded with hollow points. At this distance your skull will be a Halloween pumpkin if I shoot you." He stretched out his arm and pressed the barrel into the girl's forehead, leaving an oily halo. "So how about we all calm down?"

The girl didn't have to think long. She put her hands up and backed away. "Yeah. Okay." Her tongue flicked out, licking the blood off her lip.

Leo turned slightly to me. "Ava?"

"It's over," I said, my temporary insanity receding and the usual block of ice that had kept me alive this long growing back. Leo put the hammer up on the pistol and handed it to me, butt first. "Nobody needs a loaded gun in this place, least of all me."

Tree Trunk regarded Leo again, then turned to our driver. "It's gotta be him," he announced, stroking his braid.

"Yeah, I'm me, hoo-fucking-ray," Leo said. He slumped with a sigh onto a gold velvet sofa that was so swaybacked he sank practically to the floor. I unloaded the revolver, sticking the slugs in my pocket and the gun itself in the back of my jeans.

"Sorry," the driver said to Leo. She at least had the grace to look embarrassed. "But we've had a couple of false starts since the rumors about you started."

"Rumors?" I said, and she bared her teeth.

"Was I talking to you, bitch?"

Great. Even when I hooked up with the king of the reapers himself and rolled into town in style, I was still at the bottom of the pecking order.

"Viv," another woman spoke up, from the door. Behind her, I saw a small clot of four or five more people anxiously peering at Leo. Viv spun on her, a fleck of stray blood flying and landing on my cheek.

"*What,* Raina?" she shouted. "You going to make me put a dollar in the swear jar?"

"If I did, we'd all be rich," Raina said. She was as willowy as Viv was solid, long rainbow-colored raver braids curled in a messy bun on top of her head. She was gorgeous, like a live-action Crusty Punk Barbie with copper skin and a big silver pyramid stud gleaming in her nose. "We don't do that here," she reminded Viv. "We don't play that game."

"Personally, I'd really love it if somebody explained what the hell is happening and how it involves us," Leo said from the sofa. "Because I got a headache that won't quit and no patience left to speak of."

"When we heard the Grim Reaper had returned, some of us were happier than others," Raina said. Her accent was perfect and clipped. She could have been narrating some genteel documentary about cheese on the BBC. "Headquarters refused to believe it, and they went after anyone who advocated for trying to reach out to you. Those of us who believed banded together," she continued. "All twenty of us."

"And less every day," Viv piped up. "Gary ruled Headquarters for a hundred years and his butt boy Owen is just like him, jacked up on hair gel and energy drinks. If I hadn't shown up you two would be fertilizer and he'd still be acting like it was his right to sit in the corner office."

"The point is," Raina said, shooting Viv a poisonous look, "that while many reapers think the Grim Reaper is just a legend, we believe you. Even if you aren't him, we've been without a leader for well over a century and Owen is not the choice anyone, including his flunkies, would make if you pressed them. But kicking Owen out is not going to come easily."

"I got that," Leo said. "When he was torturing me in his basement."

"He claims there's no way you're the Grim Reaper because he has your Scythe," Raina continued.

That made Leo get quiet. Everyone got quiet, and the only sound was the wind battering the house. I flicked my gaze between Leo and Raina, waiting to see what he'd say. Reapers could choose their own Scythes, but Leo wasn't like Owen and the others. He wasn't like anything that had existed since the Dark Ages.

Which would make it easy for a douchebag like Owen to make up whatever story he wanted.

On the other hand, it also meant that he could be telling the truth.

"Well, that's bullshit," Leo said finally. "Only I can pick and choose my own Scythe."

I inhaled as a look of disappointment and suspicion passed between everyone else in the room.

"You're different," Raina said carefully. "And whatever Owen has, none of us can hold it. Only he can. I've tried to touch it and it . . . it burned me."

"Owen's talking about putting down all the hounds," Viv spoke up. "Putting us all down and just starting over. Clean house, he said."

"You have to help us," Raina said. "Go to Owen on his own terms and prove you're to lead the reapers. Otherwise we're all marked for death."

Leo started to say no, but I shook my head from behind Viv. There were hounds like Wilson, who did their jobs willingly and would gladly jump off a cliff if their reaper told them to, but I got the feeling there were a lot more out there like me, scared people who'd gotten snuffed before their time and grasped on to any second chance, no matter how shitty.

"This Owen guy grabbed us off the street," I said, to forestall Leo messing up their chances for survival now. "What makes you think he's going to agree to a nice little chitchat?"

"As long as you're around you're a threat," Raina said. "Without the Grim Reaper the next stop is the Pit, and the last thing Owen wants is a demon stepping in to clean house."

Leo massaged his forehead. "So what do you suggest we do?"

"Tell him that unless he meets and agrees to let you try and hold the Scythe you'll dime him out to your boss," Viv said. "Owen can't stand up to a demon. None of us can, except you."

I knew that wasn't true, and I also thought this was pretty

much the worst idea I'd heard in at least twenty years, but I sure as hell wasn't going to volunteer that in the midst of their little club meeting. Just because Viv had gotten us away from Owen didn't mean this group was any more stable than the suits at Headquarters.

"That's a good idea," I said to Leo, trying to put enough gravity in my voice that he'd play along for now.

"Fine." Leo stood, straightening his jacket. "Set it up," he told Raina. "And show me a place where I can bathe, get some clean underwear, and sleep."

She nodded and withdrew, and Viv jerked her thumb at the stairs. "Bathroom's on the left. There's a bedroom for you at the end of the hall." When I started to follow Leo she pulled me back. "Uh-uh. We may not be a servant class here, but reapers need their privacy. Didn't Gary teach you *anything*?"

"He taught me lots," I said, staring into her golden eyes. "Mostly how to take a beating, and how to prey on people so desperate they lose their grip on rationality and let you turn them out with shitty deals that only benefit you and your Hellspawn bosses. He was a very effective teacher."

Viv's skin nostrils flared, but she let got of me, and that was all I cared about.

Leo was running a bath into a rusty, stained tub. The water was almost as brown as the stains, and pipes shuddered from somewhere deep in the bowels of the house, groaning like a herd of dying cattle. "Classy place," he said, stripping out of his jacket and tie. I shut the door behind me and slid down to the floor, too exhausted to stand upright anymore.

"Leo," I whispered. "These people are cracked."

"'Course they are," he said, adding his pants and shirt to the pile and slipping out of his boxers. He lowered himself into the bathwater with a groan. "They've all been living like you were for a hundred goddamn years, some a lot longer. It's no small wonder they all belong in the padded room."

"We should never have come here," I said, pressing a hand over my eyes. I felt the first tears slither down my face and didn't even bother swiping at them. That was how exhausted I was. "We should have just run and not looked back."

"Ava." Leo's voice made me look at him. He smiled at me, one arm hooked over the edge of the tub. His tattoos covered every square inch of skin, all the way down to his first knuckle. He wriggled his fingers at me and I scooted across the tile and hooked mine with his.

"I never imagined I'd die at home surrounded by thirteen grandkids," Leo said. "I know when you got brought in you didn't really want it, and what Gary did to you was a violation, but it wasn't like that for me. When I got this chance, I wasn't upset. I'm glad I get more time, even if it is in a shitty farmhouse in the middle of a frozen wasteland."

"We can't do this if you take over," I said in a rush, letting out the thought that had been slowly crystallizing, since before we flipped the car over on the snowy road. "Nobody will accept a reaper and a hound. It'll make the other reapers not trust you, it'll make me have to watch my back constantly . . ."

"The other reapers are pawnbrokers from Hades who dupe assholes out of their immortal souls with a little magic talent and a copy of a necromancy text, Ava," Leo said. "Same as any other small-timer in any other syndicate. Nobody trusts anybody and everyone always has a knife aimed at the next guy's back." He leaned his head back and slid down in the water, closing his eyes in the steam. "You want the truth, being a reaper is just like when I was alive, except instead of blow, strippers, and cutting up dead bodies with power tools it's black magic, whiny middle managers, and collecting on souls."

"When you put it like that . . ." I muttered, feeling the tightness in my gut relax a little.

"Either way, I'm the boss now," Leo murmured. "And what I say goes. And what I say is you're not going anywhere."

"You're not going anywhere." Jacob Gottlieb stretched out a hand to me, his slender fingers spread.

The forest where I'd last seen him was still dark, still muffled in snow but now the fat, wet flakes didn't touch me and Jacob's voice echoed and buzzed like a bad connection.

"Phyllis," Jacob said to me. "Phyllis, you're stuck. You need to forget about what's happening there and come here."

"Where is . . . here?" Even talking was an effort. I felt drugged, like Owen had shot me up with another dose of ketamine. Was I still in the basement? Had everything since just been a trip?

"You're not in a k-hole!" Jacob shouted at me, and I stared at him. Granted, we hadn't spent much time together, but I could never picture the good doctor using that phrase. "Here!" he shouted, gesturing around him. "Kansas City. Look for me!"

"This is Germany," I slurred. "And you're . . . you're not . . ."

"Kansas City!" Jacob said again, slowly, like he was trying to order a steak in a foreign language. "Come find me! You're stuck there. We need you here!"

70

"Why?" I murmured, trying to catch a few of the snowflakes and blinking as they passed right through my palm.

"The Walking Man!" Jacob bellowed as everything started to flicker and melt like the end of an old film reel. "The Walking Man is out and none of us are safe—"

I snapped conscious, smacking my head on the dusty bed frame that was the centerpiece of the granny nightmare Viv called a bedroom. I was pinned under a number of musty afghans, Leo snoring softly beside me.

This hadn't felt like a dream a warlock or a demon could push into your head, quiet and subtle as a sharpened blade to the kidney. This felt more like a crazy person at the bus station screaming in my face and then hitting me with a stick when I ignored him.

"Wha's goin' on?" Leo muttered into his pillow. I lay back down and wrapped my arms around his waist, his stomach hard and warm under my hand.

"I had a dream," I said.

"Oh yeah?" Leo sighed. "Was it sexy?"

"They called me Phyllis," I said.

"Why the fuck would somebody call you Phyllis?" Leo said.

I stared at the blackness where the ceiling should be, and lied. "I have no idea."

CHAPTER

KANSAS CITY
JANUARY 1947

The rambling old house popped up out of the flat fields like a mushroom, looking like it had been growing there forever. The gray clapboards and mossy roof weren't anything special—the only thing that made the house unique was that it was a stop between Kansas City and wherever customers' next destinations lay. It was a place you'd forget as soon as you left. The girls working were equally forgettable. That was what I needed.

I watched the frost on the windowpane recoil from the ember of my cigarette as I looked out across the highway. Traffic was light tonight—it was too cold for all but the most hard-up johns, and even they were mostly tucked up in bed at this hour. Most of the girls, too. Even the forced laughter and tinny music from the parlor had died down. That meant it was the perfect time to go downstairs and get to work on my fourth glass of gin. Or was it the fifth? Nobody else in this place cared, I figured as I tiptoed down the stairs, my bare feet prickling against the cheap carpet runner, so why should I?

Kathleen sat on the threadbare velvet sofa counting out bills with the crisp snap of a casino teller, her puffy pink housecoat making her look like somebody had inflated her body but left her head the normal size. She barely looked up, smoke winding up from the ashtray next to her. The corpses of twenty or thirty smokes, most stained with the cheap, waxy pinks and reds the working girls favored, attested to the night's business.

"Rough night?" she said. Kathleen—"Miss Kate" to most everyone who worked here—looked like eight miles of hard road but she sounded like the nightclub singer she'd been twenty years ago. Her voice could give the wallpaper goose bumps.

"That's every night," I said, slumping into the chair by the window, the one where Kathleen usually sat one of the younger girls to watch for cops. I wasn't one to judge, but as brothels went Kate's wasn't half-bad—she didn't turn out young girls, she didn't let johns beat us, she didn't tolerate people shooting dope in the bathroom or selling it out the back door. Most important, she let me be Phyllis and didn't ask any questions about who I'd been before.

I didn't have to be here, unlike a lot of the girls upstairs. But I wasn't educated enough to be a nurse or chipper enough to be a secretary. I couldn't exactly furnish a driver's license or a VA card to get a government job. Hard to explain why someone with my name and description had been reported missing in Louisiana almost thirty years ago. If they'd ever found my body, my fingerprints would show up as a dead woman's.

Aside from finding a Clyde to my Bonnie, if I wanted to stay away from Gary I had to make money any way I could. And to stay away from Gary, I'd do a lot worse than work for Kathleen.

"Nights like this remind me of Germany," I said. Kathleen made a sympathetic noise. She'd lost her husband the first time we did this dance with the Huns, when they'd been married for less than two years.

"Shame what they did to you WAC girls," Kathleen grunted. "Real damn shame. My girl back home in Skokie, she worked in a factory. Welded plane parts to other plane parts. Kicked her ass out the door the minute the boys came back from Europe. Can't find a job for nothing now." She grunted again, slamming the lid of her lockbox and locking it with the key she kept around her neck in place of a cross. "Real damn shame."

I'd told Kathleen a few half-truths, but the basic story was right. When the war was over, we all came home—Gary and the rest of us. But after that, I'd just faded away, and for some reason he'd let me. At first I wondered if it was a game, if he was waiting for me to relax so he could show up and break me down again. But I think he sensed as much as I did that I was done. What Jacob and I had seen, what I'd seen in the camp before I found Kubler . . . I didn't think that I could break into any more pieces after Gary found me, but I was wrong.

I poured the gin I'd come downstairs for. Enough of it and I could mostly sleep without nightmares. The stuff I saw when I was awake was bad enough. Like now, with the snow falling gently, wafting down like sugar from a sifter, I could almost see Jacob's face and feel the last time we'd touched before he'd run off.

He was dead. I'd fooled myself for a while after I came back, but as more and more came out, more and more photos and film reels, and those sound recordings they played from Nuremberg almost every night during the news broadcasts, I knew Jacob was dead. The Nazis had started executing everyone they could when the Red Army and the Allies closed in. One man alone in the woods hadn't stood a chance.

The phone in the kitchen buzzed, making me jump. A little bit of gin sloshed onto my hand. "I ain't answering," Kathleen said, picking up her lockbox the way some women carried small dogs. "Gonna be some housewife looking for her husband and I ain't going to be screamed at because she can't keep his fat ass at home."

I padded into the kitchen and picked up on the tenth or so ring. "Kate's."

"Phyllis?" The voice was clipped and male, and I instantly went on guard. It wasn't unheard-of for creeps to find Kathleen's number once they'd moved on and become a pain in the ass, calling at all hours. "Phyllis Dietrich?" he said. "Is that who I'm speaking to?"

"I'm sorry, who am *I* speaking to?" I said in my best vapid tone, which wasn't all that hard with four glasses of gin warming the embers in my belly.

"I'm a friend of Lady Williams," the man said. "I'm sorry to report there's been an accident and you're listed as next of kin."

Lady. Sweet, round, blond Lady, who'd laugh at the dumbest joke the thickest john could pull out of his hat and make you laugh too, because she was just the type of nice girl who made you want to be nice back.

"Is she dead?" I said, and the caller paused for a second. We both held our breath.

"She's in bad shape," the caller said, his voice softening in response to mine going hard. "I'd get here fast, Mrs. Dietrich."

"Miss," I said. "It's Miss. Where are you?"

Lady had been driving down to Texas to see her family for the week—her dad was doing poorly, and her brother had wrapped his sedan around a tree, and they needed somebody around with a set of wheels.

"Harper, Kansas," the caller said. "We're a little speck off SR 14."

I leaned my forehead against Kathleen's mildewed kitchen wallpaper, pressing into the center of a purple cabbage rose. Lady hadn't even made it out of the state. "Are you her doctor?" I said.

"Harper, Kansas," the caller repeated. "You should come."

I didn't bother asking Kathleen if I could borrow her car. She'd just grunt obscenities at me. In a strange way, it felt good to know that the skills I'd acquired before I slipped into this life hadn't totally abandoned me. I managed to get the old Packard running in two tries and eased out onto the snowy highway. It was a little before dawn, but the sky was still all dark except for a line of flame at the horizon.

My cash lasted me to Harper, but after two fill-ups and a steak-and-eggs special at a diner that seemed to be constructed mostly of grease and stale toast, I only had change jingling in my purse by the time I pulled in to the hospital.

A charge nurse directed me down the hall to a quiet room. The curtain was pulled, and I stood in front of it, unwilling to pull it back. Lady and I were friends, but I wasn't exactly sit-at-your-bedside-during-your-last-moments close to her.

The curtain whipped back of its own accord, and another nurse, not much more than a kid, popped her head back in surprise. "This is a private room," she snapped. "Who are you?"

"I'm her sister," I said reflexively, the lie we used to visit each other in the hospital, jail, wherever Kate's girls might end up where they needed a fake family.

The nurse darted her eyes from my slender, dark-haired, five-foot-nothing frame to Lady's blond hair and curves that went on for days. "Right," she said.

I should have kept lying, but the sight of Lady stopped me. Her hair was about all I recognized—her face was wrapped in gauze, both of her arms as well. The wounds underneath were bleeding through, little half-moons all over the field of cotton. The pungent, sticky smell of iodine wafted into my nose and I choked.

The nurse, fortunately, softened at my silence. "Five minutes, all right? The doctor won't be around for ten so you'd better be gone by then."

"The doctor called me," I murmured, flinching reflexively as Lady stirred in her sleep and her gown exposed one collarbone, deep dark purple with bruises. I'd had bruises like that left on me more than once.

"No," the nurse said emphatically. "He has not called anyone. This girl is an unfortunate. She doesn't have anyone; therefore nobody called you."

"I did," said a voice from the door. It was my mystery caller, and I spun. The nurse huffed in annoyance and stormed out.

"Sorry." The man extended his hand. "Phyllis, right?"

"You're not a doctor," I said as I shook it.

"No," he replied. "But to be perfectly fair I never said I was." He gave me a thin smile that dropped off quicker than driving off a cliff. "Hell of a thing."

I moved to Lady's bed rail and leaned on it, squeezing it. "She didn't deserve this," I said.

"Nobody deserves this," the man said, standing next to me. He took his wallet out of his inside pocket and flashed a shiny gold shield. "Don Tanner. Kansas State Police."

I gave him another once-over at that. Don didn't look like most of the cops I'd run into. Then again, Kate's was rarely graced with the presence of such an august body as the state police. He was tall—almost tall enough to duck his head under door frames— and he wore his blond hair in a buzz cut that made it look almost white. He had a young face and old eyes—they were light blue, sunlight cutting through a frozen pond, and even as he looked down at Lady I could tell he was really seeing something else.

"I'm Phyllis," I said. "What do the state police want with this?"

He sighed and rubbed a palm over his head, disturbing the severe brush of his crew cut. "It's a long story."

I looked down at Lady's body again. I didn't know who'd done this, but I'd gladly get back in the saddle with Gary if it meant the means to track them down. "I've got time."

Detective Tanner shot me a look. "You're not really her sister."

I didn't look away. I was past worrying about what some human thought of me or my temporary profession. "You're very perceptive."

"Well," Tanner smiled. "I am a detective." He took my arm and I jerked reflexively, pulling it back to my side.

Tanner held up his hands. "I'm not trying to give you trouble. I just want to buy you a cup of coffee and a slice of pie."

"I'm not hungry," I snapped.

"Everyone's hungry after a scene like that," he said, taking my arm again. He escorted me across the street to an Automat, and I forced myself not to break his wrist and run.

He bought us each coffee and pie, and took a sip and bite before he talked again. "So how do you know Miss Williams?"

I stayed quiet, pushing my pie around my plate. Tanner sighed, tapping sugar into his coffee until it was fairly swamped. "Look, kid, I don't care what the two of you did together. I know what goes on with young ladies who can't make ends meet any other way. Trust me, I have bigger fish to fry than a couple of working girls."

The sugar ran out, and he frowned at the empty jar. I started laughing, and he looked up. "What?"

"You calling me kid," I said. "How old are you?" He couldn't have been much past thirty.

"Old enough," he said sternly. "And I ask again—how are you two friends?"

"My name's not Phyllis," I said impulsively. "It's Ava. But I want to be called Phyllis."

"Fair enough," Tanner said. "You read the papers much, Phyllis?"

"I have enough bad news," I said. I figured if the pie was free I might as well take a bite. It wasn't half-bad.

"About a year ago I got a call about a dead girl on the highway west of Topeka," said Tanner. "She'd been beaten and mutilated like your friend Lady. Not a fighter like Lady, though—she died without ever waking up." He sipped his coffee. "Two more like that before your friend. The last one managed to tell me she pulled over to give him a ride. He was hitching after his car broke down. I start hearing from Nebraska and Oklahoma—they got a couple dead people apiece, two men and three women." Tanner's cup clunked against the chipped tabletop. "After the last girl papers started calling him the Walking Man."

The door of the Automat swung open, letting in two hospital orderlies and a cold gust, and I shivered. Even wrapped around the hot coffee, my hands felt like they'd frozen in place.

"Your friend was just in the wrong place at the wrong time," Tanner continued. "Trying to be a Good Samaritan."

"That sounds like her," I murmured. Tanner took out a couple of crumpled ones and some change and scattered them on the table.

"I should get back. I figured if there was somebody she really wanted to see, you needed to get the call."

"You talkin' about that blonde who came in all tore up?" one of the orderlies said, hooking his arm over the divider between our booths.

"What about her?" Tanner cocked his head.

"She's gone, man," said the other, floppy locks almost falling in his coffee. "Croaked right after you left. Doc came in and she was—" He made a slicing gesture across his neck.

Tanner slumped back down in the booth. "Great," he muttered into his hand. "That's just fantastic."

I stayed quiet, not moving. Tanner rubbed the spot between his eyes, the first hint of a furrow that would just get deeper the longer he did this job sprouting there. "I'm going to request an autopsy in the morning," he said. "Not that we'll find anything. We didn't on any of the others."

He started to leave and turned back. "You want to stick around? Make sure her remains get back home?"

I swiped at my eyes. Ava wouldn't cry over a hooker she'd barely known but I figured Phyllis might. "She wasn't some unfortunate," I said quietly. "She had a family. They'll want her back."

Tanner went to go out again, then sighed, his big shoulders heaving. He looked back at me again. "You got someplace to stay?"

"I'm not that hard up," I said softly, looking at the greasy surface of my coffee.

"Neither am I," Tanner said. "Staties give me a room and meal allowance. I never sleep through the night anyway." He put a heavy hand on my shoulder. "Come on. I'll take the chair and you can take the bed."

I was tired, so tired I could barely keep one foot in front of the other. I'd been up for over a day, with the drive and Lady and every other awful thing. I followed Tanner out and to his car, an unmarked Ford that rattled when he made the left turn into the motel a few blocks from the hospital.

"Your timing belt's on the way out," I murmured, after he parked. Tanner shot me a grin—uncalculated, boyish, his teeth gleaming in the neon light of the VACANCY sign.

"You a mechanic on your nights off?"

I returned his smile, just a little. "I pick things up here and there."

Tanner stepped out of the car and got a battered cardboard suitcase from the trunk, along with a green army duffle holding a long rifle and a couple of boxes of shells and bullets. "I never could fix anything worth a damn. Much better at breaking things up, least that's what my ex-wife would say."

I flinched when he brought up his wife, and told myself that sometimes humans just did want to help. They were the only ones who did things just because it was a compassionate, *human* thing to do. Demons would as soon pick their teeth with your finger bones as look at you. Reapers would never invite a girl into a motel room for anything as innocent as sleep.

"Oh, hey," Tanner said, stopping when he saw my look. "Listen, if it makes it better she's the one that ended things. Ended them right on our kitchen table with my sergeant from back in Easy Company. Said I was no fun anymore." He turned the lock on the door and jiggled, then kicked until the door gave way. "Guess she was right."

I hesitated at the threshold and he sighed. "I'd sleep in the car if it wasn't colder'n a snowman's balls out there. I'm not going to hurt you, Phyllis. I don't pretend to know what's been done to you but I'm not interested in anything but a beer and sitting in my underwear until I pass out. Probably why Edith left me like she did."

I followed him inside, shutting the door. After a second's thought I put the chain lock on. Tanner didn't want to hurt me, that much was true. He was being way too rude, too familiar to want that. The ones who did treated you like you were special, like you were a princess, so you'd feel like you owed them something when they turned ugly. Besides, if he did get fresh I wasn't above smashing his head into the mirror in the tacky gold frame stuck up opposite the bed.

"I'm not afraid of what you'll do to me," I said to Tanner. Really, he should have the sense to be afraid of me, but that was the other heartbreaking thing about humans—they never did.

"Good," he said, stripping out of his jacket, tie, and pants in record time. His shirt landed on top of the pile right in the middle of the floor and he grabbed one of the folded towels, then headed toward the shower. The scar across his back radiated from one of the arm holes in his undershirt, tracing all the way down the back of his arm to his elbow. It wasn't raw and red any longer, just white, but I could still pick out every rough stitch from whatever field hospital had saved Tanner's life.

"Where'd you pick that up?" I asked, sitting gingerly on the bed. The bedspread itched the backs of my legs.

"France," he said. He lifted his shirt on the other side, displaying twin puckers just over his kidney. "Belgium." He turned around, lifting his leg and showing me a slim pale oval over a healed gash.

"Germany?" I guessed. He laughed.

"Tulsa, Oklahoma. My little brother hit me with a broken bicycle chain."

"You two sound close," I said. Tanner's smile dropped.

"We were," he said, and shut the bathroom door.

Tanner wasn't kidding about the beer and the sleeping. He pulled a bunch of case files from his floppy leather satchel, but he'd barely paged through the first one before the beer drew his interest. "Don't look at those," he said as he tossed them to the floor. "They'll just give you bad dreams."

I took off my dress and stockings and got under the covers, lying there until Tanner started snoring and the last fuzzy TV station had signed off for the night. My foot slithered over one of the photos when I stepped out of bed, and I avoided them as I went over to Tanner's satchel, easing the rope tie off and sifting through the layer of shirts and underpants. Spare tie, gun-cleaning kit, shaving bag. A banged-up metal first aid box. A little black dirt trickled onto my bare foot from the seam of the box and I opened it, wincing as the springs creaked.

Tanner didn't so much as stir. Then again, if I'd polished off half a dozen beers on a mostly empty stomach I wouldn't let a little thing like someone searching my bags wake me either.

Sure, on the surface I was being paranoid and ungrateful snooping around, but this wasn't what it looked like, on a lot of levels. Tanner's call hadn't been random bad luck. Lady wasn't the victim of a run-of-the-mill murderer and when I looked at the box I knew Tanner wasn't just some burned-out cop chasing said killer.

The box had held bandages and iodine at one point, I was sure, but now it was crammed with bottles and tablets of an entirely different purpose. I could recognize a warlock's kit in my sleep, but this required a little more consideration. The black dust was graveyard dirt—the staple of voodoo and folk remedies from back in my home neck of the woods. There were hand-stamped silver coins in there too, the kind Romany put on the eyes of their dead, neatly labeled packets that smelled like a restaurant, and a vial of something dark and sticky that rolled rather than sloshed. Blood, although I wasn't opening the cork to take a whiff and see if it was human or other.

I carefully shut everything back up and checked the duffel, which really did just hold a shotgun, a rifle, and a paper bag of shells.

I looked back at Tanner's snoring form, and then I got my clothes and shoes and slipped out into the cold. Whatever he was really doing here, Tanner knew too much about the world I inhabited, and that meant he might figure out what I was.

As an afterthought, I scooped up the file he'd left on the floor and tucked it into my coat. The photos I left where they were. I had plenty of those kinds of pictures inside my skull. I didn't need any more.

I walked from the motel to the hospital to get the Packard, my shoes crunching frost-covered grass. I'd intended to just get in the car and drive until I was far away from Kansas, but I couldn't shake the photos lying on the motel room floor, stark in the white light from the street outside.

A nighttime road, an abandoned car. Faces obliterated to meat, so that even dental records couldn't identify their bodies—bodies that were not just mutilated but chewed, as if he'd given up on fists and started using tooth and nail in the depths of rage.

I climbed into the car, punching on the heater and opening the plain, coffee-stained folio. Nothing in Tanner's files contained a single clue to the Walking Man's actual identity. A psychiatrist had even typed up an opinion that took three single-spaced pages to say the Walking Man had feelings of anger and despondency that he acted out on his victims. He left no hair, no fingerprints, just bloody smears on window glass and chunks torn out of flesh with teeth.

Only one medical examiner, in Tulsa, had even been able to find a definitive cause of death. There, a woman named Marge Taylor, mother of two, had stopped on her way home from the graveyard shift at a tire plant to offer a downed motorist a lift. After a beating that must have taken hours, her neck had been snapped clean as a whistle.

I sat back, looking toward the hospital. Tanner was tracking the Walking Man, but Tanner also had the tools to track things that were much worse. If he hadn't been a deep-sleeping drunk, I didn't know if I'd have made it out of his motel room. Maybe he'd already clocked me, and I'd been so desperate to believe somebody didn't have it out for me I'd fallen for the line.

My breath made a misty full moon on the Packard's window, one that froze as I turned off the engine.

If Tanner thought he was on to something more than a maniac who liked to beat women to death on the highway, what would the harm be in taking a look for myself?

I got out of the car.

The hospital was quiet, the orderly with the long hair dozing at the front desk listening to the radio. I didn't wake him, slipping off my shoes so I wouldn't make any noise on the hard floors until I got to the morgue.

Lady's body was one of two in residence, side by side on narrow gurneys. I pulled back the sheet from Lady's face. She'd died before any of the bruising had gone down. Nothing would ever make her look like herself again.

They'd taken off her gown and cut away the bandages covering her arms and torso, and I reached out to almost touch one of the deeper bite marks on her upper arm. I'd seen a lot of bodies in a lot of states, but I wanted to remember Lady.

I wanted to have something to picture when I finally tracked down the Walking Man.

I shut my eyes, breathing in the sterile smell of formaldehyde and bleach, and then I opened them and got to work. I might not have a badge and a state crime lab to help me but I'd tracked down men worse than the Walking Man with less.

Leaning close to Lady, I made myself inhale, deep. Aside from slow decomposition, all I could smell was her blood, coppery and sharp on her skin. Next the bites—a shifter would have just torn out her throat or her femoral artery to bleed her quick. They also probably would have eaten at least one of her limbs if it was a feral or a rogue pack. A hellhound like me would have a wolf's bite, angular and much deeper than these shallow tears.

These were human teeth. Sharp, but human. There were folks—from the tribes, Mohawk or Algonquin—friends of my grandmother's who believed in the Wendigo, a man who filed down his teeth to consume human flesh, transformed at the first bite into a monster that could never eat its fill.

I gently rolled Lady onto her side, checking her back, and her hair fell away from her neck. It was still in its perfect wave from the last time I'd seen her, the ends stained pink from sitting in her blood.

The front of her neck was bruised from a hand—at least twice as large as mine—wrapping around it, probably to slam her head into a hard surface and knock her senseless. But the back of the neck was free of bruises, and the mark stood out clear and black. It didn't look like much more than a pen mark, a backward lowercase r with a little tail curling off the back, but when I rubbed at it, it didn't go away.

When I touched it, I smelled the smell. That bitter, burnt, hopeless smell from the camps. The ashes that I still woke up with in the back of my throat.

I lost my grip on Lady's body as I shuddered and she slammed back onto the metal tray. I winced, hoping no one had heard. "Sorry," I whispered.

I was reaching out to pull up her sheet when her eyes snapped open, clouded over with the cataracts death leaves. Her mouth gaped, and she let out one short, agonized scream before she wrapped her hands around my neck.

We both crashed to the ground, the gurney on top of my legs. Lady snapped frantically at me, screaming, spittle trailing out of her mouth to leave a freezing trail along my face and neck. "Lady," I gasped, bracing my hands against her breastbone. "Lady, it's me!"

She whined, low in her throat, like a dog that hadn't been fed in days. That was it, I realized as she slashed and clawed at me. Lady was hungry. Hungry and so desperate she didn't even realize I couldn't feed her. Not in the way she needed.

And I had to make sure she didn't get through me to all the human residents of this hospital, sleeping in their beds like an all-you-can-chew buffet.

I braced one arm to keep her from sinking her teeth into my face and wrapped my other hand in her hair, knotting my fingers into her curls. They weren't as soft as they looked, more like a doll's hair now that she was dead. "Sorry, Lady," I muttered, and slammed her head into the metal edge of the gurney as hard as I could.

I would have crushed the skull of a living person—I think I put a pretty good dent in Lady's—but she just rolled off me, dazed, shaking her head back and forth until her bloody hair fell in front of her eyes. I scrambled to my feet, glad now that I'd forgone my shoes and kicking myself that I hadn't helped myself to Tanner's gun.

Lady howled at me again as she rose up, crouched like a mountain lion who'd cornered a deer. The full extent of her injuries was apparent—her abdomen was dark and distended from internal bleeding and there was a heavy boot print on her chest, across her left breast, where someone had held her down.

Held her down and fed her blood, like a vamp, the hound whispered to me. But poor Lady hadn't been that lucky. She wasn't a vamp, pale and sickly as a junkie looking for their next fix, kitten-weak unless they had fresh blood in them.

I'd seen something like Lady only once before, and even as she screamed, pink foam flecking her lips, I resisted the thought.

I lit on a jar of dirty instruments sitting in the deep-basin sink in the corner of the room and I lunged for them, but Lady was faster. Faster than me, and a whole lot faster than the ones I'd seen in the camps. She landed on me, slamming me into the sink so hard I felt a rib give and fireworks exploded in my field of vision. I pushed back, throwing her off me. She slipped in some of her own blood, pinwheeling and smacking the light fixture so we were plunged into darkness. Before she could lunge again, the door banged open and I saw a tall figure backlit in the hall. Lady turned on him, her mouth unhinging so wide it tore at the edges, and she screamed loud enough to rattle the light fixtures.

The shotgun was louder, and the first shell spun Lady halfway around. The second dropped her like a heap of dirty laundry and she stayed perfectly still, like someone had discarded her on the floor.

Tanner ejected the spent shell, turning to me. "You want to tell me why I just shot a naked dead woman?"

I prodded my side gently and groaned. My rib was definitely broken. "You tell me. You seem like you've done this before." The spots where the shotgun pellets had hit Lady were curling black smoke, like tiny candles, the flesh around them turning ashy and necrotic. The smell was somewhere between burning trash and rotten meat. I couldn't resist reaching out and touching her cheek, just to make sure she was as cold and dead as she'd seemed a minute ago.

"Eight times," Tanner said. "First time she almost got the jump on me. Margaret Taylor." He leaned against the wall, massaging his forehead. "The Walking Man gets 'em dancing, and I put 'em down. But I don't know why, and I think you can help me out in that area."

"Yeah, I think you're wrong there," I said as my fingers chilled against Lady's skin. Her jaw lolled open, and one of her feet trembled and twitched. "You seem like you've got this under control."

Tanner swallowed hard, grimacing at bile as it went back down. "I'm happy I have you fooled."

He shut his eyes for a moment and as he did I caught sight of something small and white inside Lady's mouth, jammed so far back in it was practically down her throat. I pulled out the small piece of bloody paper and uncurled it, my hands shaking.

Fly to me, little bird.

I shoved the paper deep into my pocket, then wrapped my arms around myself, protecting my broken rib. Protecting myself from the cold. "Tanner, trust me, this isn't something you want or need to look any deeper into. This isn't about you." The smell from Lady was overpowering, and I felt the sting of the wet, filthy snow on my skin all over again, even though we were indoors, in Kansas, miles and years removed from the camp.

"You okay?" Tanner said, then shook his head. "Dumb question. I ain't ever been okay with this and I've been doing it practically since I could walk."

"I need air . . ." I tried to say, but the words wouldn't come. I clambered up, snatching my shoes and tugging them on as I stumbled into the hall. Lady's blood squelched between my toes.

I left Tanner then, left him and the hospital, only pausing in the door long enough to pull on my coat. I made it to the edge of the parking lot, where the hissing spotlights didn't reach. If I had just gone with my first impulse to run from this town and poor Lady, I might have gotten away.

But that was a lie, I admitted to myself, because he'd been trying ever since the war ended to get me back, and he'd finally found the right girl, raised the right amount of chaos, to make me come and see what had happened, make me show myself. To stop being Phyllis and go back to being Ava.

I had just stepped out of the light and into the night beyond when I felt somebody fall into step behind me.

"Took you long enough," he said, those same slow words coming out like water droplets falling onto hot coals. "I'd think you'd want to see the man who gave you those scars, little bird."

"My scars healed," I said. "And you're not a man."

"I've left you bread crumbs all across these plains," he said. "I've been looking for you."

I turned on my heel and faced him, but he stepped back into the shadows, laughing. "So what?" I said. "You wanted my attention, you got it. What do you want with me?"

"There's only one of me," he growled. "And one of you, little bird. Together, we make a set."

I made myself laugh. It was better than screaming. How long had he been watching me? How much did he already know? "We're nothing," I said. "I'm nothing special." I spread my hands.

"The filed teeth I get. I know what some of you POWs had to do to survive during the war. But those airman's boot prints you left on my friend? That mark on her neck? I'm not what you need to worry about."

"Detective Tanner, yes," he said, inhaling like he was smelling a nice rare steak. "Without you to show him the ropes, what's to keep me from walking in there and putting an end to him? He's a tormented man. He still has dreams about the beach. About the sound of his own skin burning. About how that sniper's bullet spun him around and left him dying in the snow."

A pair of lamprey headlights came up out of the dark, a Greyhound bus putting on its blinker and pulling over. I took a hard step toward the man from the camp, the evil spirit who'd almost torn my head off. For the first time in a while I didn't feel like turning my back.

"You want me, fine," I snarled. "But Tanner's just a man, and all those people were just human. You leave them out of it or you can never see me again."

"If I have you," he said, "I have no need to make children, little bird. At least not the sort who snarl and bite, who feed on the good men like Tanner."

He stretched out his hand and laughed as the bus door swung open. "Don't worry, little bird. This is where you want to be. Not locked up in a flesh den. Not standing next to a man who sweats booze and fear. You are not any of your names. You are with me now."

I looked back at the hospital. Not just Tanner, but all the people inside, would be dead in the time it took me to grasp the huge hand and feel its ragged nails scratch over my palm.

"Good," the man said when I took his hand. "Good, little bird. This is the last choice you will ever have to make in fear."

There was no one driving the bus, and I could see nothing outside the windows as it pulled away, the man and me sitting side by side.

"Where are we going?" I whispered.

"Where the road takes us," the man rasped. "That is what we do. We ride."

MINNESOTA
NOW

I tried counting every stain on the ceiling—and there were a lot in this glorified cult compound the hounds called home—but even that didn't put me back to sleep.

I hadn't thought about Don Tanner in years—decades, really. Now he wouldn't leave me alone. None of the nightmares would. There was no cure for them except to get out of bed and move, so I nudged Leo.

"No," he grumbled, burying himself deeper under the musty blanket.

"Get up," I whispered. He pulled a pillow over his face.

"No means no, woman."

"We need to go back to Minneapolis," I said. Leo yanked the pillow away and glared at me.

"Give me a break. After that welcome? Let the raver chick down there set the meet and let me sleep."

I got up and pulled on my jeans. It was so cold even inside the house that my skin prickled all over. "Did dying make you stupid?" I said. Leo's forehead wrinkled.

"Ava, what's the problem?"

"Leo, you wouldn't let this group of misfit toys get you a cup of coffee, never mind orchestrate a meeting between you and the guy who wants to kick you out of your company parking space," I said. "For all we know, there is no split and Owen has these clowns watching us."

"If I'm getting stupid, you're even more paranoid than usual," he said, sitting up. I tossed him his shirt.

"Fine. I'm paranoid. But I'm also right." I waited, keeping one ear tuned to the sounds of the house. I wanted to be long gone by the time the guard dogs woke up.

Leo sighed, and then after a long moment he climbed out of bed and put his shirt on. I let out a tiny sigh of relief. Things were getting weird beyond the two of us—bad weird—and I didn't need Leo falling apart on top of everything else.

Downstairs, the hounds were sprawled on every horizontal surface. Viv snored softly, her Mohawk at half-mast. I opened the front door, wincing as the hinges shrieked, but nobody so much as stirred.

Uriel was right—Gary had done a damn good job making everyone who wasn't his direct hench-thug lazy, slow, and stupid. It was a wonder anything had gotten done in the past hundred years where the reapers were concerned.

"So how angry is Thunderdome gonna be that we boosted her ride?" Leo said as I tipped the keys from Viv's sun visor and stuck them in the ignition, turning them just far enough to make the radio hiss and crackle.

"If they leave the keys it isn't stealing," I said, putting the car in neutral and rolling down to the end of the driveway. Leo gestured at me.

"I'll drive. You look like you need a lot more beauty sleep."

"I need you to stop saying things like that before I get out of the car and let Owen chew on your face," I said, leaning my head back against the crusty velour seat of Viv's old-man car. My skull was throbbing.

"So what was it this time?" Leo asked, turning the engine over and putting the pedal down. We were gone in a spray of ice and gravel before I could answer.

"I mean, I've got a lot of bad dreams," Leo continued. "But not as many as you."

"I'm lucky like that," I muttered. My nightmare reels, after all, weren't supposed to include my life before I died and became a hound. Amnesia was one of the standard benefits of becoming a reaper's slave. No loved ones to miss, no memories of your usually violent and premature death to obsess over.

But I got the whole package, because I was meant to pair up with the Grim Reaper. Just like red wine and steak, that was me and Leo. A former mob cleaner and a girl whose boyfriend stabbed her to death in a swamp, reborn as Monster Sonny and Cher.

I was pretty sure I'd been right to get us away from that farm-house, but as we drove back toward Minneapolis I wasn't sure this was a good idea either. That overwhelming need to run and never stop crept over me again, until I felt pins and needles in my legs from the urge to just start sprinting.

I'd had a lot of nightmares, sure. But this particular nightmare made me feel like I wasn't really awake, even as the car groaned along the highway. I felt like I was still back there, and I shivered. I didn't ever want to go back there.

"Sweetheart, you need to relax," Leo said as we rolled to a stop across from the squat gray building. "And I mean that in the least condescending way possible. Relax and act like nothing's both-ering you when we walk in there. I don't want that son of a bitch Owen thinking he's rattled either of us."

"Well, he hasn't," I grumbled. "This has nothing to do with Owen and his alarming overuse of hair products."

"I know you better than that," Leo said. "And considering you're one of the least rattled people I've ever known, how about you tell me why you've had a thousand-yard stare since you woke me up."

"Do you even want to be the Grim Reaper?" I demanded. I felt a little bit like I was drunk—the lack of sleep and the dream hang-over making me blurt like three glasses of tequila. "I mean, what happened to the two of us just driving off and surviving any way we could? Why mix ourselves up with more assholes who are for-ever jockeying for a seat on the back bench in Hell? These people think they're living in *Game of Thrones*. What's next, pulling a sword out of a stone?"

"Ava." Leo stopped just before we went through the salt-streaked glass doors of the grim municipal building that hid the reaper's little kingdom. "These people are idiots, sure. But do you really think we'd last long out there, *surviving,* knowing what we know?" Leo put his hands on my shoulders. "Ava, we saw what Lilith was planning. We were told by a freakin' *angel* that we were meant to put things right with the reapers. To anyone who likes the status quo like our buddy Owen, there's a giant target painted on us. We don't have a choice. We have to be here."

"This blows," I said as he went inside, the door swinging back in my face. "Just for the record."

Leo was halfway across the lobby when I followed him in. The floor was scuffed with slush and boot prints, almost the same color as the nicotine-stained walls. Two elevator doors barely showed me my reflection, they were so dented and scratched. The whole place looked like a DMV from the seventies, complete with the crushing hopelessness and the surly receptionist who glared at us over a romance novel. "Yeah?"

Leo leaned down into her face. "Get Owen."

She sighed, putting a finger in her book and looking him over. "And what is this regarding?"

"Don't be cute with me," Leo said. "If you could actually do your job you wouldn't be riding a desk, so tell your friend with the cheap suits I'm here before I use your head to press that elevator button."

"Tell him yourself," she sighed, rolling her eyes and opening her book again. "He's on three."

Leo jerked his head at me and I followed him to the elevator, even though it was pretty much the last place on earth I wanted to be.

"This is way too easy," I murmured as the contraption groaned upward.

"It's always easy right up until it's not," Leo said. The door rolled back, and I felt my shoulders tense.

Owen met us, flanked by three other suits—one of them was the woman in the red dress I'd seen before. I smiled a little when I saw that her eyes were still rimmed in red.

Her lip curled back from her teeth. "What the hell is *she* doing here?"

"Welcome," Owen said to Leo. "You look well." He stuck out his hand, to which Leo shook his head, huffing a short laugh. "Come on," Owen persisted. "No hard feelings. We had to be sure you were made of the right stuff." He held out his hand to me, and I looked at it, then him, and narrowed my eyes.

"Listen, if you're really supposed to be the big man around here, far be it from me to stand in your way," Owen said. "I'm not interested in a turf war." He straightened his tie. "Between you and me, Gary made this place hell on Earth. He convinced us you didn't exist and he wasn't shy about liquidating folks who didn't hit quotas."

My instincts said that Owen was full of shit, but Leo cocked his head. "So, what, you wanna be friends now?"

"Far from it," Owen said. "I want to get back to work. If we're fighting each other, we're not out collecting. I don't want to be sitting on my ass in Minnesota any more than those malcontents who no doubt have been filling your head full of crap about how I'm a bad man." He raised his arms to encompass the low cement ceilings and the green carpet ground down under decades of shoes, the faded cubicles and the peeling paneling on the office doors at the far end of the large room. "Let's make this work, if you are who you claim. What do you say?"

"You don't want to know what I'd like to say," Leo said. "Where's this piece-of-crap Scythe I need to fondle?"

"Direct, aren't you?" Owen smirked. "That serve you well back at Coney Island or wherever you're from?"

"Oh, I see what you're doing." Leo smiled broadly. "Reminding all your boys here that I used to be human, and therefore I'm not fit to shine your shoes, and you're saying it all nice-nice so I won't put your lights out." Leo stepped closer to Owen, tapping the center of Owen's chest. "You think just because I used to have a human heart beating in here that I ain't played this game? You think a Jewish kid from Brighton Beach with a junkie mom didn't have somebody just like you trying to make him feel like shit every minute of every day?" Leo smiled, and it wasn't the genuine one he only let out around me. This was the smile everyone else saw, the hollow mask that hid his intentions. "Guys like you used to piss me off, Owen. Made me feel lower than dirt. But you know what I learned? Take away the suit and the fake watch and the hundred-dollar haircut and guys like you are all the same. Human or not, you're all weak. And you all die screaming."

Leo stepped back, adjusting his tie. "Then it's up to guys like me to mop up your blood and dump your limbs somewhere in Red Hook. Because guys like me, we're not weak. And we don't die easy."

Owen's mouth was white all the way around, but Leo had finally wiped that Ken Doll smile off his face. "Let's get on with this," Owen said, his voice tight.

"Great idea," Leo replied. "Lead the way."

Owen unlocked one of the office doors, ushering us and his little entourage of creeps inside. He held up his hand, buffed nails under my nose close enough for me to smell the clear polish and moisturizer. It smelled manly, like sandalwood or maybe men's gym shoes. I've never been very good at that stuff. "No dogs," Owen said, giving me another one of those fake smiles that practically dripped corn syrup. "Sorry, love. You understand."

"Get your fingers out of my face or you wasted money on that manicure," I said.

Owen pursed his lips. "You know, Gary would talk about you, but I never believed he'd let any of his bitches be so willful. Guess I was mistaken."

"Excuse me," Leo called from inside, forestalling my desire to choke Owen unconscious with his stupid pinstriped tie. "Either she comes in or I'm leaving and you can all sit around jerking each other off for all I care."

Owen's jaw ticked, and I felt a little bit of corn syrup dripping off my own smile at that. "Move it along," Owen grunted at me, and slammed the door, almost catching my ass in it.

He repeated the fussy unlocking procedure with a safe taller than I was, black iron bulk taking up a corner of the room. I expected the usual things people keep in safes—cash, guns, porn, big piles of paper that don't mean anything to anyone except their owners—but there was nothing inside except a black case, the kind that bad guys carry bombs around with in spy movies.

Owen removed the case and flipped the locks, looking at Leo across the dented metal desk painted that particular shade of olive green that thankfully lived and died with disco. "This is the true Grim Reaper's Scythe," he said. "It's unique because it's the only Scythe that doesn't change depending upon the reaper. If you're the real thing, you'll be able to hold it. If not . . ."

Leo waved a hand. "Yeah, yeah." He reached out and flipped the case open, pulling back the piece of black velvet covering the blade inside.

I didn't really expect anything impressive, but the Scythe was even less exciting than I'd imagined—the handle was plain, short, and slightly bulbous at the end for grip. The blade itself was flat and triangular, a little shorter than my forearm. More than anything, it looked like a railroad spike gussied up with a handle.

Leo stayed expressionless as always. The man had a poker face that would make a statue weep. "Here goes nothing," he whispered as he reached for the blade. I was the only one who heard him, and I reached out to grab his arm.

Being a hellhound doesn't really give you special senses—it more fades you out of the world than tunes you in. You disappear from normal people's radar, becoming visible only to other nightmares or the rare sensitive human. I can't sense auras, feel magic, *smell* magic, even, unless I'm the hound. If I had dog senses when I was on two legs I'd drive myself insane within a week. The world is loud, and a lot of it smells terrible.

But when Leo reached for the Scythe, I felt something shift inside me, that shot of chemicals and nausea your brain emits as an earthquake hits or a twister touches down in your trailer park.

I missed pulling Leo back by a split second. When his fingers touched the handle, he was fine, for half a breath. Then he arched backward, jittering like he'd been struck by lightning. The blade lit up molten, and smoke started to rise from Leo's palm where he gripped it, from his feet where he stood on the carpet, from his chest where the buttons from his shirt touched his skin.

A boom shattered the air around us, cracking the grimy windows of Owen's office into spiderwebs. Leo flew across the room, slamming into the concrete wall and tumbling like he was a GI Joe somebody had gotten bored with and thrown away.

The Scythe thumped on the carpet, turning the fibers into slag and filling my nose with the thick smell of burning plastic. I pressed my hands over my ears, but the feedback from the explosion just got louder, the pressure building inside my skull until I was sure blood was pouring out between my fingers. I watched Owen pick up the Scythe with the most delicate touch and place it back in the case, once he'd retrieved it from the floor. Things were going blurry, and I knew from experience I was a few seconds from passing out.

Leo pulled himself up the wall, singed and wincing but alive. He saw me, and stumbled over, lifting me without any apparent effort. He kicked the office door open and we retreated, the screaming in my head growing a little softer with every step.

By the time we got to the emergency exit I could see, although opening it kicked off a whole new set of alarms and lights. We got down to the lobby and out onto the sidewalk, into Viv's smelly car and away before I finally managed to move. When I did, I tipped my head forward and vomited onto the floorboards.

"Keep it together," Leo rasped at me. "I need you to drive."

"I can't . . ." I croaked, acid squeezing my throat. "I can't . . ."

"You have to," Leo told me. "My arm is useless. I can't move it." He reached for me with his good arm. "Ava—"

"I don't think I can," I squeaked.

"He can't hear you."

I jolted up and away from Uriel, who looked at me from Leo's former seat. "What the fuck now!" I snapped, whipping my head around. We were moving, Leo in the driver's seat, but the snowy city was gone, replaced by the flat blue sky of open fields and endless flat blacktop.

"What did you do?" I said. "You can't just drop in on me! You said Leo would never know and doing this in front of him is so fucking uncool . . ."

"You're not in front of anyone," Uriel said. "You passed out right after you upchucked everything you've ever eaten. Right now your boyfriend is trying to drive with one arm and losing his mind with concern."

He rested one arm on the open window, and I saw us passing serene fields, still pale yellow-green with the first growth after planting. Sweet air filled the car and for the first time in months I wasn't freezing cold. "Demons and psychics aren't the only ones who can drop in while you're dead to the world," he said. "We just tend to show off less."

"This is really not a good time," I said. "Leo tried to use the Grim Reaper's Scythe, and something happened. This sound . . ." I shivered, the pain flooding back into my skull. "Ever had a flashbang go off in your face? Or been in an air raid? Like that, all happening inside my head."

"In case my subtle hint about the psychics didn't clue you in to why I'm here," Uriel said, "you need to be in Kansas City. The Walking Man isn't something I was kidding about, Ava. He escaped Tartarus, and I want him back, and if you're reluctant to help just imagine how unpleasant an *actual* conversation with Leo about me would be."

"Leo's the reason I can't help you!" I said. "He's *not* the Grim Reaper, and we're in deep shit and we have to get out of Minneapolis fast." I jiggled the door handle, trying to unstick the lock. "Much as I'd love to play monster cops with you, Uriel, I have my own problems and since Leo's not the Grim Reaper, I'm not some special edition hellhound. I'm just a normal hellhound whose life is fucked, and therefore I'm off the hook."

"So your solution is to bail out of a car going sixty?" Uriel said. I glared at him, still yanking the handle.

"If I die in my dreams I wake up, right?"

"Would it interest you to know that isn't a reaper's Scythe Owen keeps locked up in his office?" Uriel said. The wind had ruffled his hair, and he smoothed it back.

I let go of the door handle, slumping. "I hate you."

"I know," he said. "Give me your word that when you wake up you'll go to Kansas City."

"Tell me what Owen's doing and I'll consider it," I retorted. Uriel massaged his forehead.

"I've fought legions of demons from Hell and you are still the biggest pain in my ass," he said. "There's six thousand other things I should be doing besides chatting with you in dreamland, so here it is: where have you heard and felt what you did in Owen's office before?"

That stopped me for a second. The pain, the bright intensity that was like holding a high-tension wire in my teeth, feeling like the air was vibrating off my skin, hitting me like a rain of gravel.

I'd met someone before, somebody Lilith had tricked me into

thinking was a soul to collect. Gary's last soul, after I'd killed Gary in Las Vegas. Except the man she forced me to find didn't have a soul, and when I sank my blade into him—

"An angel?" I squeaked at Uriel, surprise stealing the part of my voice that made me not sound like a cartoon character. "A fallen angel," I amended.

"That is your primary job, in case it slipped your mind," Uriel said. "First Tartarus, then the Fallen."

"And then you leave me alone forever," I said wistfully. "What a great day. I'm going to celebrate with a whole pitcher of margaritas."

"You love me," Uriel said, never altering his Perfect Angel mask. "And before you get nostalgic, your little buddy Azrael isn't the one who's giving Owen these toys. Azrael couldn't power a light-bulb, never mind an actual weapon wielded by a soldier of the Kingdom."

I sighed. Azrael wasn't a bad guy. Sure, he was a liar and a disgraced angel who'd been kicked out of the club for consorting with demons, but he'd always treated me fine, and I *had* shown up trying to steal his nonexistent soul. "Not Azrael. Who then?"

"Somebody with the brains to hang on to their smiting stick when they fell," Uriel said. "That's what it is, you know—it's a blade that can only be held by us. If Owen can handle it, one of the Fallen has imbued him with some powerful protection magic. Otherwise he'd fry like a squirrel on a power line."

"And because he *can* in fact handle it like he's working a hibachi grill?" I said.

"The Grim Reaper can kill anything," Uriel said. "Including a member of the Fallen. I'd say the more . . . visible . . . among their number would be extremely interested in keeping your boy down on the farm. You're a bright girl, Ava. I'm sure you can find some way to work that to your advantage."

The car slowed, gravel crunching under the wheels. "In the meantime, enjoy Kansas City," Uriel said. "See some modern art. Eat some barbecue. Find the Walking Man."

"I still hate you," I said as we rolled to a stop.

"I like to think that someday your hostility and my antipathy might blossom into a beautiful indifference," said Uriel. "Until then, do as I ask."

"Yeah, yeah," I grumbled, finally able to open the car door.

"Ava," Uriel said before my boots touched the dirt. "I am on your side. Or we're on the same side. For what it's worth."

"Enemy of my enemy," I said. Uriel nodded.

"Exactly."

"Sorry, Clarence," I said, slamming the door. "The way I see it, I've still got an enemy on either side of me."

"In that case, I'd watch my back," Uriel said, and the road vanished in a bright flare of sun off the pavement.

CHAPTER

et me get this straight," Leo said. We were parked off the side of the highway on a tiny sliver of mud that the signs optimistically called a "Scenic View" and I called a view of the ass-end of wintertime in Minnesota. "Owen's in bed with one of the Fallen, and you're leaving for Kansas City because a psychic came to you in a dream."

I nodded. Leo tilted his head back and let out the most pained sigh I had ever heard. "Okay, let's get through this fast because I think our welcome here in the Little Hell House on the Prairie is wearing thin." He patted down his jacket. "Jesus, I wish I could still smoke. Nothing like killing myself slowly to bring things into perspective."

"Dying sucks," I agreed.

"Listen," Leo said. "I'm not a jealous guy. I don't need all your secrets. But a dead serial killer from seventy years ago . . . even if he is one of the souls that took a powder from Tartarus, how is he your problem now?"

I looked out over the snow to the highway, letting the glare disguise the lie on my face. "He's a bad person, he should be in Tartarus with the rest of the dead bad people, and it's my fault he's free to wander the Midwest. *I* let Lilith trick me into opening Tartarus. *I* let her kill you. It's my fault so forgive me if I want to set one tiny part of it right."

Leo let a long line of cars go by before he spoke. "It's not your fault," he said. "None of it. But I understand why you have to go."

I turned back to him and let him pull me into his arms against the wind. "I don't have to go," I whispered. "We're supposed to stick together. Owen clearly has it out for you."

"Owen is an ass who thinks that because he's got a badass friend, that makes him an actual badass," Leo said. "I can handle Owen. Just come back in one piece." He held me at arm's length and looked me in the eye. "I can be without you, but I need you, Ava. And if you need me, I'll be there." He dropped my arms and took my hand. "Get back in the car with me. I'm from New York and I'm still freezing my nuts off in this hellhole."

"I'll be a minute," I said, giving his hand a squeeze. He would come along if I asked. Of course he would. But I couldn't ask. The Walking Man was mine. My ghost. My sin.

My unfinished business.

Even by my standards, I was driving to Kansas City based on sketchy information. A dream about a man who'd been dead for seventy years and the name of a city. I didn't even know if I was going to the Kansas City in Kansas or Missouri.

I drove south, sticking to the speed limit until it got to be around midnight, then started looking for a motel. Getting pulled over would end this adventure quick—I'd lost all my fake driver's licenses when I broke with Gary and besides, Viv had probably stolen this car once already before we took it from her.

It's not impossible to get around without an identity—not as easy as it was in the days before everything was computerized—but it still works if you follow the basic rules of the unseen and un-documented: use cash, don't leave a paper trail, and stay in places where folks are invested in not asking questions.

The motel I found might as well have had HOOKER HEAVEN writ-ten across the front of it. Half a dozen tractor trailers roosted out front, a few girls darting between the cabs that gleamed under the arthritic neon that glowed from the highway sign. Rooms by the hour, nobody making eye contact, and not a state trooper in sight.

I locked Viv's car, not that anyone would be interested in her piece-of-shit land boat, and paid for a night from a desk clerk whose red beehive was so shellacked it looked like it could deflect bullets. She mumbled around her cigarette at me about how the rooms were no smoking, where the ice machine was located, and that my room had cable TV.

"You working?" she said finally, sliding a key on a sticky plastic fob shaped like a heart across the desk. I just stared at her. Even in the dead of winter, not many girls plied their trade in dirty jeans, muddy boots, and a heavy winter coat they'd bought at an army surplus store. Even the most strung-out tweaker in the lot had combed her hair more recently than I had.

"What then? You a hit man?" She laughed, which turned into hacking, which turned into her spitting something into a tissue tucked into the sleeve of her flowery housecoat.

I looked back at the row of doors to the rooms. A girl spilled out of one, screaming and hitting another girl with her shoe. The second girl, possibly the longest-suffering person on the planet, tried to help her friend's drunk ass back to a rusty SUV where their pimp, a skinny kid with hair even redder than the clerk's, waited. I was never getting any sleep in this place.

"You can help me with something," I said to the clerk, who was still waiting for me to laugh at her joke.

"Help's not free, missy," she barked.

"I'm not asking for free," I said. "That kid out there, the one who looks like Ron Weasley's redneck brother—he holding?"

She exhaled, jamming her cigarette into an ashtray shaped like a big-mouth fish with its gullet hanging open to accept burning butts. "Depends what you need to get right, honey," she said. "And don't think you're shooting up in the rooms. I ain't cleaning up after another one of you skinny bitches can't get her mix right and OD's on the toilet."

"I just need something to help me sleep," I said. "Percocet, oxy, whatever."

She tossed her head, hair not moving an inch. "Go talk to him. Name's Ronnie."

Ronnie thrashed when I knocked on his window. I presented two twenties between my fingers and pointed to the motel office. "Lady in there said you could help me."

"Come on," Ronnie muttered, clearly not talking to me. He swung out of the truck and screamed in the direction of the office.

"Damn, Mom! You're blowin' up my spot! What if she's a cop or something?"

"She ain't a cop!" the clerk screamed back. "You don't want my help, then move out and do your business somewhere other than my motel, dumb-ass!"

I nodded in agreement with the clerk. "I'm not a cop," I said to Ronnie. "I just need to sleep."

Ronnie grumbled, fishing in his pocket for a Ziploc bag of pill bottles. "Forty'll get you four," he said. "You want a Xanax? House discount kind of a thing."

"Why not," I said. Ronnie counted out my pills, grumbling as he did.

"You got a mother?"

I shook my head. "Not anymore."

"You're lucky," he said. "Mine is constantly up my ass."

"Sounds uncomfortable," I said, and went to my room. I chased the four Percocets with some filmy water from the tap and lay back on the bed, after I put down a few towels. No way was I taking this trip on that bedspread.

After a few minutes everything got soft around the edges and that cotton-wool-cloud feeling wrapped around my brain. I tried to focus on Jacob as I drifted off, hoping that I hadn't just fallen for some sick metaphysical joke, and that I wasn't trapping myself in the sort of dream you don't wake up from.

CHAPTER

KANSAS, HIGHWAY 21
MARCH 1951

Ride the highways long enough and you lose all sense of time. Days turn into weeks turn into months. One exit after another, one mile compounds on the next until there's nothing except the lines in the center of the pavement and the horizon beyond. You can chase it, but you'll never catch it.

I'd been riding this particular stretch for a few weeks. I hadn't gotten to that place yet, where you feel like you'll cease to exist if you stop rolling along, but I could feel it creeping up with every mile, every cup of sour coffee, and every lumpy motel mattress.

I'd tried to escape him a dozen times. Really tried, and the farthest I'd ever made it was across the road. As the ice turned to mud and then to tender green blooms, I stopped trying.

He'd never told me his name. The Walking Man rarely talked, but sometimes, as we watched the miles roll by, he'd place his heavy hand over mine, on my shoulder, on my cheek. And I fought to keep still and not scream, because when you scream and panic, the predator looking you in the eye opens its jaws and eats you.

He made more of those things like Lady. At least as many bodies as my escape attempts. I always prayed that Tanner was coming behind us, cleaning up the mess. He'd followed me, that much was for sure, and I saw him once outside a diner in Oklahoma City. He looked so sad, so desperate, and my voice welled up in my throat to scream at him to get away, get away before he was killed.

But nothing happened. That was the Walking Man's real power—you could be a wailing wreck inside your own head but strangely, when he was close nothing really seemed to matter except the next mile, the next set of headlights flagged down, the next brutalized body that began to twitch and moan after the last of the life had fluttered away into the warm currents drifting in the wake of passing trucks. A thrall, but something far stronger than the kind warlocks could weave with spells and far more precise than the warm, woozy intoxication of vamp venom. Sometimes, when he was away from me for a scant few hours, I started to think about what he was, how he could do this to me when I wasn't even human, what he was trying to do over and over by making those things that would infect others like him.

Once, just as the snow was melting, I ran from him and the silent miles we shared on the driverless bus and stood on the train tracks, feeling the oncoming rumble of the Wichita line through the soles of my feet. I spread my arms when the screaming whistle filled up my ears and I waited, overjoyed, for it to be over.

But he'd grabbed me, slammed me into the half-thawed mud and gravel next to the track, wrapped those giant hands around my throat, and let me think for a second that I'd still managed it, that he'd kill me and I'd finally be able to escape.

Then he'd taken a deep breath and stroked his muddy hand down my face. "Why can you not understand that we are the same thing?" he purred in that strange flat voice. "Both creatures carved from unnatural clay. Why can you not see this is where you belong, not with Hell's dogs? Why can you not accept me and help me?"

I screamed then, and kept screaming until I vomited.

That was the last time I tried to escape. I complied, I sat by him, I watched the highway until my eyes burned. The only thing I wouldn't do was help him. I wouldn't lure the cars into stopping and I wouldn't try to help his creations find other human beings to feed on.

His rage was towering, especially when the epidemic he'd envisioned never started. I knew the forces against us were getting stronger as he got bolder and more desperate. One time, it was a family, two kids and parents, who stopped and he turned them all out into the night to feed. That time, dozens were affected and he shook the newspapers from the next day in my face, then picked me up and spun me around like we were newly married.

That lasted until the next morning, when an enormous grain elevator fire covered the front page with a picture of smoke and burned, twisted bodies that covered my hands in ink as the Walking Man raged and shouted on the shoulder of the road.

I said a silent thanks to Don and whoever was helping him. I prayed they'd never find us, because the Walking Man would hurt him and twist him so violently before he died his soul would just be a ruined thing screaming into the afterlife.

Then, it was spring and the green was so violent it covered everything in a haze of pollen and new life. And the next time Tanner found us, parked by the side of the road with our fake broken-down car, he had brought a companion of his own.

She was tall and slender, redheaded with the wide cheekbones and a narrow chin that gave her face a catlike cast. She hurt him, the Walking Man. He reeled like he'd run into a wall, like he hadn't moved since Jacob had hit him with the spell, back in the camps.

The Walking Man's wooden face shifted when this happened, and I saw the evil spirit living inside, the *dubbyuk* Jacob had spoken of.

"Ava!" Tanner shouted, holding out his hand. "Come to me, right now!"

I could have moved, but I didn't. I didn't *want* to be there; I wanted this nightmare to end so badly that I couldn't believe it was actually over.

"Ava!" Tanner shouted again. His friend's face twisted in concern, sweat working down her temples, her willowy body bending at the invisible wind stirred up by her fight against the Walking Man.

"If she's gone, you can't help her and I can't hold him off much longer!" she shouted.

"She's not gone!" Tanner screamed. "*Ava!* Move!"

A truck horn sounded from down the highway, and that snapped me into motion. I ran toward Tanner. The Walking Man screamed and grabbed for me, snatching my wrist and arresting my flight. I felt the joint pop, but his grip loosened as Tanner's friend redoubled her efforts, blood starting to trickle from her nostrils.

I swung around as the truck drew even with us, and struggled with all of my might. I'd pretty much stopped eating, and I was weak as the little bird he always claimed I was.

With the last of my strength, I yanked, he pulled in the opposite direction . . . and then I leaned toward him and let go.

He stumbled back, right into the path of the truck. His body hit the grille and was sucked under the wheels. The air brakes pumped, the truck jackknifed, and the scent of burning rubber filled my nostrils.

I fell, spent, the last of me wrung out.

When I got up, my two rescuers found nothing under the wheels of the truck, except a lot of blood—all the blood inside a person, Tanner would tell me later.

I didn't let them take me anywhere. I closed the hood of the lure car and drove to the nearest bar. All through the summer, through the wheat harvest and the first snow and the gray, stubbled fields of a new year, I took a drink as often as I breathed, and I took everything else that was offered me too. Circular bruises blossomed and grew inside the crooks of my elbows and knees like I was doing target practice with syringes of morphine. Pills burned up my gut. All of it barely kept the nightmare of my time with the Walking Man at bay, but it did—barely.

Nobody picked me up off the road that time—eventually, the faces and the screams faded just enough that I could be awake for a while without wanting to stand in front of another train. Eventually, I sweated through the withdrawals, looked in a mirror long enough to cut my hair and paint over the circles under my eyes, scraped together money for a new dress and discovered that another spring was coming on.

Now it was summer. I'd had four years to straighten up and fly right. After that day I'd cleaned myself up and gotten on a bus back to Wichita. I'd found Gary, I'd taken the beating Gary had meted out. I'd taken all the scut collections work he'd given me. I'd played the dutiful servant.

And as I'd crisscrossed the country collecting on warlocks and conjurers looking for a little more power than their share, I'd kept an eye on the newspapers. I'd befriended reporters on the crime beat, cops in every state between Kansas and California. Medical examiners, emergency room doctors, even the guys who scrape roadkill off the highways.

Every so often—not more than one or two times a year—a body would come up, beaten and mutilated and marked. He'd gotten smarter about crossing state lines so it was harder to draw a line between kills. He'd gotten better at turning them into killing machines too, at making them hungrier and more aggressive.

And every time, I'd called Tanner and he'd put another pin in the map he kept in his office. As far as the state police were concerned, the Walking Man was a cold case. As far as anyone besides Tanner and I knew, he'd disappeared as mysteriously as he'd started murdering people.

Sometimes Tanner came with me to help put down the ravenous bodies that he left in his wake, and sometimes I was on my own. But we always managed before it spread out of control. Whether it was cutting the head off a mailman in Missouri or burning down an entire trailer park full of his walking corpses in northern Texas, we kept the Walking Man's gifts to us from spreading out into the world.

But now Tanner had left word for me instead of the other way around. I was up in Idaho, tracking down a warlock with a gift for transmutation and a propensity for using that gift to pass counterfeit bills and bad checks. To my way of thinking, Gary had only himself to blame when this particular specimen tried to weasel out of his deal.

I tried to let Tanner know where I was, and even though we lost touch for months at a time, we always found each other again. But he never called on me, never made me take a detour and help him and the other humans like him. Until a few weeks ago.

The state police barracks where Tanner worked had stood shiny and new behind a big parking lot with a big flag snapping in the hot wind. I shielded my eyes from the blowing grit blooming in the field across the road. The Depression might be behind us, but this was still the Dust Bowl.

"He ain't here," the cop working the desk said when I asked for Tanner. "Out on a call. Probably won't be back until tomorrow."

"Okay, can you tell me where?" I said. The cop looked me up and down.

"Why?" he asked. "You his side piece? Didn't take him for the type."

I reached into my purse. Next to my knife and lipstick and wallet was a banded collection of cards I'd accumulated in the last four years of my side job. I picked out one for Joan Cartwright, a stringer for a paper in Nebraska. She'd been smart and a hell of a drinker—I'd liked her. If you were pretending to be someone, it helped to be somebody who wasn't repulsive.

I slid the card across to the desk cop and he raised an eyebrow. "Reporter, huh? Don't see too many dames on the crime beat."

"Well, now you've seen at least one," I said brightly. "Detective Tanner agreed to be profiled for a feature I'm doing on state policing across state lines."

I practically saw the cop's eyes glaze over, and he reached for a pad to write down Tanner's hotel address. "Knock yourself out," he said, and went back to his newspaper. The headline blared in type almost as high as my thumbprint. HITCHHIKING HORROR. In smaller type, **Has the Walking Man Returned to Kansas?**

"You have no idea," I muttered, jogging outside to catch the taxi before he drove away.

Another small town, this one almost on the Nebraska border rather than the Oklahoma one. At least this one had a train station, and somewhere to eat other than a greasy Automat.

Tanner pushed a small white plate across the table when I sat down. "I ordered you some pie."

"You're handling this pretty well," I said, taking a polite bite. I wasn't going to be tucking into any sweets. We'd been back on the trail for two weeks and there were twice as many bodies as of this morning, if you believed the cop's paper.

"Right back atcha," Tanner said. "You look . . . healthy. Healthier than you've been in a while." The first time Tanner had seen me after I'd crawled back out of the bottle, his face had told me exactly how bad I looked. For a cop, he was a bad liar. I'd gained back the weight, my scars had healed, and my skin was no longer the same shade of gray as the empty wheat fields. In contrast, Tanner had aged a decade in four years. His hair was going white at the temples and deep wrinkles that hadn't existed when I met him creased beside his mouth. Sun and stress and smoke and bad food would do that to any heartland cop, and Tanner wasn't special. Just different.

I tapped my fork on the edge of my plate. "So what do you hear?"

Tanner checked his watch. "There's another body," he said. "But that's actually not why I wanted you to come in today." He pushed back from the little cafe table. "I gotta make a call," he said. "Hang tight."

I waited, watching the train I'd been on pull out of the station across the street. There was something hanging in the air here, like the smoke from the diesel engine. It vibrated under my feet the same as the cars picking up speed as the whistle blasted a good-bye.

This was where I'd find the Walking Man again. This was where it'd finally end.

"Sorry," Tanner said, sliding back into his seat and picking up the remains of his Monte Cristo sandwich.

"Who is she?" I said, finishing off the pie. It wasn't half-bad.

"Who?" Tanner feigned confusion.

"Your wife," I said. He turned a little pink around the edges.

"That obvious, huh?"

"Well, it hasn't been long enough for a tan line on your ring finger," I said. "But the desk guy back at your barracks did ask me if I was a side piece. Implying there's a main piece somewhere."

Tanner snorted. "Six months, maybe a little more. Her name is Joyce. She's a nurse."

"Good for you," I said. "You need someone who's around to do more than help you fight off the undead."

"She knows. About my . . . night job." Tanner paid the check and handed me a photo as we walked out. It was the same mark, the little *r* and the tail, carved into the thigh of a blond woman. He did love blonds.

"Still no luck," I sighed. Seeing that thing burned me up. I was a hellhound. If there was a mystical symbol the Walking Man claimed as his own, I should know it. But it wasn't a Hellspawn language. I'd shown it to a few warlocks I'd tracked down who seemed to have more than half a brain, and they didn't recognize it either. It wasn't like I could present the thing to Gary, or worse, to an actual demon. Tanner hadn't had any more luck with the professors, ancient language experts—even the code breakers at the FBI came up with squat.

"Hang in there, Ava," Tanner said, unlocking the same rattle-trap Ford he'd driven the night we met. "I have a feeling our luck is about to change."

"*I got to* thinking," Tanner said as we turned south, bouncing along a road that wasn't much more than two muddy ruts in the snow. "The Walking Man's critters—not deadheads, not vampires. Little from column A, little from column B."

"Just like the man himself," I murmured. "Where are we going?"

"If he's not the usual sort of monster," Tanner continued, turning off onto an even more pitiful excuse for a road, "then the usual sort of professors and the usual sort of sources you can go to won't be able to help us track him down."

"So I ask again, where are we?" I said, as Tanner pulled to a stop in front of a field. A few dozen yards away, a collection of tents and camper trailers made a tight little circle against the sleet that had started to come down on our drive out here.

"To speak with someone who you've already met," he said. "That night."

My chest tightened as I thought of the redhead, all flying hair, bleeding face, and telling Tanner to let me die.

She hadn't been wrong. Tanner had just been too reckless to listen.

"Is that why you brought me here?" I demanded, following him out of the car and almost turning my ankle as my heel sank into a muddy furrow left by a trailer tire.

"She threatened to shoot me if she ever saw me again. I basically needed a human shield," Tanner said. "I was gonna make her the same offer my Joyce accepted, and when I realized it wasn't going to work out, that we were too similar . . ." He cleared his throat and turned around.

"Funny," I muttered as Don walked up to the nearest trailer and rapped on the door.

The redhead threw it open. She'd aged better than Tanner, hair straight now rather than coiffed, flipped at the ends, tied off with a smart green scarf. Her eyes filled with pure hatred as Tanner took his hat off and smiled. "Good morning, Valentine."

"You got a short memory, Tanner," the woman snarled. "You're lucky I don't want to get blood all over my trim." She started to slam the door and I stuck my foot in it, wincing as the metal edge caught my toes. "You crazy?" she shouted at me. "I said get lost!"

"We just want to talk," Tanner said. "Come on, Val."

"You lost the right to call me that when you stepped out on me with your damn night nurse," she snapped. "And you . . . why are you wasting time with this piece of highway litter? I thought you were smarter than that."

"It's complicated," I said.

"Yeah, well, when he leaves you alone at a drive-in movie concession, takes the car, and rides away into the night, don't come crying to me," Valentine spat.

Tanner rolled his eyes upward. "I don't know what you have against crying, you insufferable harpy. I imagine that's all anyone ever wants to do when you open your mouth."

"Fuck you, Donald Tanner!" Valentine spat. "Fuck you and your whole shifty pack of Irish miscreants back to the beginning!"

She shoved me back, to dislodge my foot, and then slammed the door so hard the glass inside it cracked. Tanner sighed.

"You ever spend time with these people? Travelers?"

I shook my head. "They came through here and there when I was a girl. Bear Hollow didn't get a lot of new people. Once, the mining company came through and installed road signs. People talked about that for years." I looked at the trailer, which wasn't so much red as rusty with a few silver patches left. Despite looking like a banged-up can of ham, it had new whitewalls and crisp curtains hanging in the little windows. "You shouldn't judge. We didn't live any better. Our shack just didn't have wheels."

"Who said anything about judging?" Tanner said, knocking again. "I didn't exactly grow up sipping on champagne and having butlers massage my feet at night."

This time Valentine opened the door with the barrel of a Winchester. "I'm serious, Don. No more. No more showing up, no more favors. You don't get to ask those sorts of things of me. Not after everything."

"I asked him to," I blurted. She grimaced, but the gun barrel lowered an inch.

"He's no good for either of us, Ava. I don't know you that well, but you look like you're on a better path now and he'll yank you right off it."

"Please just help us and you'll never see either of us again," I said. Don, mercifully, stayed quiet.

Valentine sighed. "I highly doubt that." She put up the shotgun and shoved the door wider. "You made me break my goddamn door," she told Tanner as we stepped inside. "Add it to the list of things you broke that belong to me."

I cast a glance back at Tanner. Whatever I'd missed while I'd been off being a good little hellhound had been ugly and it was still a gaping wound.

I turned my attention back to Valentine. It wasn't any of my business. Anytime I cared about a human, all I got was more bad dreams to add to the roster.

Valentine sat on the pile of cushions against the far wall of her trailer and gestured to a pair of folding chairs. The place wasn't half-bad—if you didn't look outside you could imagine you were tucked inside some little room in a jazz club or a hotel suite some place like Morocco or Algeria—someplace I'd never seen, and would probably never see. With some scarves, some velvet, and a lot of thrift shop afghans, the place had been made almost cozy.

Valentine lit a cigarette in a long holder and offered me one. I shook my head. Don accepted and leaned over to light it. "So how have you been keeping yourself?"

Valentine exhaled a vicious spurt of smoke. "In a trailer, next to my mother's trailer. It's been exquisite." She raised one thin auburn brow. "What do you want from me, Don? Let's get it over with."

Tanner pulled the photo from his jacket. "I didn't show you this before. It's a detail we never released to the public, but you're my last resort. I always figured it was a symbol, but now I just don't know."

Valentine accepted the photo but didn't look at it. She splayed her slim fingers against the cardboard backing and shut her eyes, letting her cigarette smolder in her free hand. "A girl," she said at last. "He prefers to start with a girl. But we all know that."

I shifted, starting to get angry with Tanner. He was wasting time with his ex-squeeze while the Walking Man was out there, waiting for me.

"I'd think you of all of God's creatures would have a little more patience with my abilities," Valentine murmured. She opened her eyes and fixed me with a look of even less warmth than she'd bestowed on Tanner. "But then again, you're not one of God's creatures, are you?"

"And what exactly are you going to do about that?" I said, fixing her with the same stare. If she wanted me to blink she was going to be disappointed.

"It's not my place to do something," she said primly, opening the file. "It's yours to hold your head up and refuse to do *every* little thing Gary asks of you."

"Gary?" Tanner ashed his cigarette into the tray at Valentine's elbow. "Who the hell is Gary?"

I folded my arms tight across my chest. She already knew I didn't like her—at least I didn't have to let her see she'd rattled me. "Can you tell us about this symbol or not?"

She studied the photo closely, squinting at it through her glasses, and then passed her fingers over it softly before putting it back in the file. "Do you read the Bible?"

"More than I ever wanted to," I said. Tanner shook his head at the same time.

Valentine put out her cigarette. "I know full well *you're* a heathen, Don. Poor girl," she said in the same breath. "She was so frightened and she died too soon." She looked back at me and sighed. "I don't like what I'm able to do. I didn't like it the night I saved you and I don't like it now. I choose to believe it comes from a decent place, but to be honest I don't know." She handed the photo back, not to Tanner but to me, holding on to the opposite edge as I accepted it. She wasn't taking my measure anymore. She was scared. "What I do know is that because of my ability I've seen a lot of monsters. A lot of evil, both man-made and not. Vampires. Walking corpses. People like me who don't make use of their ability like I do, people who only want to stand on others' necks to rise up higher."

When she did let go of the photo I started a bit, dropping it on the floor. The symbol stared up at me from the dead girl's flesh in stark black and white.

"There are two men," Valentine whispered, her eyelids starting to flutter. "Two men standing. Screaming. Fighting. It's so long ago. The world was different. Even the air tastes different, that's how long it's been. And the man, he strikes his brother down. He stands above him, and he feels . . ." She shuddered, head dipping. When she raised her head again her eyes had rolled to expose the white and her cheeks flushed pink.

"He feels as he's never felt before. He touches the wound he's inflicted. He drinks the blood of the man he's slain. He can't think about what he's done. All he can think is that he wants more."

She sucked in another shuddering breath. Her eyes slowly rolled back to the pupils. "It's not just like the Bible, but you get where I'm going with this, don't you?"

I thought of the smell, the rich burning smell, like ashes and incense and rotting flowers, that had overwhelmed me at the camp. The Walking Man's implacable gaze, the way he just kept coming, like a storm or a tidal wave—nothing any living thing could hope to stop.

"You know the story," Valentine said. She picked up the photo from the floor. "You know what this sign really means."

"You really think I wouldn't have heard of this by now?" I said. "Of him? If he were real?"

"Ava," she said. "If you're already a monster, would you want to admit the boogeyman exists? Never mind that he's gotten inside your mind once, and made you his possession." Her gaze met mine and I felt like we were both sinking into a pool of cold water, neither of us willing to let go. I felt her page through the album of my memories, like tiny scratches behind my eyes. "You're afraid of him," she said. "And I don't blame you. But pretending he's not what he really is won't make him go away."

"I'm lost," Tanner said. "Do you know what the symbol means or not, Val?"

"Not what," Valentine said, never breaking my gaze. "Who. It is not a symbol. It's a brand. A name. A mark that means these souls belong to him, have been fed to his insatiable need."

I wanted to deny her, but she wasn't wrong. I was terrified of the Walking Man. He'd made me wish for death in a way nothing ever had—not since I'd actually died. I knew all it would take was one slip, one time when Tanner and I weren't in the right place at the right time to put down those diseased things he bred, and the world would be in ashes. A whole world like what I'd witnessed in the camps.

The terror struck so deep inside me it felt like my own spine. I nodded in agreement with Valentine. "It is a mark. It's the Mark of Cain."

CHAPTER

11

THE MIDWEST
NOW

Ronnie's screaming woke me up. I'd slept in my clothes, and at an angle that made every part of my body complain at top volume as I rolled off the bed. My head throbbed in time with Ronnie's tirade of curse words.

"Swear to Christ, Mom, I'm going to come in that shit heap you call a trailer one day and chop your head off. Then I can stick it on top of the Christmas tree in my pad and have a happy fuckin' holiday!"

I picked up my boots and stepped out of my room, leaving the key in the lock. "Dude," I said to Ronnie when he spun to look at me. "Family therapy. Seriously."

He squawked when I reached out and snatched his car keys from his front pocket. "What the fuck!"Staring into his eyes without blinking, I showed him my knife. "The keys to the land whale are in my room. I think it needs a new fan belt. Leaks oil, too." If anyone was tracking me—or Viv's car—I didn't have to make it *too* easy for them.

Ronnie didn't try to stop me when I got into his truck and cranked the engine. Maybe he wasn't as dumb as he looked.

The SUV at least had a working radio and heater, and by the time I got to Kansas City I even felt mostly awake, the sharp edges of the last few days without sleep or rest chased away by the last threads of my Percocet coma.

I'd hoped the deep sleep would induce another connection with whoever was broadcasting from KC, but all I'd gotten were dreams that belonged buried, like the corpses they were. No clues to who wanted me to drive all this way. I did think it was awfully convenient that Uriel and this nameless psychic were both pushing me toward the Walking Man, like it was a blind date.

Since I was pretty sure you couldn't stick your psychic fingers into an angel's brain and work him like a puppet, I had to think that the dream I'd had was a lure, the Walking Man's latest gambit to worm his way back into my line of sight. Not even seven decades in Tartarus had dimmed his urge to stalk me. That was dedication, of the craziest variety.

Now to top it all off, I was thinking of Valentine. I hadn't thought about her in years. Crazy little witch that she was, and she'd been more right about me than anyone before or since.

That was what I hadn't wanted to betray to Uriel back in that shitty bar. I didn't know how much he knew about what Cain had done to me, how he'd made me ride with him for all those months. I'd told myself—and Tanner had told me—over and over that I wasn't responsible for the deaths. I'd been as under his spell as any of the victims. But I'd never really believed it. That was the sole benefit of being betrayed and murdered and raised as a hellhound. You stopped being prey and got to be the hunter, for once.

I'd tried as hard as I could to forget that whole period of my life—Tanner, the dead people, the Walking Man.

I wasn't surprised he was back. What surprised me was that he'd ended up in Tartarus in the first place. I wasn't sure he *could* die, never mind be locked snugly away in Hell's supermax, a place meant only for human souls.

Which technically, his had been, I guessed. Long ago.

I'd just been so glad he was gone, that I was free, when it all ended back then, that I hadn't looked too closely. Hadn't *wanted* to. And now he was back, and he was coming for me. He thought we belonged together. Both unique monsters—the hellhound who remembered she was human once and the man who remembered he was a monster.

I swiped at my eyes as sun glinted off the ice on the sides of the highway and fished around until I found a pair of mirrored sunglasses that Ronnie kept in his glove box. I was awake. I needed to stop dwelling on my crappy life choices and make a plan for when I got to Kansas City. In the annoying way of psychics, the message I'd gotten hadn't included anything useful, like an address or a name of someone I was supposed to meet.

The river glinted, chunks of ice floating below me as I crossed the bridge, and I took the first city exit with a street name I remembered. I figured a lot had changed since '51, but at least I'd be starting from a familiar point.

The Raven's Tale hadn't changed much. It was still a shitty little hole in the wall that smelled like wet paper and wetter dogs, windows filmed up with grime and a door that wailed on rusty hinges.

It was daytime, so I didn't expect Rusty to be awake. The minion sitting behind the high old-fashioned shop counter looked at me, pretending he was looking at one of the old magazines stacked in big slippery towers all over the countertop.

Technically the place was a bookshop, but that was like saying technically I was a canine. Both accurate, and at the same time missing the essential parts by a mile.

The minion looked me over. Judging by the half-shaved head of ratty black hair and the bad posture, Rusty had gotten to him sometime in the eighties. Or he could still be human, and just have crappy hygiene. It was always hard to tell.

"We're closed," he said when I got close.

"Then you should lock your doors," I said. He sighed.

"If you're a cop, you can buzz off. This is just a bookstore and whatever else you've heard is spiteful rumors generated by rival shop owners to cut into our business."

"What business?" I said. "You don't have any business. This place is deader than your boss." Up close, I caught the pungent herbal stench of dried blood and slow decay. Robert Smith, Jr. here was definitely a vamp.

"You're not a witch," the minion sniffed. "And you're not one of the kindred, so any business we *do* have, you're not a part of. Since you're not a customer, take your bargain basement, tired-out punk-rock hooker act somewhere else."

I got closer than I wanted to, already regretting what I was going to have to do. I hate touching dead things, especially when they wiggle and squirm and talk like this douchebag. I hate the whole tough-girl routine, period. I prefer to stay quiet, keep my head down, do the work, and get gone.

Unfortunately, vamps are too stupid to grasp subtlety of that level.

I grabbed the guy by the side of his head that still had hair, slamming his skull into the brass cash register that hadn't worked in the entire time I'd been coming to this smelly dump. "You know what I find really hilarious?" I asked as I knotted my fingers in the greasy tangle, using my free hand to swat away his grasping nails. "That you virus-ridden pieces of rotting meat use words like *kindred* to try to hide the fact that you are, in fact, diseased hunks of flesh who can still talk."

He opened his mouth and let out a string of curse words, and I jammed Ronnie's sunglasses into his mouth. "Now I'm going to give you a simple choice," I said. "You can tell Rusty that Ava is here to see him. That's choice one." I put my free hand under his chin and pushed to the point where his fangs scraped the mirrored glass. "Choice two is I close your mouth and you get enough crushed glass between those teeth of yours they'll be sliced clean out of your head."

He squirmed and I clicked my tongue. "Hold up your fingers."

After a long moment while his deep black eyes glared at me

with hatred, he held up one finger. "Good choice," I said, pulling the sunglasses out of his mouth. He spat at me.

"Go screw yourself, whore! I don't answer to any dogs!"

I sighed. "So you're not telling Rusty, then."

"You're not fit to look upon his face!"

"I've seen his face way too often for my liking," I said as he hopped the counter and came at me. His apathy belied that vicious, ratlike speed that vamps possess, especially if they're angry.

"Have it your way," I muttered, taking out the other thing I'd brought from Ronnie's car and pulling the tab. Road flares are pretty useful against vamps, especially older ones. They need blood to survive but the virus dries up their tissues and hair, makes them almost tinder, if they're old enough and live in a dry climate.

Robbie here wasn't old enough to be good firewood, but I jammed the flare into the soft spot under his rib cage, getting it way in there, past the muscles and into the abdominal cavity. His nasty polyester shirt smoked and crackled as he fell back, croaking out his last bad word.

"For the record," I said, brushing ashes off myself. "This punk rock hooker paid full price for her look." I kicked his limp foot. "Asshole."

Fire is the only way to make sure you kill a vamp—burn the blood and tissue, burn up the virus. Otherwise the damn thing is just going to keep getting up.

The curtains that cordoned off the back half of the building swished, and I looked up. "Setting a fire in a bookshop is very stupid, Ava," Rusty said. "Even for the likes of you."

"If you'd stop hiring mouth-breathers, I wouldn't need to burn them down," I said. Rusty cinched the belt of his bathrobe, his thin face crinkling. I could see the red of the flare reflected in the small round lenses of his glasses.

"There are many whispers behind your back these days," he said. "From all sorts of startling places."

I folded my arms. Rusty tossed back the thinning red forelock he called hair, huffing. "Well don't blame me, darling. It's that young man you're keeping company with. You and the Grim Reaper are the couple of the moment."

"Rusty, shut up," I said. The key with him was not talking too much. He quieted, then immediately opened his mouth again.

"But here you are alone, in Kansas, with dark clouds forming on the horizon. I hear of solitary souls that have spent these past dark days in Tartarus, free again. I don't hear anything of why you're here, however. Who are you after?" He sniffed as the smoke from his buddy filled the low-ceilinged space. "If he's one of my customers I will not betray a confidence. Warlocks are not your chew toys, girl."

"I'm not here for one of your shitbag customers, Rusty," I said. He threw out his arms, undoing the belt a bit and making his bathrobe flap like cheap silk wings.

"Then what, dear girl? What reason?"

"I'm looking for someone," I said, heading for the door. He shouted over my shoulder.

"If you'd just name a name, I could tell this doomed individual of your inquiry and avoid more scenes like this!"

I turned back, letting the cold air from outside fan the flames of the dead vamp on the floor. "Tell everyone."

After the show with Rusty, I realized that despite still smelling of the human tire fire that is burnt vamp, I was starving. I walked a couple of blocks and found a pancake house that had actually survived the intervening decades. It had a different sign and a different name, but the place still served greasy bacon, bad coffee, and huge plates of flapjacks.

Rusty, in addition to being a profiteering ghoul who sold knockoff magic books and spell supplies to every warlock in the two states, was an inveterate gossip. If my psychic had even a little toe dipped in the KC underground, they'd know I was here within the hour.

I took a booth by the window where I could see the door, the kitchen, and the bathrooms. I wasted one hour, then another, sucking down coffee and hoping I didn't have to use the bathroom before somebody showed.

I was well into hour three when I realized there was a man watching me. He was alone, wearing one of those canvas jacket/button-down combos popular with middle-aged dads and white serial killers. His hair, his little steel glasses, even his cheap watch was way too old for the face, which looked maybe thirty, tops. What little hair his crew cut had left was dark and he tapped his fingers nervously against his day planner, which sat next to an un-touched cup of coffee.

I set my knife down slowly, but I kept hold of my fork. I wasn't used to humans staring at me. I wasn't used to humans being aware I was in a room, unless I explicitly got their attention. And when someone *did* stare at me like that, it usually ended with them trying to put a bullet in my chest, at the very least.

But this guy didn't move. He just sat, staring and tapping like a tiny speed metal drummer. I put down some money for my food and stood up, walking over to his booth. "Can I help you?" I said, stopping just out of lunging distance.

"Not here," he said, trying to do that thing where you talk but don't move your lips. "Bathroom. Sixty seconds."

"No," I said. "Now."

"We can't be seen talking," he ground out. "There are people watching who might be very upset."

"Good," I said, sliding into the booth opposite him. "I feel like hitting somebody right now and if you play your cards right it might not be you."

"Are you insane?" he barked, grabbing up the planner and holding it in front of him like a shield.

"Opinions vary," I said. "Who are you and why are you staring at me like you do it for a living?"

He sighed, wrapping his arms around the leather book. "I heard you were in town. From Russell—Mr. Raven. I'm the one you were dreaming about."

"Oh really," I said, sitting back. He sighed.

"I'm sorry it was garbled. I've never—I'm not good at transmitting. I'm more of a receiver."

"What's your name?" I said quietly. He sighed, looking at me desperately.

"Can we *please* go somewhere private?" The finger tapping started up again and I took the fork I'd pocketed and slammed it tines-first into the table between his thumb and forefinger. He froze, eyes wide as half dollars.

"That's really annoying," I said.

"I see a lot about you," he squeaked. "You're *all* I've seen, for months. When an impression is that persistent it means I have to do something about it." He swallowed a hard lump in his throat. "I'm sorry if that makes you mad but you need to be here, now. I'm not wrong about things that I see."

I sighed. "I'm sorry. I've had a rough couple of days."

"You're Ava," he said. He jumped topics with no regard for verbal niceties. It was like trying to follow a hyperactive squirrel from one branch to the next. "I'm Henry," he said, extending his hand. "Hank. Most people call me Hank."

I regarded his hand. "Are you going to start speaking in tongues if I touch you, Hank?"

He shrugged. "I don't know. I mostly have dreams, and sometimes I can see a spirit, if it's very strong. I'm not very good with objects or people. My grandmother was better at picking up information from people and objects. She was a reader. I'm a visitor. I visit—"

"You visit other people's minds, I get it," I said. "That's cute."

"It's not really all that extraordinary when you think about it," he said. "The science of it. There are frequencies we can't hear, so why not other frequencies most people can't sense, but psychics can? I'm just open on more channels than the average person. There's really nothing mystical about it."

"Fascinating," I said.

"You and the Walking Man," Hank said. "I got that much from what I've been seeing. You're looking for him?"

"You're very perceptive in that not-at-all way," I said. "Do you have something for me or do you just invade people's REM cycles as a hobby?"

Hank took a deep breath. "I can tell you where he's going to be.

139

I can point you toward the outbreak his next victim will cause. But then I need you to leave."

I blinked. "Excuse me?" I'd been expecting a sales pitch, or at least a well-laid trap. This guy had to be shilling for Cain—there wasn't any other reason I could think of why he was all over me to validate his psychic visions. Telling me to get the fuck out didn't jibe.

"Let the Walking Man go. He won't be any more trouble," Hank insisted. "I'll keep tabs on him for you. No more of those zompire things will rise after this next one."

"Zompire?" I said.

"Zombie-slash-vampire. That's what they are, near as I can tell from reading about the last outbreak. Like I said, I'll keep an eye on him and take care of the problem."

"Thanks, guy I just met and have no reason to trust." I pulled the fork out of the table. "I guess I can just go home now."

"You don't understand!" Hank hissed, grabbing my wrist. "The Walking Man has to stay alive. I don't know why, but that's what everything is showing me. He lives, you live. He dies . . . and I can't see anything after that. And that's bad. So you kill the zompire, but you leave *him* alone, understand?"

My jaw set. I didn't like it when people tried to drag me into their shit, and I liked it even less when it involved somebody like the Walking Man. "Thanks for the advice, Hank," I said, turning my hand so I was holding his wrist, bending his fingers backward toward his forearm. "But I didn't come here to clean up his messes. I came to send him back to Hell."

He whimpered. "Why are you getting violent with me? I'm on your side! Just trying to make you understand."

"You think my problem right now is you *touching* me?" I said. "Get up or I'm going to break your hand."

He almost jumped up, and I pulled him next to me, like we were a couple. "Walk out of here with me and if you so much as let a bead of sweat roll off that square chin of yours I am going to snap you in half." I shoved us forward. "Nod if you understand."

He nodded. We walked. I shoved him into the front seat of Ronnie's truck. Hank cried out when I swerved into traffic, scrambling for his seat belt. "Why are you doing this to me? I thought you were somebody I could trust, Ava!"

"Stop talking to me like you know me," I said, hanging a U-turn and heading back toward the interstate. "Matter of fact, while we drive to wherever the Walking Man's next victim is you're going to tell me exactly how you know so much about me."

"I'm psychic?" Hank said, so dry he could have chapped my skin.

I shot a glance at him as I passed up a tractor trailer. I was going up past eighty, partly because I was angry and partly because I didn't want Hank to do something stupid like try to tuck and roll when he realized I wasn't going to obey his order to stand down like a good dog.

Hank's face was tight in response to my look. "I'm not setting you up, if that's what you're thinking."

"Funny, that's exactly what I was thinking," I said. "You really do have psychic powers."

"Look, all I know is that the Walking Man has to keep doing what he's doing, or bad things are gonna happen."

"I don't know if you've looked outside lately, but bad things are happening." I said. "They have happened and they continue to happen and they'll keep on happening no matter how many women you follow into diners."

Hank was quiet for a long time. I let him stew, let him wonder whether or not I'd really sussed out that he was the Walking Man's stooge.

"I usually see things I can actually fix," he said at last. "Missing kids. Guys planning to rob liquor stores. I have an okay relationship with a few cops I trust. Most of the time this is more like a second job than a calling. I don't know why my impressions don't give me winning lottery numbers or tell me where to find high-ranking terrorists. I figured it was a range thing. I don't pick up on stuff I can't prevent." He gulped. "But I've been having the same dream over and over. You stand above the Walking Man. You kill him. And then everything ends. Not like the dream ends—the world ends. Nuclear bombs, rains of fire, those zompire things dotting the entire landscape. I don't know why, but you killing the Walking Man starts something that ends with me and everyone I love dead."

He held up his planner, riffling the pages. I saw it wasn't a planner but a notebook, every sheet lined with meticulous handwriting. "I record my dreams and stuff in here. I've met a few other people like me and over the last year or so we've all been having this dream." He tapped the open page, deliberate instead of nervous. "I don't mean similar dreams. I mean the *exact same dream*. Except none of them knew who you were. Just me. Figured it was my job to get in touch."

I pulled over into a rest stop, putting the truck in park and gripping the wheel. "And how do you know who I am, Hank?" I was poised to do something violent, if I had to. Kill him, shut down the hotline to the Walking Man, at the very least leave him on the side of the road.

He sighed, rubbing his forehead. His perfect hair went askew. "My grandfather had abilities too. Not mine, but similar. He said if I ever ran into trouble like this, I should find you. That you could help. He said you'd know who he was because in 1945 you saved his life."

I felt all the indignation flow out of me, sure as if I'd been punched. Hank looked slightly afraid as I sagged back against the seat and put my hand over my mouth. "I'm sorry, I . . ." He reached for me, then pulled his hand back when I sucked in air. I was trying not to sob, and I was doing a crappy job.

"What was your grandfather's name?" I whispered. Hank looked at his hands.

"Jacob Gottlieb."

After that I couldn't help myself. Everything awful that had happened in the last week, all the dreams I'd had of Jacob, piled up like a car wreck. I buried my face in my hands and started to cry, big ugly sobs that ripped out of me like screams.

I felt a hand on my back after a few seconds, rubbing in gentle circles. Hank offered me a crumpled packet of tissues when I looked up. "Allergies," he said. "I always have tissues."

"Jacob . . . Jacob survived?" I choked out. Hank nodded.

"He made it through the woods and after a couple days he found a forward detachment of the Third Army," Hank said. "He was frostbitten pretty bad and his ankle was never right. He had a cane—he used to let me play with it. But he lived. Thanks to you."

I blew my nose hard. Hank looked out the window at the cars

whipping past us on the highway. "He never talked much about what happened to him in the camp. He just talked about you."

"Was he okay? After?" I said. "Was he . . . happy?"

Hank smiled. "He came here in '52 and he met my grand-mother. He got his medical license again and he was a surgeon in Kansas City for decades. Everyone loved Dr. Gottlieb. There's even an OR suite named after him at his hospital."

"He was a good man," I said. "He deserved that life."

Hank handed me more tissues. "He taught us well, me and my dad both. He became a rabbi like my great-grandfather after what you and he went through. Never saw any problem with be-ing a mystic and a surgeon. But the psychic thing was all me." He flashed an ID badge. "I'm a city engineer. Never got to the rabbi part. Guess I don't have the patience to learn all the stuff I needed to be a real live golem-making, demon-banishing badass."

I started the truck again and pulled out onto the highway. "Tell me where to find the Walking Man," I said. "Tell me everything and don't lie and maybe I'll consider listening to your *insane* sug-gestion I don't end him."

"You *have* to listen," Hank said. "Do you have any idea how rare it is for half a dozen psychics to have the same dream? Killing the Walking Man will touch off something catastrophic."

"I doubt that," I said grimly, pressing the accelerator down to the floor as Jacob directed me onto the southbound interchange.

"Why?" he said. "You of all people know there are forces out there capable of ending the world as we know it."

"Because I killed him once already," I said. "And the world did not end. In fact, it was a far better place without his poison in it."

"Really?" Hank cocked his head. "You killed him?"

"Dead as a doornail," I said. Even as I said it, though, I felt a little flip in my stomach. My grandmother used to say it was the truth trying to fight its way past the lie.

"Are you sure?" Hank said. "Because if you did maybe there's something about my own impressions I'm not getting."

"Maybe," I agreed. I felt the lie again, and I swallowed it. "Because I killed him. I'm certain."

CHAPTER

KANSAS, HIGHWAY 30
APRIL 1951

The wig itched, and a herd of sweat droplets stampeded down the back of my neck. Even with the car windows down, it was warm and wet as a sodden wool blanket. April wasn't supposed to be this hot, and I drove toward a horizon of bruise-colored sky hemmed in by charcoal thunderheads.

The gas gauge of Tanner's Ford hovered on E and I sighed, tapping my fingers against the steering wheel. I'd been driving up and down this stretch of road for almost six hours, making passes as the world got hotter and the sky got darker, just waiting. Waiting for the broken-down car and the big man flagging me down.

In the months since we'd met and talked with Val, it'd gotten easier to accept we were dealing with something old, something monstrous that the other monsters hadn't noticed, lurking way back there in the shadows.

Maybe not Cain, the character in a Bible story, but something that was primeval. A monster who was the first of its kind.

And now I was driving around Kansas in a blond wig trying to pick a fight with him, when he'd already beaten me once before without even lifting a finger.

The wig had been Val's idea. She was the reason I was driving around now. Her impression said he was going to take someone today, and after months of chasing and falling short, Tanner and I had decided to hell with it. We weren't having any luck chasing, so we were going to turn around and let him chase me.

I was who he wanted, after all. If he thought he was getting the upper hand, that he was going to have me back in his grasp when I showed up in the stupid wig, blustering like a superhero, acting like I'd caught him, he might drop his guard. He might slip just long enough for Tanner and me to finish him.

It was that, or I'd be his again. But we didn't have any other choice.

I reached over to fiddle with the radio and try to find a station that wasn't just hissing. I couldn't be alone in this silent car, on this silent road. My company was a gun in the glove compartment and a knife resting up against my thigh, tucked into my garter.

Those weren't for him. Nothing that was a weapon could hurt him. The gun was for me, if he caught me and I could still use my limbs.

The knife was a last resort.

A snatch of Bing Crosby filtered out of the speakers, only to get interrupted by the screech of an emergency broadcast. "We interrupt this program to bring you this special weather report . . ." the announcer droned, cutting in and out through the whistle of static.

I stopped paying attention when I saw the silver of a bumper pulled onto the shoulder, under a stand of cottonwoods.

I stomped on the brake, pushing on my sunglasses. No point in making it too easy for him. I waited for two heartbeats. My fingers didn't seem to want to let go of the wheel.

"Get out of the car," I murmured to myself as the cottonwoods bent and swayed in a wind that kicked up, almost obscuring the big hulking sedan parked under them. "You're not scared, you're not scared. Get out of the car."

I shoved the door open and put my feet in the dirt before I could lose my nerve and drive away. "You okay, sugar?" I called out, putting the full force of my former life as a Tennessee hillbilly behind the words.

The hulking figure bent over the engine compartment straightened up, then turned. The car was a silver coupe, the same make as the one belonging to his last victim, Tom Chavez of Austin, Texas. Chavez was a traveling salesman who moved all over the Midwest fitting aluminum siding. He'd tried to help out the Walking Man a little over three weeks ago.

"That's real nice of you, miss," he said. "You sure you're all right giving me a ride to a filling station?"

"You just try and stop me," I said, and gave him a big, broad, stupid smile. He wiped his hands off on a rag and shut the hood, taking his jacket from the open window. Were his black eyes flashing with amusement? Had he recognized me already?

"Looks like rain," he said as he got in my car and shut the door.

I gunned the engine, pulling us out onto the highway and spraying gravel all over poor dead Tom Chavez's paint job.

The Walking Man reached out and gripped the dashboard. "Don't rush on account of me."

I just had to get him to the mile marker Val had seen. Get him there, and get him into the binding hex that Tanner had set up. He couldn't be killed, but we could at least freeze him in place. Val had looked into the future for us and told us it had to be today, on this road, at that marker.

Just get him there. Less than two miles, and don't die in the process. Easy. Right.

"Really," the Walking Man said. "Slow down, darlin'. We've got all the time in the world."

I took off my sunglasses, tossing them into the backseat. I followed with the wig. "Five years is long enough for me."

The Walking Man stared at me for a long moment. I'd expected rage, that he might attack me right there and run the car off the road. I'd expected that he might try to frighten me, since I knew most of his victims died in terror.

I never expected him to smile, and I almost threw up when he started to laugh. "All this time, little bird. I never thought I'd see your nest."

I kept driving, the radio roaring and chirping with static the only sound besides the engine as I pushed the Ford past seventy. "I'm not your little bird. You're done. You're mine now."

He leaned back, hooking his arm over the open window. "I don't think so, little bird. I think you're gonna stop this car."

"Oh really," I said. He was going to try to pull me under again, look into my eyes and strip me bare and manipulate my strings, like before. I kept staring at the road, refusing to look at him. He was just a hulking shape in my periphery. A nightmare laughing at me. If he couldn't look into your eyes, we'd figured out, he couldn't pull you close and hold you. It was taking everything I had, my entire body vibrating, but I kept my eyes on the road.

"Really," he said. "You're out of gas."

I gasped as the car jerked and shuddered, the steering going soft under my grip as we rolled to a stop in the middle of the empty highway. Fat raindrops splashed against the windshield and a finger of lightning jumped between the clouds on the horizon as the Walking Man continued to laugh. He'd gone for the car, since I'd smartened up, forcing us to stop short of the mile marker.

Tanner was waiting. He'd come. He would, when I didn't show.

I let that keep me from screaming as the Walking Man spoke. "You're brave, I'll give you that. Brave as a hero from a storybook. But Theseus was thrown from a cliff by his own people and Perseus fell from Pegasus when he became too proud." His fist connected with my jaw, slamming me into the driver's window hard enough to crack it. Just as in the camp, his hands were around my neck. "And now, you are in the Minotaur's maze, except there is no thread to guide you back home. We are getting out of this car, little bird. I promised to clip your wings, and those friends you managed to con into helping you will find your body by the side of the road."

He leaned in close and that hot, burnt smell filled my nostrils and defiled what little air I had left. "I'll have the decency not to mark you as one of my children. I'm not the monster you think I am."

I squeezed my eyes shut as I also laughed, hysteria bubbling its way out of me like a kettle boiling. I wasn't going to look. He could kill me right here, choke me or beat me to death, but I wasn't going to look at him. He wasn't going to possess me again.

"Look at me," he croaked. I shook my head, still laughing, although now it just sounded like the wheeze of a dying machine, inhuman and mechanical. He grabbed my cheeks with his rough hands, crushing the flesh against my teeth. "LOOK AT ME!" he bellowed.

I would gouge out my own eyes, I thought. I would slam my own skull into the engine block and fry my eyelids shut before I'd look. The world was black and lightheaded, sounds and the smell of him, and far away the slamming of rain on the car roof.

The Walking Man reached over me with his free hand and yanked the door handle. Nothing happened, and he smashed at it more, bashing my head each time and making me see stars.

"Perseus didn't ride Pegasus," I rasped as I felt his skin heat with the rage that always lurked just beneath the surface. "It was Bellerophon. And he didn't fall from Bellerophon's back. Zeus pushed him."

"*What did you do,*" the Walking Man snarled, slamming my head into the door once more. I licked at the blood dribbling from the cut inside my mouth, where my teeth had sunk into the delicate skin.

"I didn't," I said, sliding my hands in front of my eyes. "But a friend painted a barrier spell all over this car. Up under the headliner. Door panels. Floorboards too. You can check in but you don't check out."

Tanner hadn't wanted to—had begged me, in fact, to not trap myself with the Walking Man. But there'd always been a chance we wouldn't make it to the mile marker. And I'd decided long ago that the next time we met, he wasn't getting away.

As quickly as he'd landed on me, the Walking Man let me go. "So what now, little bird?" he said. "You and I sit here until one of us dies of old age? Because here's a hint: it won't be me."

"Eventually my friends will come along, we'll cut off your head, burn you down to nothing, and dissolve the ashes in sulfuric acid," I said. "We'll put those ashes inside a barrier hex inside a hole so deep even the Devil himself can't find you, and we'll leave you there. I think that will be the end of you, old age or no."

I wiped the blood from my lips with the back of my sleeve, pressing my face into the scratchy material of the door liner to avoid looking at him. "Are you really him?" I said. "Cain? Is that your name?"

He shook his head, his nostrils flaring with every breath. "I haven't been called that in centuries. And you have no idea what I am, what I'm capable of, what this endeavor of ours is . . ."

"There is no *us*!" I screamed. "I am not anything like you, you get it?!" I tried to squirm away from his weight and he let me go. I was surprised, but I pulled myself up, spinning sideways in my seat, burying my face in my knees. "I am a hunter," I whispered.

"And for once, the bird is not trapped with you. You're in my cage now, and if neither of us leaves, that is just fine by me."

Cain lunged for me again, grabbing me by the front of my blouse and pulling me close. "You listen to me, little one—you may think you are a mighty hound sworn to that vile thing that calls himself Gary, but you are not a hound, and you do not belong to anyone but me . . ."

There was an enormous crack of thunder, and the ground shuddered, rain thrumming on the car hood so hard I couldn't see ten feet in front of us. Lightning illuminated Cain's snarl in camera flashes, and I ducked my head in terror that the glance had been enough. But all at once our brief contact was broken by a roar that sounded like the big freight trains that raced by on the tracks next to Valentine's trailer. It was so loud I felt like it could suck the air out of my lungs, like it was pulling sound and sense and feeling out of everything around me.

Cain's gaze snapped to the windshield and he dropped me so the back of my skull clunked against the steering wheel. He murmured something in a language I didn't catch, one that had to have been his native tongue, then he turned to me, no longer angry. "If you can get out of this car," he said softly. "Do it. Run. Now."

The rain parted, as if I was watching a film running in reverse. It flew upward, and I saw the funnel cloud bearing down, chunking up the highway a few hundred yards ahead. It was the biggest I'd ever seen, so wide and black it looked like the sky had grown a mouth.

I didn't argue with the Walking Man, didn't bother to wonder why he'd suddenly let go of me. All that existed was the hound's will to survive, and it grabbed the chance in its jaws and ran.

I threw the door open and lunged for the ditch next to the highway. I'd been terrified of ending up in it not ten minutes before, and now I'd never wanted to be any place more.

Road debris and sections of the guardrail started to wobble and pull away. The car scooted forward a few inches, the springs on my door howling as they were yanked the wrong way toward the pull of the wind. I clambered for the drainpipe, half full of fetid rain water, splashing into it and curling up against one of the rusty, crenelated sides as the twister screamed above me. Mixed in with the hollow howl of the wind was a scream that I took to be the Walking Man's. It wasn't a rage sound or a pain sound—it was the sound of a lost thing, standing alone when the entire world around it has finally burned down.

The storm was so loud I was sure I'd be deaf, that the sound alone would rip me apart. I felt the massive pipe shake in its stead, fighting the grip of the earth as the twister passed overhead. I tightened my body into a ball and waited to die for the second time.

Then, just as quickly as it had come up, it was gone, the ground under me rumbling faintly like the freight had moved on past the junction, going up north toward Chicago. Rainwater rushed around me, almost up to my waist, and I crawled slowly out of the pipe to find dozens and dozens of tin cans littering the roadway. Not just cans—every type of trash and muck that could be dumped on the side of the road was scattered across it. A license plate that wasn't from my car clanged as I kicked it with my toe. Papers blew every which way and I even saw the head of a baby doll, pitted and worn by weather long before the twister snatched it lying in the chaos.

The Ford was in the field on the other side of the highway, on its roof as if an errant child had stomped on it good and hard. I broke into a run, sprinting toward the crushed bulk, my feet crunching over the glittering spray of glass lying all around the body.

The car was empty. There was blood on the front seat, passenger side. A lot of it. More, in my experience, than a person could stand losing. A big, wedge-shaped chunk of glass lay in the center of the pool, the business end stained a deep arterial red.

It wasn't decapitation and a bonfire, but it would do.

Something gleamed in the backseat, and I reached in to grasp the sunglasses, miraculously unharmed and tangled in the horrid wig. I put them on and sat down in the damp grass, leaning back against the car and turning my face to the sun. The twister had come from the opposite direction of Tanner, and I didn't know how long it would take him to get through this mess and retrieve me, but I didn't care. The Walking Man was gone. Sucked up into the sky as if the hand of the divine had dropped down and snatched him its fist. Gone. Gone from the world, gone from the terror that wriggled deep in the turned earth of my mind. Erased like a stain bleached to stark white.

I had never felt lucky to be on this earth before that moment, and the feeling didn't last long, but for a few seconds I let it warm me in equal parts with the sun.

CHAPTER

13

WEST OF KANSAS CITY
NOW

The sun was just a stab wound of red at the horizon by the time Hank told me to get off the interstate. We hadn't talked much since I told him about my last meeting with the Walking Man and his voice startled me.

"Looks bad."

Up ahead, across the road, I saw a bunch of flashing lights and barricades and people in windbreakers with big yellow letters on the back standing around gesturing and yelling, mostly at each other.

A state trooper flagged me down. "Road's closed," she said,

shining her light on Hank and me. "Going to have to turn around and go back to Route 41 if you're headed into town."

"Can you tell us what happened?" Hank said. I could have slapped him. You didn't just start asking a cop questions at a road-block.

"Looks like some kind of industrial accident," she said. "Probably nothing, but you know how the three-letter brigade gets. All that money from Homeland Security and not a terrorist to spend it on."

"Thank you, Officer," Hank said. "We'll be on our way."

She smiled—actually smiled—at Hank and stepped back, gesturing where we should turn around. "Drive," Hank said. "Drive away and observe the speed limit."

"Because I was going to drift-race the ATF down the highway . . ." I muttered. Industrial accident my ass.

"This is all wrong," Hank said. He was flipping pages in his planner so fast they fluttered like wings, and he was pale and panting.

"I'll say," I said.

"No," Hank said sharply. "I saw us coming here before all this happened. Before the quarantine, before he actually attacked anyone else."

"Back up," I said, taking the turnoff for the town the trooper had mentioned. "Quarantine?"

"You did something!" Hank shouted, slamming the book shut. "Something changed and I don't know what's going to happen now!"

"Hank, I like you," I said, gripping the wheel. "But if you keep yelling at me I'm going to leave you on the side of the road for the zompires."

"Look out!" he screamed, and I swerved as I almost hit a blond woman waving at me frantically from the shoulder. I hit the brakes, and we fishtailed to a stop a few yards past her.

"Don't stop!" Hank barked at me. "Things are already messed up enough!"

"This?" I said as I opened the door. "This right here? It's reminding me of all the reasons I hate human beings." I walked back toward the woman, who blew out a huff of relief when she saw me.

"I'm real sorry about that," she said. "I can't get a signal and I ran my damn car off the road swerving to avoid one of those things."

I took her in by the glow of her car's one headlight. The other was crushed up against the cement liner of the drainage ditch next to the road, and a little steam whispered out from under the hood. She was tall, stocky, hair in a pixie cut that flopped over one eye. She was pretty striking, but her looks weren't nearly as interesting to me as the shiny shield clipped to her men's leather belt. "Things?" I said, and she chewed on her bottom lip.

"I hit my head," she said. "I don't know what I'm saying."

"The dead people," I said, figuring the worst thing she could do was shoot me or call me crazy. "If you saw one we shouldn't be standing out in the open. It's sort of like throwing sandwiches at attack dogs."

"Only one I saw up close is wrapped around my front axle," she said. "Had a bad thirty seconds before I realized I hadn't killed somebody."

She gestured over to her car and I approached the ditch, realizing the hiss I was hearing didn't come from the radiator. The thing trapped under the car had been a teenage girl at one point, I was fairly sure. Her bloody, stained jacket had the name of a high school on it.

The mark was plain as day on her forehead.

She smelled me, and her mouth lolled open, thick black tongue flicking out. She moaned, one arm trying to reach for me, but her elbow had been knocked out of joint and it flopped uselessly against the concrete.

"What agency are you?" the woman I'd almost hit said, coming to stand a few feet behind me. "Not law enforcement. No fed would drive that shitty truck. You one of the folks setting up the big tents? The CDC or whatever?"

"Or whatever," I echoed, still staring at the thing trapped under her car.

"So what do we do?" she said. "I'm not a person who can't admit when she's out of her depth. I am out of my depth, out in the ocean with the fucking waves crashing over my head."

The thing under the car snapped its teeth, gurgling as it tried to worm its way out from under the hulk of metal. The spine had to be severed, but that hunger lighting it up inside didn't care.

I looked back at her. "Cut off the head and burn the body."

"Riiiiight," she drawled. "You do see this badge? You do realize that even if I wanted to, I can't go all Van Helsing on a civilian?"

"Van Helsing used a stake," Hank said helpfully. "Also he's not real."

"Get back in the car!" I snapped at him.

The cop reached into the backseat of her car and withdrew a coat and a satchel full of files. Avoiding the thing under the wheels, she slid through the front passenger window and retrieved three spare clips for her pistol, shoving them in a pocket. "You can take me into town. The staging area for the quarantine is there."

"There's the small matter of the walking dead over here," Hank said. I bored into him with my standard death glare, but he seemed not to notice. "You should definitely listen to her, Ms. . . ."

"It's lieutenant," the cop said. "Lieutenant Beatrice Valley, KSP. And I don't need to listen to any whack job telling me to burn bodies. What I *need* is to find whoever is heading up the quarantine because I have something they need to see."

"Okay," I said. "Okay."

"Thank you," she muttered testily, climbing into the front seat and forcing Hank to sit behind her. He gave me an alarmed, bug-eyed look and I shook my head. This might be all wrong and it might not, but it was definitely all bad and getting a closer look escorted by a badge couldn't hurt. Rushing in headlong was not something that kept you breathing for any length of time. I preferred to prowl around, scout the perimeter, poke and prod a little before I dove in, especially to a pool of Cain's latest and greatest edition of the zombie apocalypse.

I pointed Ronnie's truck down the road toward the town. It was like any other pin-size map speck you'd drive through at seventy miles an hour—fast-food joints and gas stations in the outer ring, a big-box store, and a mile or so farther a downtown that had been dilapidated and shut down long before the Walking Man showed up. A temporary chain link fence topped with barbed wire stopped us, guarded by two guys in ill-fitting uniforms. The local National Guard, I guessed—they didn't look comfortable enough to be regular army.

Valley flashed her badge, but that didn't get us anywhere. "No local PD. Homeland's taken over," one said. "It's a biological attack."

"Yeah, I'm a state trooper, not a doughnut sucker, and I'm pretty sure it's not the kind of attack you're thinking of," Valley said, leaning across my lap. "I need to speak to whoever is in charge. Preferably somebody with 'Doctor' in front of their name."

The guy in the uniform looked at Hank and me. "What about you two?"

"They're with me," Valley snapped. She was mean enough, because after some garbled talk on the radio, the gate rolled back and I pulled forward into the no-man's-land between an inner and outer fence. Inside, I could see green tents, temporary floodlights on poles, and a big white tent with one of those plastic antechambers eggheads set up when they were convinced they were dealing with something contagious.

I felt my insides sink another couple of feet. All of these people were probably going to be dead soon, if nobody figured out what they were dealing with.

I waited for the second gate to open, but instead something slammed into my window, and I saw myself looking into the barrel of a rifle. The guy holding it *did* fit into his uniform, and the patches let me know that he wasn't just regular army, but the kind of guy they send in only when shit has well and truly hit the fan.

"Out!" he hollered, then ripped open the door and grabbed me by the collar, throwing me on the ground. Looking across under the car I saw Valley get the same treatment and heard a yelp as a third soldier manhandled Hank.

"What the fuck are you doing?!" Valley was yelling. "I am a Kansas State Police officer!"

I stayed quiet. I didn't fight the zip-tie handcuffs and I tried not to flinch when somebody shined a light in my face and patted me down for weapons. All they found was my pocket knife, which they took away before marching Hank and me to a metal hut near the white tent and shoving us both inside. They took Valley somewhere else, with her hollering protest all the way.

"This is just perfect," Hank said, pressing his hands over his face when the door slammed and locked. The hut had a few metal benches bolted to the walls, and some lockers that were all shut up tight.

"That we're trapped in the center of an outbreak or that we're being held prisoner in a locker room?" I said. "Because if things go south, a place with a lock on the door is a lot better than a tent."

"I told you this was all wrong," he grumbled.

"And for the tenth time, I didn't do anything!" I yelled. "I didn't *ask* to be here, Hank, unlike you. You had a chance to stay home like a normal person and instead you went chasing after things that have nothing to do with you."

"If the world turns into a buffet for the undead, I think it will affect him, Ava," Uriel said. I whipped my head to look at him, where he stood in the corner of the locker room.

"Look who decided to show up," I said. Uriel looked toward the door.

"Not what either of us expected," he said. "Things are moving a lot faster than I thought."

"I doubt any of this is a surprise to you," I muttered. "You've got that all-seeing-angel thing going on."

"Ava, I'm hardly omnipotent," Uriel said. He started to say more, then glanced past me at Hank. "What's wrong with him?"

I turned to see Hank's mouth working like a hooked bass as he stared up at Uriel. "Holy shit," he said. "You're an angel."

Uriel looked back at me. "He can see me?"

I shrugged. "He's psychic."

Uriel narrowed his eyes at Hank. "Stop looking at me. Staring is very rude."

"So are you going to let us out of here to kill the zompire army or what?" I asked Uriel. "I assume that's why you're here. You can save the pep talk. I get what my job is."

"You misunderstand me," Uriel said. "This is not the Walking Man's design. I don't believe he's even here any longer."

"Then what?" I demanded, massaging the point between my eyes with my thumbs. "Enlighten us, oh great sage."

"This is noisy and frightening, but this isn't the end I would expect from a creature like him," Uriel said quietly. "There isn't any point to this."

I looked up at him. The light was down to a single flickering bulb and Uriel's profile looked like it was carved from the same stuff as the metal walls around us. "This is a distraction," I said.

Uriel nodded. "I can help you get out of this town, but between the Kingdom's weapon ending up in the hands of a reaper and this, you need to do what I asked and stop the Walking Man." He leaned in so only I could hear him. "Stop him and you stop the Fallen pulling his strings. If you could kill them both I'd appreciate it."

"You got a tornado in your back pocket?" I muttered. Uriel frowned, confused, and I waved him off. "Never mind."

"What do you want to do about the walking crew cut?" he said in the same soft tone. "I say leave him to a vacation in Guantánamo Bay."

I rolled my eyes. "Be nice."

"Angels aren't nice," he said. "Have you even read a single page of the Bible? We are judgmental and avenging and occasionally we destroy the earth with floods, but we're not nice."

"I'm freaking out," Hank stated. "I have asthma. You can't get me excited like this . . ."

"Hank, you better calm yourself," I snapped as something banged on the outside of the shed. "Because the next thing that comes through the door might be way worse than an angel."

Valley stuck her head through the door, and I was almost glad to see her. "Hey," she said. "I managed to convince Mr. Male-Pattern Baldness in the windbreaker I'm not a threat to national security, but the bad news is you two are quarantined."

"What?" Hank exclaimed as one of the soldiers ushered us out. "But we're not sick!"

"You'll be tested and then you can go about your business," Valley said. "Oh, and if you have ID, strap it on. They're real sticklers around here."

She was still holding the satchel, and I realized the files poking out of it were bent and stained, their edges yellowing, type so smeared with age I couldn't read the tab headings.

Hank cleared his throat behind me and I turned around to

shoot him a fresh dose of death glare. "Sure thing," I said to Valley. More huge, uniformed guys with M-4s strapped on marched us to the white tent and shunted inside with half a dozen other people who weren't with the military or the police. One of them had on a fast-food uniform, and a pair of men wore matching jumpsuits covered in grease stains. Their names were embroidered above their hearts. "Well, hey," one of them said. "Looks like we're getting some new party guests."

"Sit tight, you two," Valley said. "I'll be back soon."

The girl in the uniform looked up at us. "So what are you in for?"

"Wrong place, wrong time," Hank said. She sighed.

"All of us were too stupid to listen to the evacuation order. Or let their *boyfriend* talk them into staying." She glared at the shorter of the two jumpsuit guys and he heaved a sigh.

"Baby, how was I supposed to know a stupid emergency broadcast would turn into this?"

"You're an idiot!" she shouted. "This is just like when you promised we'd go to Branson for my birthday and you got drunk at the dog track and bet it all because the dog had the same name as your mom!"

He started to yell back, but his jaw just lolled, a little drool coming from it. "Oh, that's cute," his girlfriend snarled, before she swayed and fell over, limp as a severed limb.

I didn't last much longer—just enough to see the six strangers and Hank drool, sway, and pass out. I tried to head for the door, but it was down a corridor, one that twisted and turned, impossibly long, and the door shrank until I could put it in the palm of my hand.

The floor wasn't a floor anymore but soft tropical waves, and puffy white clouds coated my vision as it swayed gently. I let out a short giggle. A hellhound who could walk on water. That was something you didn't see every day.

I saw the shapes approaching, shadows on my perfect, warm little world, and I let them lift me up and take me away, not really caring where I ended up.

Cool droplets peppered my face, and I felt wet earth pressed into my cheek. My vision swam from the gas and all I could see were two pale tree trunks nearby. I wanted to stay in the woods, feeling the rain. I wanted to let go and sleep.

The trees swayed, but there was no wind. I blinked, and felt something sticky coating my eyelashes. I smelled rusty metal and realized that the wet on my face wasn't rain, and the pale stalks in front of me weren't faraway trees, they were a pair of human legs, close up.

Without moving, I rolled my gaze up and saw a naked woman standing over me. Deep scratches marked her torso, like she'd crawled through a barbed wire fence, and blood dribbled from her mouth in a steady stream, pooling at her chin and spattering me.

I dug my fingernails deep into the soft ground under me, willing myself not to move. The creature let out a deep, pained wheeze, scenting me to see if I was alive or like her. As she crouched, reaching out a hand to scrabble at the leather of my jacket, I tensed every muscle. I was going to have to be quick, and hope that Cain's children didn't have the same taste for hellhound blood as for human.

While she muttered and poked at me, more droplets hitting me like I was under a faucet, I scouted my surroundings. I was in a yard, in front of a dumpy ranch house that had probably gone up around the time I last saw Cain. All the houses around us were dark, and the street bore the sort of litter left behind when a neighborhood clears out in a hurry. A sheet of newspaper blew against the flimsy picket fence separating the yard from the street, and the creature jerked up, hissing at it.

I sprang up, changing on the fly and hitting the dirt again on four paws. I dug in with my nails, clearing the fence in one spring and sprinting down the center of the street.

Behind me, the creature screamed, and an answer echoed off the slope-roofed houses around us. I put my head down and ran faster. I didn't know what had happened back in the enclosure—I didn't know if Hank was alive, where Valley was, why we'd all been gassed. Maybe they thought we were infected. But if that was the case, why dump us back in town?

I got my answer when a much shriller, more human scream caught me from down a broad avenue outside the little neighborhood, and I saw the girl who'd cussed out her boyfriend inside the tent go down under a pile of three creatures. I stopped, padding silently on the asphalt, but there was nothing I could do. They'd already ripped her throat out, cupping the blood in their hands and slurping it like dying men in a desert. The air filled with the scent of new pennies and the stench of unwashed, decaying flesh.

I didn't feel sorry for the girl as I growled and drew back into the shadows of a filling station on the corner. She'd be awake soon enough, and just as ready to rip my throat out.

"Ava!"

I swung my head around, snarling. I could talk, but it was in hellhound language and it all sounds the same to humans. Hank peered out from the door of the filling station, pushing it open an inch or two and beckoning me inside. "Hurry!" he said as the creatures let out a series of hoots, already raising their heads to scent for the next target—and turning right toward Hank. I trotted inside, turning to shove the door shut with my snout. Hank's shirt was soaked, pits to waist, and he probably smelled like a rack of baby-back ribs to the things in the street.

"Thank God it's you," he said, turning the lock. "Everyone else is dead."

I whined, looking at the window as the three creatures were joined by the one who'd been testing out the idea of eating me back in the yard. They started creeping toward us in a wedge shape, like how wolves hunt. If I knew my apex predators, there were probably two or three more on the roof of the station, waiting for us to run out the back.

"Okay," Hank said. His voice was shaking, as were his hands, and he pressed them over his face. "My head hurts so much," he muttered. "Okay. What do we do?" He looked at me, and I looked back, wishing to everything that he could understand me. Or that Uriel would swoop down on a bolt of lighting, or that Leo was here.

I needed Leo. It was a physical need, deep in my gut, and it made me whine. If he was here, we'd be fine.

"He's not," Hank said, surprising me. "But I am, and between the two of us we have to get out of here. So what do I do?"

I blinked. I didn't realize the whole mind-reading thing worked when I was a hound, but maybe we weren't so screwed after all.

I bumped the front window with my nose, where the creatures were almost within spitting distance. They wanted us to run, so they could chase us down. Adrenaline pumping through our blood probably made it that much sweeter.

"So we gotta fight our way out?" Hank whispered. "Because I'll say right now, I hate zombie movies. I am totally the guy who gets eaten immediately. I'm not prepared to battle the undead."

I didn't need Hank to fight—he'd probably just get in my way—but I did need him to be ready to run. I'd make sure the creatures' attentions were on me.

"How?" Hank asked. I bumped his hand with my nose, and he shivered. "Cold," he said. "I mean . . ." I kept my eyes on the fleshy part of his hand. He sighed heavily. "Go ahead. I trust you."

I took his palm gently in my jaws and bit down just enough to start a good flow of blood. Hank grunted, but he didn't flinch. I made sure the blood was smeared all over my head and back, and then I looked up at the door lock. Hank flipped it open, and I sucked in a breath.

When the door opened I exploded outward, giving the creatures no time to swarm me. I hit the biggest one in the chest, taking him to ground and tearing into his neck with my teeth. The blood tasted terrible, clotted and rotten, and I fought the urge to gag as I shook one, two, three times until I felt the vertebrae snap.

Another creature hit me from the side, pinwheeling me off the first. This one wore shreds of a jumpsuit. He landed on me with his full weight, snapping but only getting a mouthful of my fur. I flipped us, slamming his skull into the pavement hard enough to crack.

The last two were smart enough to try to rush me from both sides simultaneously. I ducked, swiping one in the torso with my claws. It tripped and stumbled into the other creature. I bit down hard on the Achilles' tendon, crippling it, and when the other one swiped at me, I latched on to its forearm, so hard I felt my teeth connect through the loose, rotting skin and muscle. This one had been out here for a while, and had a smell to match, but it also took the longest to go still after I'd ripped its throat out.

Turning to check the darkness and the roofline for other moving shapes, I jerked my head at Hank, who broke out of the door running and headed for a truck parked askew across the boulevard, abandoned with the keys still inside.

I followed him, until he tripped and went down. He let out a cry, and I saw he'd tripped over the waitress's body and was floundering in her blood.

"It's okay!" I yelled—well, snarled. "They have to bite you to infect you!"

Hank scrambled up, using my fur for purchase, but before we'd moved a step the waitress's hand locked around his ankle. Hank screamed, and she returned the sound, rearing up and locking on to his arm.

I put my full weight on the waitress, cracking a few ribs and ripping her away from Hank. I bit down, tearing into her already ruined throat and crushing part of her jaw in my haste to make her stop moving. She gurgled and went still.

I looked back at Hank. He was standing there, his shirt shredded, holding his arm as if it didn't belong to him. He stared at me, his pupils expanding with every breath. "She . . ." he said, staring at the deep, bloody half-moon in his forearm. "It hurts . . ." he said mildly, and started to sway.

"Hank!" I barked, jumping up and shoving my hip against him to keep him upright.

"I'm dead," he said, his voice still calm and detached, like he was telling me he'd gotten a paper cut. "I'm infected. I'm dead."

"Don't freak out," I said, as much to myself as him. I breathed out, blinked, and opened my eyes back at human height.

"Holy shit," Hank said. "You think I'd be used to seeing weird stuff by now, but that was . . . the weirdest."

I didn't asked him what it looked like when I changed. I'd never seen it and I really didn't want to know.

"But that aside," Hank said, "I'm dying."

"You're in shock," I said. "That's why you're so calm about this. But I need you to stay calm when I tell you what's going to happen next."

I looped Hank's arm over my shoulder and dragged him back toward the filling station. "Does it strike you as odd," he said, voice slurring, "that we would be drugged and dumped in a town full of killer zompires by the government? I mean, I know it happens all the time in movies but this is not a movie . . ."

"It does," I said, kicking at the garage door until it rolled up a few inches and I pushed it the rest of the way. "But right now I have more important things to think about, like you not dying."

"Oh, I'm definitely dead," Hank said. "I know these things, Ava. I have precog . . . precog . . ." He shivered and went limp against me, and I lowered him as gently as I could, stripping off the rest of the ripped shirt. The flesh around the bite was already going blue-black, and soon the infection would stop his heart, and jump-start it as something new and terrible.

I dumped out the garage's ancient first aid kit, grabbing all the bandages I could find. I tied off Hank's arm with rubber tubing, as tightly as I could, and yanked the coffeepot off the warmer, putting one of the metal disks from the grinder in its place.

Hank's eyes fluttered open at the crashing. "What are you . . ."

"Listen," I said. "The only way you live is to stop the infection, and the only way to stop it is to cut off the path to your heart."

Hank looked over at his arm, which was turning purple. "I can't feel it . . ." he said. I put my hand on his forehead, looking into his eyes.

"I need to cut off your arm."

Hank immediately started screaming. I tried to block it out as I knelt on him, pinning his shoulders with my full weight. The garage at least had a crop of power tools—if I'd had to do this by hand, I'm not sure I could have. "I am so sorry," I whispered as I picked up the saw, pressing the power button. Hank was lucky, in a way—he'd pass out from the pain after a few seconds. He didn't have to see the aftermath, smell the blood, or inhale the smoke from the burning stump after I pressed the hot metal circle now sizzling on the coffee machine over it to cauterize the wound.

I wasn't stupid. I knew even as I slumped back, coated in Hank's blood, with burned fingers and shaking hands, that his chances of survival were pretty minimal. But he could just die. He didn't have to wake up one of Cain's creatures.

Picking up the bandages, I wrapped the stump as tightly as I could. Hank's breathing was ragged, his eyes dancing back and forth under the lids. I'd seen a lot of men die of a lot less on battlefields, which this undoubtedly was. I was still fighting the pull of the Walking Man, even now. He was reaching out to me. Picking off people around me one by one until I gave in.

I wasn't giving in this time. I put Hank on one of the rolling carts and opened the door again, in time to see headlights sweep across the street. I tensed, but there was only one black SUV, and one person inside.

Valley opened the driver's door but paused when she saw the two of us. "What the hell did you do to him?" she said.

"Why do you assume I did this?" I grunted, rolling Hank toward the car.

Valley leaned down and felt Hank's pulse. "Just a crazy hunch."

I started to tell her we should get in the car and get the hell out of here but before I could, Valley straightened up, lifted her boot, and put it on Hank's neck. "Now how about we're both honest for a minute?"

My stomach sank. I guess I had my answer about why we'd all ended up out here.

Valley didn't speak as we faced one another. She just pressed down harder on Hank's windpipe, until Hank's mouth worked like a fish thrown up on land.

Shapes moved in from all around, from the street and the houses and the fields beyond, naked corpses moved by the sheer force of their hunger. The smell of stale blood permeated my nose.

"So he got to you?" I asked Valley.

She flinched, just a little. "He is not the reason I'm here."

I tried not to show any fear as I stared Valley down, and the creatures moved in around us, surrounding us. The one nearest me let out a sad sigh as she ran bloody fingers through my hair. Her torn-up nails caught and pulled at my scalp until I jerked my head away.

"My reasons are not hunger and madness," said Valley. "But brotherhood. You'd understand that, if you weren't working for the bastard set on exterminating us."

"I'm sorry that you got kicked out of the special angel club," I told Valley—or whatever her name actually was. The Fallen kept personal details like that close to the vest. "But I am only interested in myself and the few people I care about. I don't care what kind of vendetta you've got against heaven, or Uriel. Leave us out of it."

Valley laughed. "Oh, and speaking of your golden boy upstairs—don't bother screaming for him. This whole town is packed so full of death magic thanks to Cain that he might as well be looking for hay in a haystack."

I clenched my jaw so hard I drew blood from my own lip. I was so angry I wanted to scream. I could feel the hound clawing its way up my throat. It didn't want to scream, it wanted to tear and shriek and howl. It wanted to fight back. I pushed it away.

I shut my eyes and wrapped my arms around myself. This was how it always ended up for me. I could try to break away from what I was, but I was always going to be the one who had to bend to someone else's will, to keep myself or somebody innocent safe and alive.

Sure, I could strut around like I was the Grim Reaper's personal badass, but now I was going to knuckle under to another psycho control freak who'd decided I was fun to torture. And I was going to do it willingly, because Hank didn't deserve to be here with me.

"Promise me that you'll get Hank help. Leaving him alive for now isn't good enough."

Valley gave a cold sigh, colder than the wind whipping up. "Azrael said you were a sentimental piece of work. Way too many feelings for a hellbeast."

"Promise me or I'm going to slit my own throat," I said. "And somehow I think that my delivery is a condition of Cain helping you people out with your Armageddon."

Her square jaw ticked, and I knew I was right. "Fine," she ground. "He'll be good as new in a few hours."

I stepped away, letting the dead press around me. "I'm all yours," I whispered. Maybe this time it would be different. Maybe I wouldn't fall back under Cain's thrall. Maybe this was a good thing—if the Fallen who'd given Owen a fake Scythe was working with Cain, and Valley in turn was helping them, maybe I was the one who was really in control.

The crowd of dead moved, and I was forced to move with it, until I felt hands on my arms and legs, bearing me up and moving me along without my feet touching the earth. A tear slipped out of my eye as I realized the truth—I had never been in control. I was just a piece of flotsam on a tide I couldn't fight. Drifting inexorably back to Cain's side. Back where I belonged.

We moved for miles that way. I tried to keep my eyes on our direction but after a while it was hard to see anything except the mass of bodies. There had to be a couple hundred of them, and eventually it became too much effort to do anything but look up at the black sky, slowly fading toward a weak gray first light.

A sudden chatter of rotors cut the silence, and the mass of dead rippled and stirred. "The army is taking over the quarantine,"

Valley said from somewhere close but invisible to me. "Or if they aren't they will be shortly. People get so upset nowadays. Entire cities wiped off the map by flood and plague, back then. Bodies as far as the eye could see stinking and bloating under the sun. The flies would be so thick you'd think they were the air." She breathed deep, letting out a satisfied sound. "The air is very clean here. I like the cold. Where I am from in the Kingdom, it was a hot place."

"The place you're going is supposed to be pretty hot, too," I muttered.

"Fighting is always such a waste of energy and yet the small things always refuse to give up," Valley said. "The army will quarantine this town. They'll contain this for a while, keep it a secret, but eventually it will get out. It will spread. And then this beautiful cold place will be just as the deserts were. Covered in corpses. Dirt soft with spilled blood. Sky clouded with flies."

"Sounds like you have everything you want, then," I said. "Lots of dead people and lots of live ones who are miserable because of you. The ultimate temper tantrum, am I right?"

"You think we're angry at the *Kingdom*?" Valley laughed. "We couldn't care less about those still sitting under the thumb of the Host. We hate *humans*. The people who get to live never knowing that behind the veil, all of this is happening. Creatures like you and me watching them with envy, because they are happy and their lives have an ending." She slid into view, her hair glowing gold against the sunrise. "But not anymore. Now their world looks to them like it does to us."

I stayed quiet, and she grinned. "No more fighting?"

"No," I said. "Just thinking I used to find Uriel kind of nutty for wanting you exterminated. Now I completely understand his desire to spit-fry every last one of you."

"Feel like you might still win while you can," Valley said. "Keep hope alive. Once Cain has his prize, you'll never see a sunrise like this again." She stroked my cheek. "He's missed you. He can't wait to show you how much."

We passed through another town, another main street. Windows were broken out. A car had crashed into a hydrant, windshield spattered with blood. Somewhere far away, a burglar alarm whooped and droned endlessly. I focused on staying still, on not screaming. If I started, I wouldn't stop.

The sun was up, but weak, when the dead finally stopped. We were far away from the highway now, in an empty field surrounded by a half-tumbled cyclone fence. A sign too rusted and riddled with buckshot to read lay on its side, but I guessed this was some kind of government property. Lilith had once taken me to an old missile range, when she'd tried to use me to open Tartarus. Maybe Cain had similar proclivities.

Valley stopped, waiting absolutely motionless. She had the eyes of a snake, unblinking, devoid of any life. The dead lowered me to the ground and I realized I was on a pitted ribbon of asphalt painted with ghostly white letters. An airfield, I thought, and heard a groan as an ancient antenna radar swayed in the wind, a few hundred yards away.

Then my vision blacked out and he was in front of me. "You returned," Cain said to Valley.

"And I delivered," she snapped. "Now get back to work. The quarantine barriers are going up faster than your little science projects are reproducing."

"Patience," said Cain. "As in all things, Dantanian. Patience."

"Great," Valley said. "Now she knows my name."

"Not to worry," Cain rumbled, crouching and lifting my head with his massive hand. I couldn't struggle, was too tired and sore to even move. I didn't bother shutting my eyes.

I'd always known I'd end up right here, back under his control. It was like the last decades had been a great dream, and now I was awake. I knew he'd never stop looking for me, and that eventually, like all good hunters, he'd run me to ground. "You're not going anywhere," he intoned. "Are you, little bird?"

"Must be nice," I whispered. Valley wasn't wrong—even though I'd accepted I was probably not leaving this place alive, I couldn't resist fighting his thrall. "You get a free ticket out of Hell and all of this is waiting for you. It's like coming home from prison to a hooker holding a birthday cake."

Cain let out that rock-crushing sound he called a laugh. "I want nothing, little bird. And I have received nothing. I have not been in Hell."

"What are you talking about?" I said. "You escaped from Tartarus like all the rest of the damned souls. That's why you stopped. Because you died on the highway in that twister."

All of a sudden the dead drew back, ten or so feet, like startled roaches fleeing from a light. Cain stood to his full height, teeth bared. "You stupid creature. You think the wind can stop me? The storm? Any force of nature? Nothing will remove me from the world. Least of all you."

His foot flashed out, and I felt as my skull got trapped between it and the asphalt. The last thing I saw were the dead closing in again, hands lifting me up as if they were taking me away to my funeral.

When I snapped to, everything was bright instead of dark, dry instead of damp and cold, and I could hear my own heart throbbing so deep I vibrated all the way down to my toes.

"See?" Valley's voice cut through my fog like a weed whacker outside the window cuts through your Sunday hangover. "I told you she wasn't dead."

"I get that the know-it-all thing is a big hit with the meat bags at the Kansas SP," said a voice I didn't recognize. Or rather a voice that sounded vaguely familiar but to which I couldn't put a face, like a familiar radio announcer doing the weather. "But if you could cut it out, I'd royally appreciate it."

"Bite me," Valley said. "I get Cain's chew toy, I make nice-nice with his creepy ass, now you get busy with your end. Need I remind you that all of these moving pieces you love to shove around the board all have the potential to get us skewered on the end of Uriel's sword."

"You guys are cute," I murmured, trying out a whisper. Talking hurt. Everything hurt. I was used to waking up in strange places with strange bruises, but when I tried to open my eyes all I saw was a couple of blurry streaks and a blinding light that make me squinch up my face in self-defense. I tried moving and found that my wrists and ankles were immobilized. When I wriggled, a chain rattled.

"You're chained good, Rover," Valley confirmed, her voice drawing closer while another set of footsteps retreated. "Prison shackles. The kind that they used on chain gangs."

I tried opening my eyes again. One whole side of my face was swollen, so that explained the blurriness, but from what I could see lying on the concrete floor, we were in a windowless room. Shelves lined the walls and a couple of caged bulbs lit up their contents. Lots of cans, lots of metal ammo boxes. A cot was across from me, moth-eaten wool blanket arranged with military corners. The shelves on the other side were full of books and questionable antiques. Taxidermy animals dressed in little costumes—cowboy, chef, scary clown. A jar full of animal teeth, a tangle of those weird monkey puppets with the cymbals. The walls that weren't covered in shelves were squeezed with taped-up newspapers and drawings on the backs of book pages. The drawings weren't of anything pleasant. The whole effect sort of looked like the place had been decorated from an estate sale held by the Manson family.

The only way to the outside I could see was a metal hatch-style door, and a hallway beyond. A shadow blinked out of view. Whoever Valley had been chatting with was making themselves scarce.

Valley patted me on the cheek again. "The chains are just a precaution. Your boy here might have his own ideas." She walked away too, and metal screamed on metal as the hatch shut. There was movement from the corner of my eye and Cain's shadow blotted out the feeble light. "Still chirping," he said. "I don't know if you're spirited or simply stupid."

"Votes are split," I tried to say, but he grabbed me by my hair and yanked me up, unlocking my chains with a big old-style skeleton key. I whimpered, and he shook me like a toy.

I struggled against him as he pulled me down the hall, but I didn't have any luck getting away until he let go of me, shoving me into a metal chair in a bare-bones kitchen. "I'm not going to hurt you," he said, slamming around a dented kettle and lighting a burner under it.

"No, why would you?" I said. "You *already* hurt me. The hurting's done, and I know you're capable of a lot more so why don't we just get to why I'm down here and how many sweaters you're gonna knit from my hair."

"You know, you did me a favor that day," he said. "That day on the highway. I was a lost soul. Full of rage, centuries of it. When I came out of that storm . . ."

I held up my hands. "No offense, man, but bad poetry is not making this bunker experience any better."

"Silo," he said. "There are missile complexes all over the Midwest. Once they housed dozens, to make the missiles fly. But one by one they were abandoned. I found my way here a time after a tornado."

The kettle started to rattle and spurt, and he turned down the flame, reaching for one of the rusty metal tins above the stove and pulling out a tea bag. "I meant what I said. I don't want to hurt you. When I saw you and that man in Buchenwald I was full of rage. Burning alive with it. But now I don't feel anything toward you. I ordered you brought here so that you and I could speak without you being in harm's way."

"Ah, so I can leave whenever I want?" I said. He shook his heavy head.

"Of course not."

I felt the pull of the thrall, heavier than ever. Before it was like being drugged—that detached, pillowy softness of being above it all. This felt more like I was pinned to a board, being examined by something massive and curious.

Either way, whenever I thought of running my mind darted away from me, like a fish slipping through your hands underwater. I couldn't even focus long enough to see if the kitchen door was open or shut. My eyes always jerked back to his face, and his power over me made all of it just fine.

"You drink tea?" he said. I stayed quiet, gripping the cold edges of the chair. It was freezing in the kitchen, even with the stove going, but he didn't seem bothered.

"I give you my word that I'm not going to harm you," he said. "I just can't allow you to fly away, little bird. And your companion— he is human, and humans are not even birds. They are rabbits, or rats—small things, easily scared, easily panicked. From the hawk's view, they are all the same, small things scampering over the ground."

"You'll forgive me if I don't believe the guy with the army of dead people outside just wants to chat with me," I said. "And don't punch me again, but you sound exactly like a guy who's spent sixty years living in a missile silo."

"I was alone long before that," he said. "I was alone from the moment I struck down my brother. The moment I stood and felt the earth under my feet soak up his blood."

He stared straight ahead through the steam from the kettle, and I could tell he wasn't looking at the wall, or me, or anything else around us. "But now all that's done. All that rage is like a bad dream. Now you and I will stay here. Until it's over." He pulled a metal mug off a hook and set it on the counter with a clack. "Truthfully, I'm glad it's all done. I have no wish to see what the dead do when they walk. I'm not the same man I was when you met me."

"You do sound different," I allowed. "You're talking and not threatening to kill me and everything I love."

"You love nothing, just as I do," he said. "That's why I don't mind waiting here with you. You won't weep at what happens up there."

"I don't understand," I said, although the churning in my stomach said I understood pretty well. "You're talking like we're going to live down here together. Don't you need to be up there, you know . . ." I flapped my hands helplessly. "Leading your zombie army?"

"It's not an army," he said. "It's an extinction. And we're just to wait here. Wait until it's over. That's all."

"Until *what* is over?" I said. The kettle started to scream, and Cain turned his face to me.

"Everything," he said. "Nobody up there can escape the ones who've been marked. It might take a few years—even a decade— but what's that to us?"

He smiled to himself as he put the tea bag in the mug and reached for a shelf of jars. "Do you take honey?"

I looked down at my hands, shaking my head. I'd had a lot of bad moments imagining what would happen if the Walking Man caught me again, but this went beyond any of them.

"Why would you do it?" I said, after he thrust the mug into my hand. "Why would you help two insane Fallen destroy the world?"

"We all do what we must," the Walking Man said. "This is my part to play. I am just glad that you are here to play your part with me."

He reached out to touch my face, and I flinched back, but after a heartbeat his power took over and I felt myself lean forward into his palm. "I knew," he whispered. "From the first moment I saw

185

you in the camps. A thing made by the angels, constructed of the same clay as I was. A companion for all the dark days of my time on this earth."

I shut my eyes, feeling tears shudder down my cheeks. "I wasn't made for you," I whispered. "I am a hound. I was made to stand beside Death, not stand behind a bitter, broken soul like you."

He turned his hand and struck me as easily as the tornado had picked up the car all those years ago. I went flying off my chair, hot tea splashing my pants leg, and landed hard on the cement floor.

I licked at my lips, tasting blood, and he stood over me, frowning. "You are not for the reapers," he growled. "You want Death? *I* am Death. And you will be with me forever."

He lifted his hand again and I flinched, curling into a ball and waiting for a blow to rain on my back. Nothing came, though, except the scuff of his shoes and the slam of the heavy door.

I lay there for a long time, breathing ragged. I felt the last bit of rationality in me struggling to escape like a wriggling rabbit in a snare, but I held on to it.

I'd flinched when he'd touched me, and when he'd struck me. I hadn't been able to do that before. I'd just been a doll, totally under his power. Now there was a thread still pulling me away from his influence. It was tiny, and fragile, but it was there.

I reached out and took the sharpest fragment of the shattered mug, sliding it up my sleeve and tucking it against my skin. I'd flinched.

That was enough.

CHAPTER

I lost count of days much faster with no sun and darkness to at least give me a sense of time passing. All the clocks in the place were long drained of power, so I passed the time by counting heartbeats, steps, words Cain spoke to me.

Mostly he wanted me to sit with him, close to him so that we shared body warmth, while he stroked my hair and whispered the same stories over and over, of battles he'd seen and blood he'd shed, of the time he'd first seen me in the camp. I wasn't stupid—he was batting me around, wearing me out, waiting for the moment when I'd finally break in half.

He was gone for long stretches, too, and while I could never quite wrap my mind around the concept of finding a way out of the silo—any thoughts he didn't want me to have simply wouldn't stay put, like the words to a song you can't remember—I did start stretching out my chain to its maximum length, little by little. I mapped every inch of the silo—which wasn't much. Most of it was taken up by a vast empty bay, at least four stories high, where the Titan cruise missile had once waited on its cushion of rocket fuel, nose cone pointing toward the stars. The kitchen, a bunk room, the big room Cain had turned into his weird habitat—aside from them and a small medical room the rest was just corridors and hatches.

There was an escape hatch somewhere, I knew it. A long, dark climb to the surface, but an escape nonetheless. And while I couldn't begin to think of opening the little door at the bottom of the missile bay marked FIRE ESCAPE and seeing if the ladder was intact, or the shaft still open, I held on to the location of the door like I held on to my own name.

I also held on to the broken shard from the mug, hidden in my clothing. Hoping that when the time came I could use it like I'd planned.

The Fallen who'd been with Valley had never returned, and I'd never seen her again, although I could always tell when she'd paid a visit because Cain would come in and slam the door, make his footfalls heavy, and snap at me. "Why do you look so sad?" he demanded once. "This is where you're safe. I am who protects you. Why do you look as if you've lost something?"

After the slap that had broken one of my teeth, I'd never mentioned Leo again. But I made myself remember him, whenever I felt myself slipping or my memories fading. I made myself think of his face, of his voice. I pictured every tattoo and every scar, over and over. I did it with everyone I knew—my grandmother, Uriel, even Gary got his chance to star in my struggle not to lose my memory in the face of Cain's thrall.

I had my eyes shut, listening to Cain drone on about the smell of blood and the buzz of flies, or whatever he was on that day, when I suddenly couldn't take him stroking my hair any longer and grasped his hand, sitting up to look at him. "Why don't you just make me do what you want?" I asked.

He frowned, his craggy brows landsliding together. "What do you mean?"

"You brought me down here to be more than a maid," I said. "You could force me to do anything you want. Why haven't you?"

"Poor creature," he said, stroking my palm. I fought not to yank it away. That was getting easier, the pulling back, and I didn't want to let on. If his power over me was fracturing, I wanted to be ready when it snapped entirely. "You have been forced to do a great many things, no doubt," he rumbled. "But when you submit to me it will be a true union. We are meant to be, little bird. I wouldn't taint that for anything in the universe."

I settled back, but I kept my eyes open. However he dressed it up, he needed me to give in to him willingly. I'd bet it wasn't for any of the romantic crap he spouted. There must be something about this fucked-up dance of his that required a willing partner.

As long as I could hold out, I could get out of here, I realized.

"One day, Ava, you will say you love me," he whispered in my ear. His breath was sour, like he'd gone a long time without brushing. "And when we join it will be the greatest day this burning world has ever known."

I smiled and let him pull me back into his arms. This time the urge to fight him off and run was almost irresistible. I thought of the fire escape and held it in my mind. I thought of Leo waiting at the top, holding out his hand to pull me into fresh air and sunlight.

As if someone had reached between us and sliced a rope, the hold Cain had on me was suddenly gone. He let out a sigh, and I almost panicked before I realized he was just settling back onto his cot.

"My head aches," he said. "I'm tired of stories. I will sleep now."

I didn't move, just lay back to press against his chest. "I'll stay," I said softly. He grunted, then let out a contented sound.

"We will only sleep. Until you come to me."

"Until then," I agreed, reaching up and touching his face. I stayed very still when he shut out the light, matching my breathing to his until I was sure he was asleep.

Moving by inches, sure it took me at least an hour, I worked the shard of pottery out of my sleeve. He'd rolled on his back, snoring soft and steady. I felt a hum in the air all around me, like the currents in the air right before the tornado had hit. The darkness holding its breath. Whatever was going on, why he was sleeping and why I'd finally been able to overcome his thrall, I was going to use it. I knew I wouldn't get another chance.

I sat up and swung my feet over the edge of the cot, leaning over his sleeping face and examining the choppy planes one last time. I lifted my hand, the edge of the broken mug biting my palm, and his eyes snapped open.

"Little bird—" he said, and I slammed the shard into his eye with all my strength. The pottery snapped in half when it hit his orbital bone, the sharp end buried deep in his eye with no way to pull it out. He screamed, heaving up and clawing at his face. His eye was a bubbling mess of blood that gleamed in the darkness. I didn't stick around to deliver another blow. I just ran.

I kicked open the rusty door to the fire escape and grabbed the ladder, climbing for what seemed like miles, shaking and sweating, until I finally butted up against a rusty hatch. I heaved and beat on it, letting out a scream. I couldn't have come this far only to get stuck because the last jerk-off to check the silo door forgot his oil can.

The hatch finally gave way, wet snow and mud raining down on my head as I climbed out and flopped into the cold wet, sucking down the freezing air.

It was just starting to get light. Far off I could see spotlights and hear the grunt and clatter of heavy all-terrain vehicles. For a moment it was like being back at the Rhine during the last push into German territory, cold and wet and loud. I had the insane thought that somehow I'd never escaped the camp, that the last fifty years had been a dream planted in my mind by Cain.

Then a Black Hawk helicopter swooped low over the field, the roar pushing away my panicked thoughts as it headed for the swarm of spotlights on the horizon. I slammed the hatch shut and cast around frantically for something—anything—to keep Cain from getting out. The rusty cyclone fence was only a few dozen yards away, and I grabbed one of the broken posts, jamming it into the hatch handle as tight as I could. Then I ran. I ran until my lungs felt like two saw blades and my heart was hammering so hard to push blood through my veins I saw double.

I reached a stand of cottonwood trees, bare in the cold, and fell against one, sucking and gasping until I could stand up straight again. I tried to move but my fingers dug into the bark. The hound wanted to make sure nobody was behind me. No one and nothing.

I waited, in the cold, silent dawn, listening to my own heartbeat. I didn't hear any hissing and groaning, so I peered out from the tree trunk to confirm I was zompire-free.

I was standing at the edge of a rest area, near the county road Hank and I had used to get into town. How long ago had that been? Now there was a big orange sign propped in the center of the pavement, CLOSED BY ORDER OF CDC. I was sweating bullets in the cold, shivering, and my hand was sliced and bleeding freely. I went into the little bathroom shed at the edge of the asphalt and washed it carefully. I had to stop putting blood in the air, on the chance there were any of Cain's offspring roaming. I tore off the bottom of my shirt to bandage the cut once I'd cleaned it, like I had a hundred times before, except this time I started crying.

Making yourself stop sobbing isn't really a trick. Bite your lip hard enough and you can be distracted from almost anything. Tasting my own blood, I looked up at the ceiling. There was a dead moth in the light fixture. Outside the door I heard a scuffling, and I froze, shutting off the water and turning to the door. I heard a low voice, muffled by the door and the wind.

"Ava?"

It was him. He'd gotten out, he'd found me, and if I looked at him he'd take me back, and this time I'd break and I'd give in and I'd be his.

I picked up the dented trash can and used it to smash the mirror over the sink, holding up the longest, wickedest shard of glass. "Come on!" I screamed at the door. "Step in here and I'll put this in your other eye!"

The door swung open. The black shape standing in the gray first light outside looked me over, his face falling. "Oh, Ava," Leo ground out, his voice breaking. "What happened to you?"

I swayed, and dropped the glass. Seeing him sent all the blood out of my head, and Leo rushed across the room to catch me as I fell, both of us going to our knees.

"You're not real," I sobbed, trying to fight him. "You're not going to make me say yes."

"Ava!" Leo grabbed me by the shoulders, then pulled me to him, pressing me against his chest. His shirt smelled like aftershave and cigarettes, and like it had been on his body at least two days longer than it should have been. He felt warm, and strong, and I sobbed hysterically, my whole body shaking. It was a trick. It had to be. It was all a trick of Cain, to make me think I'd escaped when I hadn't.

"You got out," Leo whispered. "It wasn't easy, taking down those barrier spells, but you got out. You ran before we could get to you."

"You're not here," I whimpered, but Leo just held me tighter.

"The conjuring will work its way out of your system in a few hours," he whispered. "Do you trust me?"

I couldn't even respond anymore. I was so cold I couldn't feel my limbs and I shook like I'd just been tossed into a frozen lake.

Leo lifted my hand, unwrapping the cut on my palm, and touched the bloody spot. With the blood on his finger, he pressed it to my forehead, murmuring. I felt his spell settle over me like a blanket, warm and prickly, but the frantic churning of thoughts in my head quieted, and with it, my body stopped shaking.

"Leo," I managed, looking up at him. He looked so tired, even paler than usual, his face drawn tight. He hadn't shaved, or combed his hair, and he had a small moon-shaped cut healing at one side of his mouth.

"Yeah, it's me," he said, relief relaxing the tightness in his jaw.

"I'm so sorry," I said, starting to cry again. It was like a floodgate in me—I couldn't close it. "I left you alone. I should have protected you . . ."

"I'm fine," he said. "All I cared about was getting here once I knew you were in trouble."

"You found me," I choked out, going limp. Something Leo had said before, when I was still convinced this was a fever dream, suddenly flicked back into being. "No, you said 'we' . . ."

"If you're going to complain about how long it took," Uriel said, "understand that I can't just snap my fingers and break magic as powerful as Cain's." He stood in the door, his arms folded. "But I do owe you an apology. I underestimated his desire to keep you near him."

I looked back at Leo. "You . . . and him . . ."

Leo nodded. "We got here as fast as we could. I'm just sorry it wasn't sooner."

The glance he traded with Uriel confirmed my worst fear. "If Uriel went to you to help me . . ." I breathed. "Oh, shit."

"You and I have a long talk ahead of us," Leo said, pulling me to my feet. Uriel rushed in, shocking the hell out of me, and took my other arm, supporting me like I was his feeble old grandma and we were on our way to church.

"I'm sorry . . ." I whimpered, but Leo cut me off.

"Not until you're strong enough."

"It wasn't her fault," Uriel said, surprising me again. He was going to have to quit that. My heart couldn't take it with the state I was in. "I ordered her to . . ."

"You stay out of this," Leo said, and his voice was colder than the prairie blizzard outside. None of the Leo I knew, who could be warm and even funny. This was the Grim Reaper, Death himself, speaking to an angel who'd trod all over his territory.

"Don't be cruel to her," Uriel said before he let go of me at Leo's car. "She's had enough of that in her lifetime."

He was gone when I looked up, and Leo and I were alone. "Get in," he said, helping me into the front seat and buckling my seat belt. I looked up at his face, which wasn't angry or cold but simply blank, careful not to give away what he was thinking.

"Where are we going?" I said, thinking it was pretty much the only inoffensive question I could ask. Leo slammed my door and got in the driver's seat.

"Far the hell away from here."

We didn't speak for many miles down the highway, but this time it wasn't the comfortable silence I could endure.

I peered out the windshield as we pulled up in front of a lot of blinking neon and last-ditch drunks stumbling out into the dawn. "What is this?"

"Indian casino," Leo said. "My dad used to have meetings here sometimes with the godfather from Denver. Neutral ground and all that."

I tried to climb out of the car but my legs were shaking too badly. "Leo . . ." I tried again, but he just held me up as we crossed the parking lot and through the smoky lobby and got into an elevator.

"Wait," he said. "Until we're alone."

The hotel room was the nicest I'd seen in decades, but I couldn't appreciate it. "I need to wash up," I told Leo, aware that my skin was itchy in the way you get when you haven't showered in a few weeks too long. Now that we were alone, I would have done anything to avoid the conversation we had to have.

"Ava . . ." he started, but I flipped on the bathroom light.

"Oh Lord," I breathed as I saw my reflection. I looked dead. My cheeks were hollow and my skin was streaked with dirt. My hair hung in stiff, greasy chunks. I pressed my hands over my eyes, and my stomach growled in response.

"When was the last time you ate?" Leo said quietly, coming behind me to help me strip out of my filthy jacket and overshirt.

"I don't remember," I said. "I guess if you're immortal you don't think about stuff like food and water. Or need to bathe."

Leo turned on the shower hot and helped me get undressed the rest of the way. "I'll order you some food," he said. "I don't know if we can salvage these clothes."

"Burn them," I said, getting in the shower and sitting down, pulling my legs up to my chest.

Leo went out and while he was gone the bathroom filled with steam. I sat for a long time watching black water slowly turn clear again as I washed layers of grime off my body.

"How long was I down there?" I said when the door opened again.

"Couple weeks," Leo said. "Angel boy came fluttering around, freaking out because he couldn't find you and one thing lead to another."

I shut off the water and stood up stiffly. Leo wrapped me in a towel and helped me to the bed. He'd ordered a rare steak and stood by the window while I ate it, watching the pink halo of neon flash below us on the marquee.

I set down my knife and fork when I was done, and looked at him. "I didn't want to lie to you."

"Then why did you?" His shoulders were a perfectly straight line, drawn taut as a rope.

"I . . ." I felt sick, the food a knot in my guts. "I couldn't tell you what was happening. Uriel said if I did he'd . . . he'd make things very bad for both of us."

"You could have told me anything," Leo said. "Anything in this world and it wouldn't have mattered. I could have accepted it and we could have moved on. But to keep something like this from me? That you're on the Kingdom's payroll?"

I shut my eyes tight, almost hoping that I'd wake up inside one of Cain's nightmares, back in the silo.

"I am so sorry," I said finally. "But that was before, when I didn't know what was going to happen with us. I didn't think you'd be very happy."

"That you're a bounty hunter turning in Fallen scalps?" Leo growled. "God fucking *dammit,* Ava! Out of all the shit that happened to us, this is the *one* piece you should have told me!" He swept the room service tray off the bed, shattering dishes and sending the silverware flying. I curled into myself, shaking.

"You know what the worst part is?" Leo said after a long time. His voice was far away, and he had his back to me again as he stood on the other side of the room. "I needed you. These past weeks. It's not getting any better with the other reapers and I really needed you. But you couldn't be straight with me. You couldn't let me help you. You think so little of yourself, so little of *me* and what we have that you willingly go with the Walking Man and leave me choking on your dust."

I opened my eyes at that, sitting up. "Willing? You think I put myself through that again on *purpose*?"

"Why else?" Leo snapped. "Because it sure wasn't to kill the Fallen. It wasn't to get rid of Cain. You must have a reason that you don't care to share with me, Ava, because normally you're a lot smarter than this."

"Fuck you, Leo," I said, jumping up from the bed and dropping my towel. A bag from the hotel boutique sat on the side table and I dumped out the new set of underwear, jeans, bra, and shirt, yanking the tags off.

"Where do you think you're going?" Leo demanded as I wriggled into the outfit. It hung on me, and I could see my hip bones sticking through my flesh. If Leo could look at me and think I'd gone through this of my own accord, then he could go piss on a live wire.

"Anywhere you aren't," I said, grabbing up his overcoat from the chair by the door. "Because if all you can do is whine about how I was shacked up with Cain after what you've seen, then you have your head so far up your ass there's nothing I can do to help you."

"Ava, don't walk away from me!" Leo thundered as I opened the door.

"Go order around somebody who gives a shit," I said. "I'm not your bitch."

He didn't have anything to say to that, and I let the slamming door end our conversation.

I boosted a no-frills granny coupe from the edge of the long-term parking lot, screaming onto the highway before security or the cops could catch up with me. I stopped to swap the plates once, but I kept driving until I got to the hospital that was both closest to the town we'd been in and the nearest to the quarantine zone. Hank wasn't there, and I tried six more hospitals before I finally found him.

At least Valley had held up her end of that bargain. Hank was in the ICU, and I glanced at his chart because the nurses were way too busy to notice me, even if I wasn't hard to spot. He had an infection, his kidneys were beat up from it, and he'd lost enough blood to be in a coma. But his eyes fluttered when I came up to his head, and he gave me a weak smile.

"I know I should thank you," he said. "But all I can think is that I used to be right-handed, and you chopped off my fucking arm."

"You're welcome," I said, putting a hand on his forehead. He sighed, then frowned a little.

"Why are you so sad?" he asked.

"You got a couple days?" I said. Hank laughed.

"I'll be okay. I might even get out of here with the rest of me still working if I can kick out this infection."

"You know, I should be pissed at you too," I said. "You walked me right into a trap."

Hank mumbled something, but he was drifting off and I leaned close. "What?"

"He said 'now you know what you need to kill the Walking Man,'" a voice said from behind me. Uriel leaned against the door frame, devoid of his usual company-man smirk.

"You have some goddamn nerve," I told the angel. Hank

moaned a little in his sleep but morphine could apparently block out even angelic visitations. Lucky bastard. "He was never in Tartarus," I said. "You knew and you sent me anyway because that's just how it works for me. How the world sees me."

I'd never felt like it was really the end before. When I'd been tempted to give up, something kept driving me forward. It was the hound. It was trying to survive even when I'd been tempted to throw in the towel. But now I was free, and the hound had no reason to stick around.

Uriel clenched his jaw and then visibly made himself relax. He stood tense and awkward, like he didn't know what to do with himself, which was a first. "I did know," he said at length, like the words were being yanked from him with pliers. "I knew he was never in Tartarus. And I knew it wasn't as simple as bringing in an immortal serial killer who liked to spread chaos."

He gestured toward the highway beyond Hank's window, choked with Humvees and emergency relief trucks. "But I didn't know about this. This was not my doing." He relaxed again, and I realized that was what Uriel looked like when he told the truth. "I am fighting a war, Ava. I would never sacrifice a good soldier on something as petty as a fugitive hunt." He took my arm, pulling me to my feet. "I wasn't after the Walking Man."

"Cain," I said. "Let's just call him what he is. Even if he isn't the guy from the story he's definitely an original son of a bitch."

"Cain is a rabid dog," Uriel said. "I'm after the person pulling his leash."

"You are so stupid," I said. "All of you, in the Kingdom, looking down on the rest of us. Like we're vermin to you. Things like Cain don't have a leash, not really. They can't be reined in."

"Sure they can," Uriel said mildly. "You just have to find a bigger, meaner dog to do it." He folded his arms. "Did you learn anything in your time with him?"

"Other than that he'd spent sixty years in a silo and he was ending the world in a plague of zompires?" I thought back to Cain's implacable speech, as if he'd been anticipating the telling of my fate for the whole stretch of decades since the tornado swept him away. "He fixed me a lot of tea. Oh, and he told me I was made for him and that eventually I would willingly submit to being his companion until the end of days."

Uriel looked out at the highway as a green Humvee rolled by. "We should go," he said. "There's too much of a chance the Fallen are out there and neither of us needs to run into any of them right now."

"There is no 'we' anymore," I said. "I'm going to go beg Leo to forgive me, and if he takes me back I'm not leaving his side again. I'm going to get as far away from the start of the end of the world as possible." I started to walk out, but Uriel's cold voice stopped me.

"This isn't the start," he said. "It's not even the prologue." He came to stand next to me in the door of Hank's room, looking out onto the ward of the wounded and the dying, beds shoved close as graves. "As far as world's ending goes, we're well into the first act."

I stared at him, an entirely new sort of hopelessness creeping through me. Why did I have to be here? Why couldn't I have just died at twenty-six like I was meant to?

"Cain fell off the radar and I was grateful," Uriel said. "Truthfully, I was preoccupied with what was happening in Tartarus. But he wasn't gone. He'd been leashed, and what I want is whoever is holding the other end. You should want them too." He patted me on the shoulder. "They're the same person who gave that sword to Owen and put your boyfriend over a barrel."

He sighed. "I was hoping when you showed up gunning for Cain, it would force the man behind the curtain to step out. But I underestimated both how powerful and how obsessed with you Cain was. So—and this is the first and only time you'll ever hear this from me—I am sorry. I got you involved in a fight you couldn't win, and I had no right to do that."

Another heavy vehicle rolled by outside, shaking the floor under our feet, and Uriel frowned. "Now we *really* need to go. You need to be back in Minneapolis. Leo will forgive you. Death is not petty."

This time I was the one to stop him. "So what about this? The Fallen and the plague and all?"

"We keep looking," Uriel said. "We keep shining a light into corners looking for the Fallen who started Cain on this path and eventually they run out of places to hide."

"That's a lousy answer," I said, but Uriel shrugged.

"Nonetheless, it's the only one I have. And don't get any ideas of coming back here," he said. "You're not as expendable as you used to be. You're not a game piece. You're *the* game piece. You could do a lot of damage." He reached for me, and I felt the air being sucked out of the space around my body.

"Don't!" I screamed but my stomach dropped, like when you miss a step coming off a sidewalk, and when I opened my eyes I was standing on a street corner in Minneapolis.

"Remember what I said," Uriel told me. "Take it seriously. I'm not the enemy here. Keep Leo safe. The Grim Reaper is one of the few things that can stop Cain and the Fallen. Once he has his Scythe, anyway."

A car honked at me as I swayed too close to the traffic, and when I looked back Uriel was gone. He'd left me in front of a motel that the epithet *fleabag* would be too generous for. I kicked the snow. "Son of a bitch goddamn fucking angel."

"Amen, sister." A bum on a bus stop bench grinned at me and offered me a slug from a brown bottle wrapped in a paper bag.

"Sure, why not," I said, and slumped down next to him. He looked me over.

"You look like seven kinds of hell, child." I drank the vile, fiery liquid that was inside the bottle and handed it back to him.

"I've had a rough night."

"Boyfriend trouble?" He took his own pull off the bottle and coughed, spitting something brown into the snowbank. "Feels like this winter is never gonna end."

"I wish it was that simple," I sighed.

"Never is," the bum said. "But don't you fret. Sooner or later all this'll be gone and it'll be spring again. Always liked spring. Cold traps you in. Makes it hard to move from place to place. Like the earth is tryin' its hardest to keep you pinned."

I waved off the bottle when he offered it to me again. "You're pretty smart for an old drunk guy."

"It's six A.M.," he grunted. "I ain't that drunk yet."

"Ava?" I snapped up to see the last person I wanted or expected looking at me like she'd just stepped on a big pile of dog droppings.

"Viv?" I said. "What are you doing here?"

"Not sitting on a bus bench day drinking, for a start," she said, hefting a brown paper bag of food.

"Where's Leo?" I said, standing up and brushing snow off my jeans. "Why aren't you with him?"

Viv sighed, looking up and down the block, and then jerked her head at me. "Come inside. It's not safe out here."

"Good luck, sister," the bum called as I followed Viv into the motel. "See you in the spring."

Viv slammed and locked the door behind me, peeking out the blinds before she dumped her groceries and glared at me. "Look who decided to come back."

I sat down on the bed. Sticky comforter or not, it was better than anything I'd slept on recently. "Don't!" Viv snarled. "This is my room, not yours. You're not my boss, and I don't owe you shit."

"Fine," I said, moving to the hard chair next to a little table holding cardboard ads for a strip club and a wing joint. "You don't owe me and I don't owe you but I've had a really shitty morning already so I might just decide you're the person I beat repeatedly in the head to deal with my emotions surrounding all this if you keep shit-talking me, Viv. And because I'm not a sociopath, I don't *want* to start punching people for no good reason, so how's about I take a chill pill and you start acting like you're housebroken?"

Viv growled, and I didn't even look at her this time. After what I'd seen in Kansas, she was about as intimidating as a Chihuahua in a pink fluffy sweater. "Is Leo here? And where's Raina and all of them?"

Viv rubbed her hands over her face. Her Mohawk drooped and she looked like she hadn't slept since I'd left. "They found the farmhouse," Viv said. "Owen's goons, I mean. Some of us got away. Raina . . ." she sighed. "Raina didn't make it."

I felt sick. I'd let Leo convince me he'd be fine without me, but that hadn't been true. I'd let myself get lured away. I'd let our enemies divide us.

It turned out that Uriel's little trick had gotten me back to Minneapolis way ahead of Leo, and Viv was so relieved that she let me stay in her crummy motel room while I waited for him.

"Can I ask you something?" she said as I unwrapped a toaster pastry and shoveled it in my mouth. I was still starving.

"Do you think Leo can take down Owen?" she said. She cracked her knuckles as she talked, staring at them. "I mean, we're all hiding and scattered and Owen and them are still at headquarters, with all the ledgers, doing all the collections . . ."

"Leo can take down Owen," I said, putting a stop to her ramble. "The Grim Reaper can kill anything."

"Not if he doesn't have his Scythe," Viv muttered.

I got up, ignoring her doomsaying. I was tired of waiting, and tired of feeling like shit for what I'd said to Leo. And for what he'd said to me.

I'd fallen into the trap again—my own trap of being passive Ava who was afraid of all the walking ghosts dogging her steps.

That wasn't me anymore. As I got dressed, I pointed at Viv. "Do you have any friends left inside Headquarters?"

"Maybe a few hounds . . ." she said hesitantly. "But none that will risk their lives."

"All I need is a face-to-face with Owen," I said. "Preferably a surprising one."

Viv's expression went slack. "Are you crazy?" she demanded. "The last time—"

"This won't be like the last time," I said. "Can you do it or not?"

She nodded. "I don't like it, but for the Grim Reaper's hound, we'll do anything. You know that."

I did, and I felt almost lousy exploiting their loyalty, but I was done watching my life expectancy circle the drain while the world went to shit. I could do something for once. I could not be afraid of what might happen and just fix things for Leo and me.

I tried calling Leo's burner but it sent me straight to voicemail. I left him a message telling him to get his ass back to Minneapolis and then aimed my stolen car toward Headquarters. I didn't feel shattered and exhausted anymore. I felt clear. Maybe it was the sleep and food after two weeks being held hostage. Maybe I was just so far around the bend I was past caring about what happened to me.

I kept trying Leo, all the numbers I had for him, leaving messages where I could. He was going to piss himself when he found out what I'd done, but it wasn't like he could get any angrier at me.

Viv's hound friends were good as their word—the door was unlocked and stairs were where they said. I just hoped they weren't currently being tortured for their efforts.

The floor of offices was quiet this early in the morning, and only one light was on. I hung back, staying silent, and waited until Owen crossed the hall, whistling to himself, and pushed through a swinging door. I followed noiselessly, catching the door before it could swing back and stepping into an executive washroom that looked to be designed specifically for coke binges and hookups with your assistant. Lots of gold, black, everything reflective.

Not that Owen noticed me as he stood at the urinal, still whistling as he shook himself off and adjusted his briefs.

"I wouldn't have pegged you for tighty whiteys," I said. Owen yelped and spun around, his pants falling to half-mast.

"What the fuck!" he screamed.

"It sucks being accosted in the bathroom," I said. "Trust me, I know."

Owen started to laugh as he zipped up his pants, shaking his head. "You little whelp bitch," he said. "You are in so much fucking trouble. I am going to take you apart."

He took a step toward me and I snarled. The sound rolled around the little bathroom like we were inside a thunderhead, and Owen stopped, fear swimming up into his eyes for the first time. "You can't touch me," he said, but his voice held about half the sass it had a second ago.

"That's where you're wrong," I said. This time it was my turn to take a step. "You know good and well what happened to my first boss. Gary. The one who doesn't have a windpipe anymore."

"So what?" Owen said, just above a whisper.

"So the Grim Reaper needs his Scythe to become Death, it's true," I said. "But I don't need a Scythe to kill, Owen. And I don't need Leo to kill one punk reaper who's gotten a big head. I don't need a reaper at all." I bared my teeth. "I can take care of you all on my own. And nothing would make me happier."

Owen backed up then. He stumbled over his own foot and fell back into the urinal, scrabbling for purchase. "I'm sorry!" he shouted. "Okay? I'm sorry! It wasn't my idea!"

"I think it was at least partly your idea," I said. "Because you're a venal little bastard who wants power but doesn't want to work too hard for it."

"It's true," he gasped as I kept him pinned against the piss-stained urinal. "I am a bastard . . ."

"Shut up, Owen," I snapped. He clamped his lips together, his eyes wide and his jaw quivering. "Leo needs to prove he's the Grim

Reaper," I said. "No argument there. But you don't need to be around when he does. This game you're playing is making me real fucking mad, so how about you stop hindering and start helping before I decide to turn you into a human sprinkler the way I did Gary?"

I was so tense I was vibrating, not sure how much longer I could keep this up. Threatening people really takes it out of you, whether it's pretentious vampires or asshole reapers.

"You can talk now," I said when Owen just kept staring at me.

"What do you want?" he squeaked.

"I want to know where you got that angelic blade, for a start," I said. "And the name of the Fallen who gave it to you. Then I want the spell that lets you handle it."

Owen cocked his head. "You want to use it? Why . . ."

"Because there's an immortal monster who I have a power-ful desire to stab until he is dead," I said. "Name. Spell. Now." I snapped my fingers in his face.

"The spell is on the inside of the case," he said in a rush. "Just write it anywhere on your bare skin and you can handle it for a little while. Too long and it'll burn, even with the magic."

"Great," I said. "Now tell me which Fallen convinced you to keep the Scythe from Leo. And tell me where it is."

"I don't know," Owen said, swallowing so the tendons in his neck stood out. I shook my head.

"Not good enough."

"I gave them the Scythe and I don't know where they took it!" Owen said. "Why would I *want* to know?"

"So you can get a pissed-off hellhound off your ass?" I said. Owen sighed.

"Not a problem that I ever anticipated, let me tell you. I am a Reaper."

"And you're doing a shitty job," I said. "If you can't give me a where I'll settle for a who. Tell me the Fallen's name and somebody will take care of them."

Owen narrowed his eyes. "Fallen is way above your pay grade, doggie."

I slammed his skull hard into the porcelain, and he yelled. "I didn't say I was going in guns blazing, moron."

Owen held up his hands. "Okay, okay. They contacted me about a month before I heard about your little, heh, dog-and-pony show . . ."

"You're pushing it," I warned him. "I want the name of the Fallen and it's the last time I'm gonna ask you."

"Fallen," Owen said, letting out a small giggle. "Yeah, the Fallen. It's—" He choked, his face twitching, and a little black blood dribbled out of his mouth.

"Shit," I said, backing off from him. Owen's eyes rolled back as he fell to the floor convulsing, and then they snapped open again, pure black like they'd had ink spilled in them.

"Owen?" I said cautiously. He shook his head mechanically.

"Guess again."

I raised my chin. "Who are you, then?"

He let out another one of those high-pitched laughs. "I know something you don't know . . ."

There was something about the voice, even filtered through Owen's smarmy mouth. It cut right to the center of me. It was a frightening voice, one I'd tried hard to forget over the past months with Leo.

"Come back and see me, Ava," it said with Owen's tongue. "And maybe I'll give you what you want. Maybe. If you have something I want in exchange."

The door to the bathroom banged open before I could say anything else and Owen went limp, eyes open as he stared up at the ceiling. The black drained away, and his chest rose and fell slowly.

Leo crossed the floor and stood between us, head swiveling. "What did you do to him?"

"Nothing," I said, shaking off the shock of what I'd just seen. "I mean, I beat him up a little but that was not my doing. Why are you here?"

"You left me like fifty messages," he said. He bent down and felt Owen's pulse. "He's alive," he said. "What a shame."

I looked at Leo and stayed quiet as he stared at me. "I don't even know what to say. You come busting in to the one place you shouldn't be and—"

I grabbed his face in my hands and kissed him, hard. After being gone for so long I just needed him to know that I had cared I'd been gone, that I was sorry. Leo returned my embrace after a minute, wrapping his arms tight around me. "I'm sorry," he muttered into my hair. "I was a dick before."

"You think?" I said. He stepped back, holding me at arm's length.

"It's not that I don't appreciate the initiative. But kicking in doors isn't really your style, so what's going on?"

"You were right," I said in a rush. "I should have stayed here and helped you. It was a stupid move to let Cain take me again."

"Yeah, it was," Leo said. "But not the stupidest thing either of us has ever done, so let's just forget it."

"Somebody wanted you without a Scythe," I said. "They took it and hid it so you couldn't stop what Cain set in motion. They tried to sideline me by giving me to him. And Owen was gonna give me a name, until he went all *Scanners* on me."

Leo waggled his fingers in front of Owen's slack face and glassy eyes. "Yeah, nobody's home in there."

I shrank inside my coat, even though the bathroom was stuffy. "I thought this would at least get us some answers."

"Doesn't look that way," Leo said. He stood up, rubbing a bit of the sticky blood that had come from Owen's nose on his fingers. "This isn't a Fallen, either," he said, sniffing it. "Demon magic smells."

I pressed my hands over my face and then gave Leo an agonized look. "It can't be."

"She did say she'd see you again," Leo told me. I shook my head, still unwilling to believe that my luck could get this much worse.

Lilith, Gary's demon BFF.

"Assuming this is Lilith," I said quietly, "what could she want?"

"I think there's only one way to find that out," Leo said.

"Okay," I said, squeezing my eyes shut. "Let's go ask her."

Leo decided that there was no way to disguise the fact that I'd put Owen in a coma, so he called in the other reapers, who stared at the two of us like we'd just taken a leak in their morning coffee.

"Why?" the one in the red dress asked. "Owen just wanted you to prove yourself. He was *protecting* us."

I was pretty sure the only thing Owen had been protecting was his own ass, but I held my tongue. A mouthy hellhound was just gas on the fire with this many reapers.

"You assholes listen and you listen good," Leo thundered as the voices crowding the little room grew to a roar. "I tried to jump through Owen's hoops, and I came to him today to let him step aside with no hard feelings, and this is the result. If anyone else wants to test me then come on ahead."

The group of reapers went silent at that, all looking at each other.

"But you can't hold the Scythe," the one in the red dress ventured. "You don't have any more right to lead than Owen or Gary did."

"You all know that Scythe is bullshit," Leo said. "What I'm hoping you don't know is where Owen stashed the real deal, because if one of you does, you're probably looking at life with eight fingers or less." He scanned their faces, and nobody could meet his eyes.

"I don't have any illusions that one of you will try and take me out the first goddamn chance you get," he said. "In fact, I'd be a little disappointed if you didn't. But Owen's out, I'm the Grim Reaper, and now I want you to stop all this shit and go do your goddamn jobs."

After a long second, the red dress reaper and her friend Polo Shirt nodded. "Fine," she said tightly. "Seeing as how you iced the only one of us willing to stand up to you."

"You want some, sweetness?" Leo asked. "Come here."

Shockingly, the red dress suddenly didn't want to mouth off anymore. A couple of reapers collected Owen and the rest milled around nervously, watching Leo and me.

"What now?" I murmured to him.

"You need to chat with a demon, right?" Leo said. "This is one of the few places in the world with a direct conduit to Hell." He snapped his fingers at the nearest reaper. "Show me the conduit."

There are places in the world where things are thin—places of suffering and disasters, places where bombs ripped the atomic structure of the human world apart. Those places are nexus points where all the balls on the table line up with the cue—where you can hop from one to the next without expending enough power to collapse a star. The Nevada Test Site was the only one in North America I'd been aware of before all of this. It was a far cry from an empty basement room in Minneapolis, but it had the same feel, of standing in a place so empty even the air had deserted you.

I wasn't one hundred percent sure how transiting the conduits worked, just sure that it *did* work, because the last time I'd been taken to Tartarus for my trouble. I'd gone willingly, too—I'd been looking for Leo. He'd died, and I wasn't ready to let him go.

I still wasn't.

The other reapers refused to even go into the room with us, and I didn't blame them. It looked like a room, but it clearly wasn't—passing through the door sent prickles all over my body.

"Only Gary used this place," said Polo Shirt, before he slammed the door behind us. "And you're not Gary."

"Well, that's something," Leo said, flicking on the row of lights along the low ceiling.

"Are you sure about this?" I said. Leo shook his head.

"I haven't been sure of anything since I woke up a reaper." He reached out and squeezed my shoulder. "But you're here. I'm not worried."

The lights flickered as we stepped into the center of the room, and I felt a harsh wind, not borne from any place we could see, slide over my face and through my hair. One by one, the bulbs in the ceiling started to blink out.

"Here we go," Leo murmured.

I waited. Lilith had told me things weren't over between us and if there's one thing demons are good at, it's grudge holding.

More of the bulbs blinked out, faster now, and the wind kicked up icy and smelling of ashes. When the last light went out with a pop of glass, I heard an expensive shoe clack on the cement behind me.

"It's pathetic what some women will do for their man," Lilith said. I turned around, one eyebrow going up.

"I'm pretty sure I'm speaking to the person who staged a jail-break in Hell just to get her boyfriend back," I said.

She walked over to me, and I instinctively backed up. It was like standing in front of a cobra wearing human skin—something about the way demons move, too fluid and quick to be anything flesh and blood. The eyes too—they never blink, not even the ones who spend a lot of time pretending to be people.

"What do you want, Ava?" she said, the hiss of her voice blending with the wind. "And what's with the muscle?" She looked Leo over, her tongue flicking out. "Didn't I kill you?"

"It didn't take," Leo said. "Now how about telling me where my Scythe is before I peel that pretty fake face off and see what you really look like?"

"Just because I can't kill you again doesn't mean you frighten me," Lilith drawled. "But if it's a dick-measuring contest you want . . ."

"I got your invitations," I said. "Both of them. You might not have convinced Owen to hide the Scythe but you kept me from finding out, so what do you want?"

"I want things to be the way they were before I ever laid eyes on you," Lilith snapped. "But not even I can go back in time, so I'll settle for fucking with you until the end of time. Have a nice day."

She turned and started to walk away, but I spoke up. "I'd think after what Gary did to you, you'd want payback as much as we do."

"Fucking Gary." Lilith sucked in air between her teeth. "He's one soul I'd love to tear to shreds."

"Too bad reapers don't have any," I said. Lilith brushed a strand of platinum hair away from her eyes, which glowed blue even in the starlight.

"You got a big set of brass balls, Ava, I'll give you that much." She buffed her nails on her black suit jacket. "But what makes you think I'm not just in this to watch the world burn up and you along with it?"

"Because if every soul that comes to Hell bears Cain's mark, then you and every other demon are shit out of luck," I said. "You might hate me, you might visit my dreams and snuff Owen just to torment me for crossing you, but you need the damned or the lights go out in Hell. Whoever set Cain loose this time, they don't care about you or any other demon. If there's no world out there, you'll be in the dark, alone in Hell with the other demons, and the Fallen will have won."

I waited as she sized me up, her nostrils flaring. Demons hated the Fallen even more than the angels, if that was possible. Lilith knew what it was to be a Fallen's slave. She couldn't be on their side in this.

"Fine, you make a good point for a glorified purse dog," she sighed finally. "Step into my office, both of you." She pointed one perfect pale finger over my shoulder and I blinked when I saw a door in the middle of the barren sand. It was just there, like one of those fake tunnels the Coyote paints for the Road Runner. As much time as I'd spent around demons, I'd never get used to the way they could grab reality by the hair and twist its neck around. It made my stomach roll, like I was at the top of a carnival ride.

Lilith opened the door and the next thing I knew we were standing in the kind of office you usually only see on TV shows about bratty teenagers in a prep school. Lots of leather furniture, a tray of expensive scotch on a side board, paintings of boats on stormy seas, and a nice big chair for Lilith to sit in, setting one red-soled foot on the desk as she sat and looked up at Leo and me.

"Demons are so literal," I murmured. Lilith cocked her head. She favored the business bitch look when she was wearing human skin, and her black pantsuit was so sharp it could have sliced me. Her high-collared shirt showed just a hint of skin and her hair was loose and blown pin-straight.

"I don't know the Fallen's name," she said. "No one knows the name of every angel expelled from the Kingdom. But I did spend a lot of time serving them drinks and pretending to laugh at their jokes. I could easily find out."

"For a price," I finished. After hearing Gary give the pitch for ninety years, I could recite it in my sleep.

"Well, of course," Lilith said. "Don't worry. I'm not going to ask you for the head of John the Baptist. It'll be something manageable."

I didn't believe her—because who in their right mind would believe a demon, never mind the evil queen among their ranks of screwing people over? "I'm through owing people," I said, but Leo stepped up.

"What do you want?"

I stared at him, trying to bore into him with my eyes and let him know this was a bad fucking idea. Lilith looked between us, tapping her forefingers together. "Now, this is interesting. The big bad man is willing to deal, and the scrappy sidekick has grown a spine."

"Go fuck yourself," I said, tugging at Leo's arm. "Come on. She doesn't know anything."

"Cain is pals with a Fallen named Dantanian," she said. "Looks blond, corn-fed, pretends to be a cop? We thought she and many others who left Hell were dead until just now, when you two went to Headquarters and started making a ruckus."

"So?" I said.

"So I have that dead list, if you have what I'm after," Lilith said. "One of those is the Fallen who's remaking the world in their very own zombie image, and it's not a long list."

"It's not worth it," I said as Leo leaned in. "Leo," I exclaimed in a whisper. "Whatever it is, it's too much."

"It's not too much," he said. "The world is ending, Ava. You said it yourself. I need the Scythe. You need me to have it." He looked back at Lilith. "Besides, without us, there's no damned souls flowing into this bitch's coffers. So whatever she wants, it'll have to leave us in one piece."

Lilith returned his wide fake smile. "More or less, darling, yes." She picked up a silver letter opener from her desk and pricked her own finger. "Now you."

"Hell no," I said, and Lilith rolled her eyes. "I need to tell you a story and since you're the last person I want to chat with I'm just going to show you." She waggled her finger at me. "Come on, Ava. It's just a little blood. Far from the worst thing you've done."

I shut my eyes, willing myself not to vomit as she touched her finger to my lips. It wasn't the power line I was expecting to bite down on, though. It was numb and soft and warm, like I'd downed that handful of Percocets all over again. Things went bright and fuzzy around the edges and when I could see again Lilith was on the ground in front of me. No more thousand-dollar suit, no more flawless manicure. Black crescents rode high under her eyes, pushed down by tears. Someone had given her a fat lip. I guessed it was the guy standing over her, just a shadow and a pair of feet.

"You want to raise your voice to me again?" he said. His voice was sharp and angry and Lilith's breath hitched when he spoke. Lilith was afraid of him. I watched, helpless to move or look away.

"N-no," Lilith said softly. "I'm sorry."

"Damn right you are," the shadow said. "Now get up. Do it again."

Lilith put her hand up to touch her bloody lip and he reached down, slapping her hand away. "Are you stupid? Or just defective?" He grabbed Lilith by the arm and yanked her upright. "There are a dozen girls who'd take your place. Do you want to be out there on your knees, scrubbing or sucking? Is that what you'd prefer?"

"No, please!" Lilith cried out as he shook her. "I'm sorry . . ."

The angel grabbed her chin and pulled her close, his face coming into the light. He was beautiful, but he was also even more waxen and dead-eyed than Lilith. "I decide when you're allowed to wipe the blood off your beautiful skin. Only me. I'm your entire world. I won't be denied. Soon we'll be out of this Pit and then nobody can deny me. The world will end in ashes, Lilith, and if you're smart you'll be standing next to me instead of tasting them in your mouth." He smiled when he finished speaking. His eyes were blue, almost white, and his eyebrows blended into his pale skin so that he looked like he almost didn't have hair, just a halo of white. He was so pale I doubted sunlight had ever touched him—unnaturally pale.

As I stared, and Lilith sobbed quietly, he turned toward me and the smile stretched wider, wide as a snake ready to swallow me.

I came back to the real world with a crash, and immediately fell over, retching and clawing at my stomach and throat. I felt like fire ants were crawling from my throat to my belly button and biting every inch in between. I tried to talk and only desperate hacking sounds came out.

Leo swooped in to hold me up and Lilith leaned over her desk to get a better angle. "Oh, Ava, did that poison not agree with you?"

I was starting to black out, and I tried sticking a finger down my own throat to make myself puke, but my mouth was dry as the ashes I could still smell everywhere.

"The humans you love so much have that saying," Lilith said. "About life giving you lemons? Cute, and I can see the humor in it. To go from one of the top men on the totem pole to some . . . some . . . *trailer park* on the outskirts of the Pit? All because some hellhound got her panties in a twist over a worthless piece-of-trash mob hit man who would have died before forty anyway?" She shook her finger. "No, no, Ava. Not how I roll. That's another human saying. I like that one better."

"If she dies there won't be a place in Hell you can hide from me," Leo snarled. He stroked my face and brushed a few beads of sweat off my forehead as my throat closed up. I couldn't breathe at all now, my chest a furnace, every muscle in my body seizing.

"What are you going to do about it?" Lilith purred. "*You* don't have your Scythe." She refocused her shark's eyes on me. "Imagine how happy I was when you showed up. It cost me nothing to show you that face. You will never put a name to it because you are a fool and you always have been."

She straightened up, brushing a speck of lint off her pants. "In the few seconds before you die from anaphylaxis, know that you were never anything but a dead girl living on borrowed time, Ava. And know that I was the one who ended your bonus round in the game of life." She waggled her fingers. "Bye now."

CHAPTER

A person can survive an average of three or four minutes without oxygen before brain death starts to set in. If you drown in cold water or stop breathing from a nasty shock, maybe a little longer. There are cases where people spring back to life after fifteen or twenty minutes, with nothing beyond a little memory loss.

I tried to keep that in mind as I thrashed on the freezing concrete, but it was hard to keep much in mind beyond the indescribable pain.

If I'd been turned into a hellhound by anyone except Gary, I'd probably know demon blood was poisonous. I wouldn't be on a basement floor suffocating. I wouldn't be a lot of things.

But I wasn't dying. I'd gotten the suicidal impulse out of my system the first time I'd gone to Tartarus. I'd wanted to die for a long time and actually living for something was terrifying.

Especially since I was coming close to being dead again.

I flopped on my stomach. I couldn't see much, blackness pervading my vision, but I didn't need to see for this. I used the last tiny gasp of energy I had to let go of the hound's leash, let it roar out of my throat, and let fresh cold air in as I howled into the blackness.

I still didn't make it far on four legs, but at least whatever was in my system was a little more compatible with the hound than my human body. I felt drunk and wobbly but at least I could breathe. Things were still pretty blurry and I sank down on the basement floor, exhausted. I wanted more than anything to just shut my eyes and sleep, but I sat and panted and tried to fight off the poison. Bile roiled around in my stomach and I finally did vomit. After that, I just couldn't keep my eyes open anymore.

When I woke up, Leo was leaning over me, stroking my hair. His face went slack with relief when he saw my eyes were open. "I told you not to trust that bitch," I whispered. My throat was burning from vomiting but I felt better than I had any right to.

Leo handed me a bottle of water and I chugged it while he passed a hand through his hair. "That isn't what we need. We're in this together, remember?"

I pressed my hands over my eyes, wishing the buzzing from the basement lights would just stop. "I'm sorry," I said. "Can we please just go somewhere aboveground?"

Standing, my knees started to give out and he held me up. "You *sure* you're okay? You did just take a hit of demon blood."

"I'm fine," I muttered as we headed for the door. "If I let Lilith take me down I'd die of embarrassment."

"I mostly can't believe we went through that and she didn't even give us a name," Leo grumbled. "All that just to fuck around with us."

"Lilith would level a small city for the sake of petty revenge," I said. "She's relentless that way." I leaned against the wall once we were out of that room, away from the conduit, when the pressure on my skull had eased a little. "And besides, she didn't give me nothing." I cracked a tiny smile. "I saw what he looks like. The Fallen."

"So, what are we gonna do with that?" Leo said. "Pass out sketches to all the Hellspawn we come across?"

"No," I said. "But I bet if I described him to Uriel we'd get a name."

I thought Leo might actually be happy that I'd figured out how to find the asshole who'd taken his Scythe, but he started shaking his head instantly, pacing away from me down the hall.

"You're done," he said. "You're not the Kingdom's unpaid hitter. Uriel and you are done being besties."

"I think that's up to me," I said. Leo punched the metal door, the echo reverberating down through my feet. I flinched away from him, bracing for a blow and then hating myself because I knew it wouldn't come from Leo. Gary really had fucked me up.

"Dammit, Ava," Leo snapped. "I know how these guys work. I *was* one of those guys. When you got somebody who's good at what they do but doesn't know they can stiffen up their spine and tell you to go to hell, you squeeze 'em until there's nothing left.

Then you put a bullet in the back of their head and find a nice quiet landfill in Jersey to leave 'em."

"And I was someone who hunted down the dregs of humanity for a demon," I said. "I tracked people down relentlessly and I killed them. I'm no stranger to doing the unpleasant thing, the thing that's necessary to survive whether it's ripping out a warlock's throat or taking twenty bucks from some john so I'd have food for another week." I folded myself in, digging my fingers into my own rib cage as I hugged myself. "I know that Uriel's using me, but hunting down the Fallen is a necessary thing. Look what they've done here, with one angry monster who's willing to be manipulated."

"It's the way he used you!" Leo shouted. "It's that he took something that wasn't his and put his fingerprints all over it."

I slammed my foot into the floor. "Stop it."

"No! You need to get it through your head that Uriel isn't any different than Gary or any of those johns, because until you do you're just setting yourself up to be used over and over until you finally get killed!" Leo's face was red and a vein in his neck pulsed.

I didn't have anything else to say, so I turned my back on him and broke into a run. Leo yelled, his voice distorted by the low ceiling, "Ava! Ava, get back here!"

"Fuck you!" I screamed, turning on him. I wanted to be feral for once. I wanted to be the one out of control, the one people were afraid to get close to. "I'm not yours, Leo! That was the fucking point! I killed Gary and I ruined everything but I am *not. YOURS.*"

I flapped my arms helplessly. "And really? If I have to explain that to you now, I don't think we ever worked."

"You're right," Leo said without hesitation, and reached out to stop me. "Look, I am an asshole. I died an unreconstructed douchebag. I just . . . the thought of some other guy hurting you just because he can . . . I swore I'd stop that from happening if I could. I didn't mean I own you. Nobody owns you. If you want to walk away right now I won't stop you." He let go of me and backed off. "I'm sorry."

I stared him down for a long time, until my heart had stopped pounding. "You're lucky I don't feel like fighting with anyone else today."

"I feel lucky," Leo said quietly. He looked almost scared, which I'd never seen before. "I really am—"

"I don't want you to apologize," I said. "I want you to help me stop this. Not your opinion, not your proclamation, your help." I looked at him. "If we're as equal as you say, we can stop this."

He relaxed, looking more like the cocky bastard I knew, and I relaxed a little too. I didn't like it when people like him acted vulnerable. It made me think we might all be screwed. "I hate to break it to you, Ava," he said, "but I don't think you're equipped to take out one of the Fallen. I don't know that I am either, not without any actual backup from my so-called colleagues."

I thought about Cain's face when he'd talked about how we were all just going to stay in the silo and wait out the eradication of humanity. He hadn't looked angry. He'd looked happy.

"I think we can get the Fallen to come to us," I said. "If you can calm down and play nice with Uriel. If we can figure out who he is."

"Fine," Leo grumbled. "Then what?"

"Then we take away his toy," I said. Leo raised an eyebrow.

"Kill the Walking Man?"

I nodded. "For a start."

CHAPTER

18

Leo was skeptical of my plan. *Skeptical* wasn't even the right word—he complained all the way back to Kansas. I would have been more annoyed but it was actually kind of nice—just the two of us in the car, like it had been before we'd gotten to Minneapolis and stepped on the hornet's nest.

"So you want to go *back* to the bunker where the crazy undead serial killer held you prisoner and bust him up?" Leo said. "I get this right?"

"That's the short version," I said. The roadblocks were much farther out now, and the real army was here, with convoys on the highway and Black Hawks overhead. I could see the chaos seeping out in the pinched face of the woman who handed me a cup of crappy to-go coffee at the truck stop and the thump of the rotors overhead, the random checkpoints set up by local police.

Leo burned a fake ID getting us within the quarantine zone and back to the hospital where Hank was recovering. I made him wait outside when I went in—I didn't want Hank to flip his wig when he met the Grim Reaper up close and personal.

"Ava," he said, smiling at me. He looked stronger, but he was still pale and full of tubes.

"I need to ask you something," I said. "It's a lot, and I understand if you can't do it." I looked at the steady blip of his monitors. "There's a chance you'll die."

"Is there a chance you'll die as well?" Hank said. I nodded. He sat up in bed, his face crinkling with pain.

"Then say it."

"Your grandfather did something to the Walking Man the first time we ran into him," I said. "He actually managed to slow him down. Do you know how to do that?"

Hank chewed on his lip. "Jacob was a powerful mystic. He had talents that I just don't."

"Anything would help," I said. "Even a word, a spell . . ."

Hank shook his head. "It doesn't work like that. It's not like conjuring, where you can read from a book and smear some blood on the ground and be good to go. You have to have the talent and you have to be Jewish." He swung his legs over the bed, his slippers whispering against the linoleum. "And since you're neither of those things, where are we going?"

I tried to stop him, but he waved me off, limping over to a wheelchair and flopping down. "Are you okay to be, you know . . . outside?" I said. Hank shrugged.

"I'm as healthy as anyone who got their arm chopped off by a power tool," he said. "I managed to survive the virulent infection that filthy auto shop floor gave me, and I'm not craving the blood of the living. Overall I'd say it's a pretty good day for me to go be heroic."

"You really don't have to do this," I said. Hank shook his head.

"I do, though. You forget, Ava, I can see how this all ends."

He didn't say anything more as I wheeled him into the corridor, except to grunt when Leo joined us. "Who are you?" he said as we walked out the sliding doors into the freezing wind.

"Leo," he said, and left it at that. I was grateful. I figured if we lived past Part One of my half-assed attempt to save the world I could properly introduce the two of them.

We all made it to the fence around the bunker, Hank leaning heavily on Leo, but I stopped them there. "If he sees anyone besides me, he's going to go nuclear. Let me get him outside."

Leo chewed on his bottom lip for a second, and then sighed. "Yeah. I really fuckin' hate this but okay."

I stood on tiptoe so I could kiss his cheek. "I'll be fine."

He touched the spot with the tips of his fingers. "It's not you I'm worried about, dollface."

I mimicked the touch and tried to show him my most confident smile. He returned it. I turned and headed for the bunker. I could still lie to Leo when I needed to. I didn't feel good about it. I wanted one person I couldn't lie to, one person who saw all of me, even the ugly parts.

The walk to the bunker seemed a lot shorter than the crazy

sprint away from it a couple of days ago. Still, the stone of dread I'd swallowed was just as heavy.

The light dusting of snow was still disturbed from where I'd run. I removed the broken post, stomped on the hatch, and waited. After a few seconds it popped open, hydraulics groaning in the cold. There was nobody there, just darkness. I sighed and climbed in, feeling the stale, humid air ruffling my hair.

Cain met me at the bottom of the hatch. The lights were off, and in the soft red glow of the emergency bulbs he almost looked human.

"Little bird," he said. "You look almost happy to see me."

"Speaking of birds, you're a strange one," I said, getting straight to the point. "I couldn't figure you out at first—you're a necromancer, clearly, or started as one. I don't know what kind of convoluted sequence of bad luck you had to go through to end up like this, but if you've been at it this long you must enjoy it."

Even though every survival instinct I'd managed to pick up told me not to, I took a step toward him, under one of the red bulbs, letting him see me. "But then I remembered when I woke up in the employ of a reaper. My soul wasn't my own. Not even my body was my own anymore. I was alive but I felt like I was on strings and someone else was pulling them. I thought about how a hundred years of that made me feel and then I multiplied that by an order of ten."

Cain didn't speak. As far as I could tell he wasn't even breathing. "You're the boogeyman," I said. "But even you have a boss. You don't want this any more than I wanted to spend a hitch collecting deadbeat souls. But I know what you do want."

Cain's rasp startled me. "Do you?"

"You want to die," I said. "That's why you were so happy when you thought the world was gonna go tits-up. You want it to be over."

"I don't see how this is important," he said. "It doesn't change anything. The Fallen will still do what he has planned to do and he will still usher in a spring thaw with the fire of a reborn world."

"You don't have to be here to see it," I said.

"Nothing can kill me," Cain muttered at long last. "Don't you think I've tried everything?"

"Every thing like you knows what will end it all for them," I said.

"Why do you care so much, little bird?" he sighed. "This world has offered both of us nothing but pain. I tried to save him, you know. The man I slew. And when I couldn't I tried to use my gift to bring him back but all it brought me was a thing with his face, and I have been walking this earth with that nightmare for a thousand years, and a thousand more."

"I guess I'm not as jaded as you," I said. "This world sucks but it's all I've got. I died, and I got a fucked-up second chance, and then I got a real one. I was tempted to waste it and give everything and everyone the finger but I'm here. There's a fallen angel trying to end the world. I guess it's good I'm here because of that."

Cain reached for my face, and I jerked back. "No," I said. "I'm as good as my word, but we're not doing this again."

He could still use his thrall on me and I'd be stuck here. I dropped my eyes and backed up to the ladder. "If you want what I'm offering, then you have to do as I say for a change."

I turned and climbed, faster than I had the first time. Being back down there in that stale air was nauseating and I sucked in a long breath when I was topside.

Hank straightened up when I came to the fence and nodded at me. Leo's jaw tightened. "What if he doesn't come out of that hole?"

"He'll come," I said. "He wants me too badly not to."

Hank gripped the chain link to stay upright, and as we watched, Cain's shadow emerged ahead of him in the pale sunlight.

"Holy shit," Hank murmured.

"You have no idea," I told him, as Cain approached.

"You can't kill me, little bird," he called. "Not even your man there, Scythe or no, can do it."

He reached out his hand, and I felt the tug before I could look away. "Now forget them, and come to me. We will live out the end together."

I started to walk, unable to help myself, when Leo's hand clamped down on my shoulder. "Ava," he said quietly. "It's all right. You don't have to do that."

"She bends to my will," Cain called to Leo. I groaned. The inability to walk was painful, the compulsion to obey like an ice pick through my skull.

"She bends to no one," Leo said. "But I care about her and I protect her, so if you want her, then come and get her." He considered and then added, "Dickhead."

Cain stalked across the frozen ground, coming on like a tank, and I felt a scream start to form in my belly, but then he stopped, jerked, and clawed at his body.

Hank let out a sigh of relief as his power took hold of Cain, dragging at him like hooks sunk into his skin. "Thank God," he said. "I wasn't sure that would work . . ."

Cain let out a scream of rage, and I used his distraction to push the thrall off me, like I had back in the silo. "I lied," I called over his wailing. "I don't have the faintest idea how to kill you. But I do know that if the Fallen holding your note can't use you, sooner or later they'll deal."

I looked at Hank. "Those barriers will hold him?"

"Yeah," Hank said. "They will."

"Now it's your turn to be staked out as bait," I said to Cain. "And for what you did to me, I hope it takes your boss a long fucking time to show his face."

Cain raked his hands over his face, like he was trying to claw his own skin off. "I will tell you!" he shouted. "You were right. I know how I can die. I was the first of my kind. In the beginning all life and knowledge sprouted from a tree. The first of its kind. A stake carved from the tree can kill anything that walks, no matter how old."

"Really?" I said. "A stake? From an old tree."

"Not any tree," he said. "It has a lot of names from a many different peoples. I only know it as a story. I have looked and I have never found it. Once you've been mortal, even if you aren't any longer, a veil drops. I think only things that never stepped on the earth are meant to know."

"This is bullshit," Leo murmured. I nodded.

"Probably. Let's find Uriel and get this over with."

"You can't turn away from me, little bird!" Cain shouted. "You will return, and you will beg to stand by my side!"

"I'll keep that in mind," I said, and turned my back on him.

It was a strange feeling, walking away from the boogeyman after he'd occupied such a huge space inside my head, but Cain wasn't that. Not now. Not ever again.

"You should get back to the hospital," I said to Hank when we reached Leo's stolen car. "We can take it from here."

Hank started to get in, then looked back at me. "It won't end the way you want," he said. "I can't see what's coming for you, or for Leo. That should scare you. It should make you stop trying to do whatever it is you're doing."

"Hank," I said, "I know this is a dumb, shitty plan, but it's all I've got."

"I know," he said sadly. "That's part of what frightens me."

CHAPTER

19

"Let me see if I understand," Uriel said. I'd convinced Leo to let me meet him alone, and to not try to beat the crap out of him the second he showed up. "You staked out Cain as bait for the Fallen and you want me to do . . . what exactly?"

"I want you to tell me who the Fallen is based on the look I got," I said. We were standing out of view of Cain, in the shadow of the trees that blocked the bunker site from the highway. It was after dark by this point, and freezing, but Uriel didn't even shiver. I did. "I want to know what we're up against."

Uriel sighed. "Back up and explain to me how you saw this bastard's face but don't know who he is." He massaged his temples with one finger, stopping when he caught me looking.

"You're putting out a lot of fires," I said, using his line.

Uriel blinked once. "But this is the only one threatening to burn my ass."

I started to tell him about Lilith, and her games, but Uriel stopped me. "You know that was incredibly stupid, right?"

"I figured it out when I almost died choking on my own puke, yeah," I said, glaring at him. He held out his hand. "It's best to simply show me."

I looked at his hand, then at his face, my own displaying my distaste. "After what I've been through?"

"I'm not tricking you, Ava," he said impatiently. "I value you. I'm not a psychopath who hurts people for the enjoyment of it. Let me take a glance at your memory and I'll tell you if I recognize him or not. Either way . . ." He nodded toward the bunker, where Leo stood watch over Cain, who was still letting out long, inhuman cries into the wind. "Good work," he said. "I do believe this new alliance with you and Mr. Karpov was the right move."

"Don't tell Leo," I said, slapping my hand into his. "He hates your angelic guts."

Letting Uriel into my head wasn't like Hank, or Lilith, or anyone else who'd poked around in there. It didn't feel like an intrusion so much as a connection, like our hands had extended into our two minds and we stood side by side in the same room Lilith had shown me.

The Fallen looked even more frightening now that the haze of Lilith's blood had worn off, pale as the snow under our feet back in Kansas. His eyes were that strange, animal gold that only angels possessed but the rest of him was freakishly pale.

I looked over, starting to realize Uriel was beside me. More shocking, though, was the look of fear on his face. "Oh shit," I said, as he shook his head, his usually neutral face contorting in anger. "What? Who is he?"

"I thought he was dead," Uriel said softly. "I was so grateful."

I stepped back, reflexively trying to shield myself with Uriel. "Who is he?"

As quickly as it had slotted into place, the connection between us broke, and we were standing in the snow again. Uriel rubbed his forehead. "Somebody I'd very much hoped I'd never see again."

"Well, he's got Leo's Scythe, Cain, and a good jump on the apocalypse," I said. Uriel sighed, looking cold for the first time.

"That sounds about right." He blew into his hands. "His name is Belial. He was one of the angels who led the rebellion in the Kingdom. He was supposed to have died in the Fall."

"Looks like you got bad intel," I said quietly. Uriel turned around and hit the tree behind him, so hard the wood splintered around his fist.

"We have a list of *every* Fallen who survived," he said. "If he's here then he's kept himself hidden for a very long time."

"Yeah, well, Cain claims he can only be killed by a magic tree branch, so you're not the only one who's heard some wacky shit today," I said.

"What did you say?" Uriel grabbed me by the shoulders, and I squeaked. Leo started toward us but I held up a hand. "Tell me *exactly* what he said," Uriel demanded.

"He said in the beginning there was a tree, and that they were both the first of their kind, and only a stake carved from the wood could kill him."

Letting go of me, Uriel stalked away, then back. He looked

almost human, his face flushed and his hair falling in one eye. "That's how he did it," he said. "Belial. It's where he's been and where he's keeping the Scythe." He threw his arms out, laughing. "I'm so stupid!" he shouted, turning around in the few snowflakes beginning to drift down.

Leo came up beside me. "So has Clarence finally cracked?"

"I heard that!" Uriel shouted. "I heard that and I don't care, because you two beautiful creatures have solved the biggest mystery currently plaguing me!"

He came to me and held out his hand. "Belial will be here soon to see what's become of his pet, and you and I have work to do before he does."

Leo stepped between us. "Whoa, pal. She's not going anywhere with you alone."

Uriel regarded Leo, and Leo stared him down. I could have told Uriel he was going to lose that contest but then he coughed and looked away anyway. "I assure you I'll return her in the same condition she is now. Neither you nor Ava have anything to fear from me."

Leo sneered, and I nudged him. "Stop. You want this to be over as much as I do."

"Sure," he said. "Doesn't mean I got to suck up to the heavenly host over there."

Uriel returned Leo's shitty smile. "'Because I would not stop for Death, he kindly stopped for me.'"

Leo ground his teeth and Uriel patted him on the shoulder. "I know you were too busy slinging crystal meth to pay for your mother's own habit to pay attention when they covered Emily Dickinson in your English class. Look her up. I think you'd enjoy that poem."

Uriel guided me away before Leo could haul off and stab him in the eye. I pulled away, frowning up at him. "You're a dick."

"It's one of my many charms," Uriel said. "If we're going to save the world together, Ava, you should learn to love me as I am."

I rolled my eyes. "I cannot wait."

Traveling between the beads on the string with Uriel wasn't anything like when Lilith had taken me to Tartarus—I didn't pass out in pain, there was no jerk of my atoms separating and re-forming in another place—just a quick "Watch your step" from Uriel as we left the field, a click like a flash in my eyes and I stood alone with Uriel in one of the white sterile halls like I'd woken up in after he'd pulled me from Tartarus.

"Nice," I said, turning in a slow circle to admire the shiny floors and walls and soft recessed lighting. "You get a big new office after the Lilith thing? Company car? Parking spot to go with it?"

Uriel led me down the hall to a blank set of double doors. "We're not in my office."

A single light shone down on us when he pushed the door open, the purest and cleanest sunlight I'd seen in a long time bathing a heavy silver pendulum, as big as my fist, swinging back and forth. Sand flowed from the tip with a soft hiss, spreading in thin, even lines over a white marble floor veined with lines that looked random, but as the sand connected them turned into roads and highways, rivers and borders before the sand shifted and showed another part of another world, miles away from the first.

The light reminded me of the sun on the mountainside where I'd grown up, the only time anything around me besides the woods and the river looked clean.

"We're in the Kingdom," I breathed.

The pendulum swooped by me and Uriel pointed. "You know the Three Fates? The line that can show you anything, including when and where your life will end?"

I nodded. "I thought that was, you know, three old women."

"Yeah, and the tree was in an apple orchard run by an ornery snake in some versions," Uriel said. He pointed at the center of the room. "Stand there. The sand is—I don't know. I'm old but I'm not that old. There's a lot of things in all the spheres older than I am. It works, though."

"Are you sure?" I took a tentative step into the room, my boots ringing on the marble, waiting to see if I got electrocuted or just burst into flames like a bad guy in an Indiana Jones movie.

The pendulum swung around me and a line started to form almost immediately. "I don't know how to do this," I whispered. "I'm uncomfortable around this sort of thing. Angels. Demons. I just want to keep myself safe. Myself and the person I need to protect. It's my *job* to protect . . ."

The outline got thicker and fuller, connecting the black veins of the marble. The veins flowed and re-formed like they were alive, like I was standing on the back of something massive and cold-blooded.

I almost screamed when Uriel came to stand beside me, looking down at the shape. "Any luck?"

The outline was unmistakable now, and I almost wanted to laugh looking at the square-boot shape with the star-shaped scribble at the toe end. It was either laugh or scream. "Of course it would be there," I said, as vines and cypress roots and moss and rotted, rusty iron fences played out all around the map.

Uriel frowned. "Louisiana?"

I sighed. "Yeah. Louisiana is where I died. And for some reason fate just won't let me stay away."

Uriel looked without expression at the overgrown mound of brick and iron that had been a plantation house. Not a single drop of sweat coursed down his perfect hairline, even in the heavy heat of the swamp.

I tried not to look. I'd seen it all. The cypress roots and the heavy blanket of greenery were the last thing I'd seen.

"This isn't really the place you died," Uriel said. "You know that, right? This place looks different to everyone who visits it."

"Are we even supposed to be here?" I said, stripping off my jacket as sweat soaked through my top.

"Nope," Uriel said. "Places like this are strictly off-limits to angels. I'm going to have some very unpleasant conversations when I get back to the Kingdom."

He patted me on the shoulder. "But this is way more important, so let's find the tree, find the Scythe, and get the fuck out of here."

We slogged through the mud for what seemed like hours. The old plantation where I'd died wasn't anywhere near this large. This swamp just kept going, getting murkier and hotter until I was panting trying to move in the heavy air. "We could have used Leo," I said, leaning against a cypress root and wiping a handful of moisture off my face. "A locator spell would be nice about now."

"I don't think putting all three of us in one place is smart," Uriel said. "You and I can be replaced but the Grim Reaper is needed."

"Yeah," I muttered. "I'm used to hearing that."

We walked in silence after that, until the land started to tilt up, mud instead of dirty water squelching under our feet. The long gray curtains of moss parted, and Uriel cocked his head.

"I thought it'd be bigger."

The tree was little taller than I was. The trunk bent to the left, and the gray and gnarled branches looked almost dead. Only a few leaves clung to the ends of the smallest twigs, wilting in the heat. What really got me was how green everything around it was. It wasn't just the green of a hot, moist environment. There was grass, and flowers, all the most brilliant colors that almost hurt my eyes. Bluebells cascaded down the bank, crushed under our feet, and thorny vines loaded with roses tugged at my hair. Even the air was sweet, no longer like sucking on a wet rag. Sunlight filtered down through the haze, catching every droplet in the air and casting tiny rainbows down around us.

"Wow," I said quietly, because what else can you say when faced with a primal force?

"It's really beautiful," Uriel said quietly. "More beautiful than I ever thought."

I tore my gaze away after a moment, even though I hated to let go of the feeling of calm and certainty that pervaded the air around the tree. "We need to find the Scythe," I said quietly.

Uriel blinked. "Yeah," he said. "Sorry. Even we don't see things like this very often. Life in the Kingdom is pretty dull, really—"

I turned back when his voice trailed off, and saw him standing still. His face went slack, and his gaze dipped, like I'd just profoundly disappointed him. His mouth turned down in a sad frown and then his knees buckled and he fell in the mud, the black-green muck splashing up onto his dove-gray suit like he really had been shot in the wing and crashed to earth.

Gary smiled at me, holding a short black blade carved from some kind of gleaming stone or glass. "Ava," he said, a grin spreading across his face like kudzu. "We really have to stop meeting like this."

CHAPTER

No matter who you are and how much you face death, sooner or later fight-or-flight is going to fail you. One day your body will betray you and your mind will take wing, leaving you frozen and alone.

I froze while Gary laughed at me, twirling the blade in his hand like it was a baton and he was leading the Asshole Parade.

"Don't look so hysterical," he sighed. "You always reacted so badly to the slightest bit of untoward news." He pointed the blade at my chin. "I'm not going to hurt you, Ava. It's going to be just like it always was. You do as I say without arguing or I'll liquidate you." He leaned in. "And if you think demon blood tastes iffy, angel blood will really fuck your day up."

I finally got my mouth to work as, grinning all the while, he waved the black knife at me like it was a damn metronome. "You look pretty good for a dead guy. Better than you ever did when I worked for you."

Gary shrugged, spreading his arms. "What's the saying? 'Rumors of my death have been greatly exaggerated'?"

"You know what I missed the least about you?" I said, crouching to check on Uriel. "You thinking you're witty."

Uriel was in bad shape, making a gurgling sound when he tried to breathe, his face drained of all color. His blood was mingling with the mud underneath him, trickling down toward the water. "Ava . . ." he rasped, reaching for me.

Gary stepped on his hand, crushing it into the mud. Bones cracked and Uriel let out a strangled scream. "Did I ever get the chance to tell you how much I hated you?" Gary said. "Never mind. I figure a Grim Reaper's Scythe to the lung gets the message across."

"You are such a dick," I said, trying to turn Uriel and see if I could stop his bleeding.

"And you are so predictable," he said. "You fight even when you've lost. I think I could cut off all your limbs and you'd still try and bite at my ankles."

I couldn't do anything for Uriel. His breathing was fading away and his eyes were going glassy. I wanted to cry, or scream, but I was damned if I'd let Gary see me do either one. Instead I turned on him with a growl. "I'm so going to enjoy shoving that Scythe through your eye."

Gary let out a laugh. "You're cute." Then he hit me, how he always used to, a hard cross to the jaw that dropped me and exploded lightbulbs behind my eyes. My hands sank into the muck, next to Uriel's still form.

"I'm sorry," I whispered to him, as Gary stood over the two of us. Uriel blinked slowly, his eyes downcast.

"Annoying little shit of an angel," Gary said. "Like that kid who always wants to be the milk monitor. Look at me, look at me, I've got the biggest stick of all up my ass." He put his foot on my chest, pressing me down into the mud, and grinned. "Bring back memories?" he said. "Ava the little waif, stumbling barefoot through the swamp to her death?"

Uriel's fingers brushed mine, and I felt the twisted lumps of his broken knuckles. He blinked at me again, and I realized he was trying to look at Gary's foot. I shook my head as Gary stepped on me again. "You'll die . . ."

"You know, after I'm done here I think I'll pop over to Kansas, pay your irritating little boyfriend a visit," Gary said. "This Scythe can kill anything. Including the Grim Reaper. Won't there be a lot of feathers fluttering in the Kingdom after I ice their big man downstairs."

Uriel gritted his teeth as a little blood dribbled from his mouth, and nodded at me. I linked my fingers with his, then looked up at Gary.

"Gary?" I said. He leaned down, stepping on me so hard my ribs creaked.

"Yes, doggie?"

"Shut the fuck up," I said, and squeezed my eyes closed as Uriel popped us out of the hot, wet swamp and back into freezing air.

Gary looked around at our new surroundings, seeming almost surprised. "What kind of half-assed stunt is this, now?"

Uriel's eyes drifted closed, and he went still. Against the Kansas snow, his blood was much redder, almost the color of the roses twined around the tree back in the swamp.

"I thought you'd be pleased," I said, heaving his foot off me. "We're here to see the Grim Reaper, just like you wanted."

Leo was already starting toward us at a run, and Gary smiled at me. "Okay, gotta hand it to you, kid," he said. "That was a pretty sweet sacrifice play." He turned and gave Leo a look, and Leo stopped in his tracks, gasping, and then went flying back against the fence.

"Aww," Gary said, pulling a mock sad face. "Denied. I was hoping for a little song and dance but I guess I'll just stab him in the chest and get it over with."

"How did you survive, Gary?" I blurted, clambering to my feet as he started for Leo. Talking was literally the only weapon I had left, so I started jabbering. "I saw you die. You bled out in a parking lot. I still had your blood under my nails when I packed up to get the hell out of there."

"Ava." He sighed, as if I were a very stupid small child. "You of all people know death isn't as permanent as it looks. But seeing as you were never too bright, I'll play."

I held up my hands. "You made your point. I get that you want payback but Leo is the Grim Reaper. You kill him and you throw the entire universe out of alignment, Gary."

"But that's the first mistake you made," he said with a sarcastic lilt to his voice. "I'm not Gary."

"No," I said. "You're Belial. Fallen pretending to be Hellspawn, hiding in plain sight. I get it now. It's very clever, yay for you."

"Wrong again," he said, flipping the Scythe over his knuckles. "Belial's just a name I picked up from a dead angel. Figured it was as good a cover as any, but the Fallen are dull. And whiny. Bunch of sad navel gazers, all of 'em."

I swallowed, not moving, still blocking him from Leo, who thrashed against the fence, letting off a string of curses. If this thing really wasn't Gary, douchebag reaper with the fashion sense of a blind librarian, *or* Belial, asshole Fallen with a penchant for beating on demons, then what the hell was he?

Whatever he was, I was afraid of him, but I made myself keep standing there, because for some reason it was keeping him from Leo.

"Aren't you going to ask me what I am, with that little southern belle tremor in your voice?" Gary smirked. I felt my lip curl reflexively.

"All right. What the fuck are you?"

"Pick a shapeshifter," Gary said. "A trickster, a god with a thousand faces. I'll answer to any of those."

"You expect me to believe," I said, "that you are not Hellspawn or even an angel but an ancient god of something?"

"Used to be," Gary said. "So long ago even the stars have forgotten I exist. Everyone else is gone. They faded out and gave up. But I'm a survivor. What you might call adaptable." He pressed his foot into the earth and the snow bubbled, hissing away. The grass under it sprouted green, then withered and died, all within the space of a breath. "I started seeing signs a few centuries ago. I went to the Garden and prepared for the end times at the world tree, as you do, and . . ." He poofed his fingers out. "Nothing. So I figured it was my job to get the ball a-rolling, and I started looking for things like me. Other survivors, and adaptors. Your boy Cain over there was my best find by far."

"Cain, the Scythe, and a little bit of unrest in Hell was all I needed," Gary said, standing. Black frostbite spread out from his feet, climbing over everything, including Leo, who moaned. "All I needed," Gary repeated, "until you got cute. I don't know why that bag of bones over there couldn't keep you with him in his love bunker until it was over but I swear, Ava, there is literally nothing that can stop me, so give up, lie down, and let the world die like it should."

"If the world dies, you die," I said. "And I *know* you aren't suicidal like Cain."

Gary shoved me out of the way, landing me on my ass in the frost, and advanced on Leo, pulling out the Scythe. "You're so small-minded, Ava. Worlds come and go. Only I'm eternal. I'll be just fine with whatever's left, and I sure as hell won't make a mistake like you again."

I jumped up and ran at him, leaping onto his back as he swung at Leo. He staggered under my weight and swung around, driving the Scythe back into my shoulder.

I let go when he did. The blade felt like running into a brick wall. The pain dropped me, and I watched snow start to drift down around us, thick and furious. Not snow, I realized as a few flakes landed on my tongue as I panted. Ash. The same kind of burning ash I'd tasted in the camps.

Gary looked down at me and shook his head. "I'll always be the alpha dog, Ava. That's the natural order."

He reached down and patted my head, cool hand pressing on my sticky hair. "Good girl. There's a good girl."

I curled away from him, trying to work the knife out of my shoulder while I played at flinching. It felt like it was burning my flesh off, stripping me down to the bone, but it finally popped free. I convulsed slightly and Gary chuckled, giving me one final pat.

He's not Gary, I reminded myself.

"It'll be better than you think, Ava," he said. "It's a cycle. As natural as birth and death. The new world kills the old. That's what my people believed, back in the day."

He kicked me over onto my back with his foot and picked up the Scythe. "Nice try, by the way. You were always secretive and sneaky. Guess that's why I liked you."

"I hate you," I choked. "It'll almost be worth it to see the world end just so I don't have to listen to you anymore."

"Don't know how you missed it," Gary sighed. "The signs are all there—the dead rising, the Grim Reaper taking his seat at the head of the table, demons walking the earth, angels turning their backs on it." He rocked on his heels, crunching the frost like a happy little boy as he faced me. "And you, my pet, will get to see it all. Before I kill you, again."

He stood up and whirled away from me, heading for Leo. "But first, I've got a bone to pick with the guy who stole my seat."

I was dying. The hit from the Scythe was killing me, surely as Lilith's poison blood or the knife wound I'd gotten when I'd been human and died for the first time. The fire wasn't just in my arm now; it was in my chest and everywhere, and I thrashed, spitting blood into the snow. Soon I'd be as still and cold as Uriel, all alone in the cold. Cain would get to watch every one of us die with that smug, satisfied look on his face.

I flopped onto my other side as I convulsed, and looked at Leo, who met my eyes as Gary advanced on him. "It's okay," he whispered. "I'm not scared, Ava. It's okay."

Gary lifted the Scythe, and I didn't even think, I just let go. If I was going to die, I wasn't going to die a sad little broken body in the snow.

I was a hound, and that was how I was leaving this earth.

My feet crunched heavily over the snow and I was still trailing blood, but I took one step, then another, letting out a low snarl that rattled the frost on the chain link fence. I was going to look at Gary as I died. I was going to let him know he hadn't beaten me down, not in the end.

"That's cute," Gary said. "What are you gonna do, bite me? Better think on that one, Ava. Bad doggies get a smack on the nose. Bad doggies—"

I lunged at him, slamming into his chest with my full weight, shoving him backward, until his arms windmilled, and I sank my fangs into his shoulder and kept pushing, until I felt the impact of something solid thumping into Gary's back. Got him in the left lung, in my semi-expert opinion.

He raised the Scythe, his face finally twisting into the real one, the hateful, spite-driven mask that couldn't pass for human on its best day. "You bitch," he rasped. "You can't kill me—"

I locked my jaws around his wrist and bit down with all my strength. I bit through skin and muscle, tasting the bitter, battery-acid blood that burned my tongue and throat. I shook, ripping at the tendons and finally crunching through the two bones that held Gary's hand to his body. Gary let out a scream, a real one, and his hand thumped into the snow, the fingers relaxing on the Scythe's handle, letting it slide out of his grasp.

I fell back, landing on two legs. Gary was close behind me, and he slammed me back into the ground, his one good hand wrapping around my throat.

"You're dead," he snarled. "You just don't know it yet. That wound will burn you up." He shook me by the neck and spat blood in my face. "How does it feel to die alone again, Ava?"

"She's not alone," a voice said from above us, as my vision blurred. "She's got me."

Somebody kicked the Scythe to me as Gary spun around, distracted, and I jammed it into his neck with all my strength, where the fat vein pulsed under the skin.

Gary swayed back and forth, like a tree in a gentle wind, and then he toppled off me, releasing my throat.

Leo skidded to the ground next to me and wrapped his arms around me. "I'm okay," he said as I let out a long, shuddering gasp. "Biting him got him to let go of the hex. I'm fine. It's over."

I looked past the bulk of his chest at Gary. I've seen plenty of people die, but this was different. The life drained out of him, but slowly, as if the Scythe were drinking down the forces that had kept him alive this long.

I pushed away from Leo, getting to my feet, and went over to Gary's body. Leo tried to stop me but I shook him off, kneeling in the bloody pool next to him and pulling the Scythe free from his neck. His blood fountained over me, dousing my upper body, and he gave one last shudder as his heart stopped and the blood along with it.

I staggered back to Leo and put the Scythe in his hands. "I'm your hound," I said, raising my voice over the howling wind. "You're the Grim Reaper. Now we both have what we need."

Leo folded me into his arms again. He was warm, and I was so slick with blood I felt like I'd slipped underwater, going down and down until the blackness swallowed me.

CHAPTER
21

Uriel was where I'd left him, lying in the snow. He was pale—corpse pale, blue around the edges, and I shivered as I touched his skin. It was cool and lifeless. I put my hand on his face. "I'm sorry," I said. "I was wrong about you."

Leo stood at a respectful distance, and I looked back at him. "Leo," I said softly. "I don't feel so good . . ."

I swayed, and fell over on Uriel. I couldn't stop myself. The wound from the Scythe was filling me up with poison and there was no controlling my muscles anymore.

This time wasn't like the last, when there had been panic and confusion. This time I was almost glad. Saddened to leave Leo, but so glad the pain was almost done . . .

"Do you mind?" Uriel muttered at me. "You're small but strangely heavy."

I started, barely able to lift my head. "You're not dead."

"Not yet," Uriel said. He rolled his head to look at Leo. "Reaper. You need to release what the Scythe is holding. We're dying because it's sucking the life force out of us."

Leo looked down, stroking his fingers over the Scythe. To his credit, he didn't waste any time with a bunch of questions.

"Hold on," Uriel said. "This is going to hurt like a bitch."

Nothing he'd said could have prepared me for what came next, though. If being stabbed had felt like a truck, this felt like a freight train. I arched like I'd been shocked, and fell over, feeling myself twitch as I convulsed. I couldn't even scream, it hurt so much, and thankfully I blacked out for a few seconds before I came to, looking up at Leo.

He smiled at me. "How was it?"

"Fucking awful," I said, sitting up. I still had a hole in my shoulder you could drive a compact car through. Uriel also tried to get up, making it to one knee.

"On the bright side," Leo said, helping me to my feet, "you both look better than he does."

We all regarded Gary for a moment. A light layer of snow had already covered his body, covering the wounds and the ugliness.

"Who was he?" Leo said.

"Belial was just an alias," Uriel said. "If he was really something as ancient as all that . . ." He shrugged. "There are a lot of mysteries left in the folds of the universe. Things even the Kingdom has forgotten. I don't know what he was."

"He was adaptable," I said.

"He was a fucking asshole," Uriel said, making it to his feet with a groan. "And he ruined my suit."

I looked to Leo, and then to the figure behind the chain link. Cain was still watching us. I don't think he'd blinked since we'd shown up. "Leo," I said quietly. "We can't leave him alive."

"Yeah, I know," he sighed. He turned to Uriel. "I know you just came back to life and all, Clarence, but we need one more favor."

Uriel dipped his head. "You want to go back to the Garden." He beckoned when we didn't step closer. "Well, come on. I don't have all night."

The sun was rising, somewhere behind the gray snow clouds, when we returned, Leo holding the stake we'd cut from the tree. He and Uriel stopped at the fence, though, and he turned the stake over to me. "This is yours, darlin'," he said. "You earned it."

I sucked in a breath and then ducked through the cut in the fence. I could feel Hank's spell gently curl away from me and then close behind me as I crossed it and stood before Cain.

"I didn't think you'd come back," he said.

"But I did," I said. I held out the stake, balanced on my palm. "And now you have to hold up your end of this deal."

Cain stretched out his hand, then drew it back. "Will you do the honors?"

I shook my head. I didn't want to be a part of this. It was sad, and private, and it wasn't mine.

He nodded after a moment. "I'm glad I didn't see the end," he murmured. "When Belial told me . . ."

"He wasn't Belial," I said. "But you knew, I think. You've been around a long time. Even when you were alive, you were a powerful warlock. Probably the most powerful I've met."

"I wanted to die," Cain said. "I still want to. I wasn't thinking straight."

I put the stake back in his hands. "It's your time," I said. "Past time." I started to leave, and then turned back. "Do me a favor. If you change your mind—come back to me. Because I'll make damn sure that thing goes in your heart."

Cain nodded, and then reached out and grabbed my hand, positioning the stake between his ribs with the other. "I told you we'd be together in the end, little bird. We could take this and slay the Grim Reaper and—"

I leaned into him and shoved the stake up and between his third and fourth rib, angled into his heart. "You don't know me," I whispered. "And you don't own me. And your time's up."

I walked away without saying anything else. I didn't want to see his end. I walked west, past Leo and Uriel, toward the big orange scoop of sun sitting on top of the snow, and stared into it until my own vision dazzled me. I told myself that was why I was crying, and not any other reason at all.

CHAPTER

22

Leo caught up with me on the other edge of the field, the far one beyond the silo. We were on a short cliff above a frozen river, the water hissing and crackling below the surface. "That was him on the highway," I said, putting my head on his shoulder. "Cain. Trying to get to me before we even hit Minneapolis."

Leo breathed big, his chest raising and lowering me. "I am not looking forward to going back to all that mess. I always hated office politics. Why I became a cleaner and didn't fuck around trying to be the boss like my old man. I liked working with sulfuric acid and a fifty-five-gallon drum a lot more than coworkers."

I looked up at the sky, the faintest hint of blue showing behind the iron-bellied clouds that scudded over the plains. "At least Lilith put your main competition in a coma," I said. Leo snorted.

"I should send that witch a muffin basket."

We were quiet for a long time after that, Leo keeping his arm tight around me. I was glad to be under it. Things had been shitty and scary and chaotic for way too long, even by my standards.

"Do you think he was right?" I said. "Gary—or whoever—I mean? Do you think the world is really ending?"

"You're the one who grew up in the Bible Belt, kid," Leo said. "Signs and portents and all that. What do you think?"

I wriggled closer to him, until his arm could almost circle me. "I've been around awhile. Things are different now. It's not like an apocalypse—more like a virus. All the things Gary said are happening. Maybe it's not so much an end as an overlap. Maybe there's too much for the barriers to handle. Who knows what tipped it over?"

"Lilith sure didn't help," Leo said. "Or Uriel using you to do what he didn't have the balls to."

"Ease up on him," he said. "He saved my life, and he got you your Scythe. He's not so bad."

Leo grunted, but he didn't say anything.

"If things can't support their own weight they implode," I said. "Maybe all of what happened this past week or so is us starting to see the cracks in the wall."

"So this is how the world ends," Leo said. "With a whimper. A little hairline crack."

I replayed everything Cain and Gary had said to me. How I was like Cain. I was meant to be here, now, at this precise moment. Not because I was unlucky. For a reason. And it didn't have to be the reason Gary or anyone else picked. I didn't have to be a sign or a portent. If I wanted, I could be here to shore up the foundations. To keep the walls from cracking.

I watched the clouds roll back from a daylight sky as Leo gave me a squeeze and went to start the car. I watched sunlight touch ground it hadn't in weeks, starting to melt the ice, and then Leo honked the horn and I turned and jogged back to the car.

Spring would come. It might be slow and muddy, but eventually it would be like winter had never fallen at all.

Leo shook his head as he pulled out onto the highway, heading north to whatever was waiting for us back in Minneapolis. "Just a little crack," he said again.

I patted his arm, and watched the road. In a strange way, I owed Gary a thank-you, wherever he was.

He'd finally gotten me to stop waiting for the world to end.

I squeezed Leo's hand as he accelerated, pushing the car to the limit. "Not if I can help it."

About the Author

Caitlin Kittredge has written sixteen novels for adults and teens, including *Black Dog*, the award-winning Iron Codex trilogy, and *Coffin Hill*, published by Vertigo. Caitlin spends her time in Massachusetts fixing up her 1881 Victorian house that she shares with several spoiled cats and a vast collection of geeky ephemera.